ADVANCE PRAISE

"Jill Orr's delightful, laugh-out-loud debut is the perfect mix of mystery, humor, and romance, anchored by an endearing heroine you can't help but root for. A fun, fast-paced read with a satisfying mystery at its heart. Perfect for fans of Janet Evanovich."

— **Laura McHugh,** award-winning author of *Arrowood* and *The Weight of Blood*

"Orr's debut mystery is a fun romp populated with peculiar characters. [We] recommend it to new adult fans or admirers of Janet Evanovich's Stephanie Plum capers."

— *Library Journal*

"Riley 'Bless-Her-Heart' Ellison is a breath of fresh air—a funny, empathic, Millennial heroine. She kept me turning the pages well into the night."

— **Susan M. Boyer,** *USA TODAY*–bestselling author of the Liz Talbot mystery series

"Who knew obituaries could be this much fun?"

— **Gretchen Archer,** *USA TODAY*–bestselling author of the Davis Way Crime Caper series

"What a fun, quirky, mystery! This was exactly what I needed to comfort me during these uncertain times. I can't wait to give this to all my girlfriends for their beach vacations."

— **Whitney Berger,** The King's English Bookshop, Salt Lake City

"An extremely fun read! Regina H., Personal Romance Concierge, may be my favorite new literary character of the decade."
— **Anne Flett-Giordano**, author of *Marry, Kiss, Kill* and Emmy-winning writer of *Mom, Frasier,* and *Desperate Housewives*

"Jill Orr will make you laugh, make you think, and steam up your reading glasses with this funny, smart, and romantic mystery debut. *The Good Byline* is an engaging story that will keep readers wondering whodunit and how'd-they-do-it until the very end."
—**Diane Kelly,** award-winning author of the *Death & Taxes* and *Paw Enforcement* mysteries

"In this irresistible page-turner, Jill Orr delivers a funny, smartly written mystery featuring a charming heroine and appealing setting. I can't wait to join Millennial Riley Ellison on future adventures—and misadventures!"
— **Ellen Byron,** award-winning author of *Body on the Bayou* and *Plantation Shudders*

"Jill Orr's Tuttle Corner is absolutely charming, and you'll want to hang out more in this Virginian small town with Riley and her cast of friends. The methodical local reporter, Will Holman, is a standout, and here's hoping he will appear in more of Riley's mystery adventures. Fans of Hannah Dennison's Vicky Hill series will devour this debut!"
— **Naomi Hirahara,** Edgar Award–winning author of the Mas Arai and Ellie Rush mystery series

THE GOOD BYLINE

A Riley Ellison Mystery

By Jill Orr

Prospect Park Books

Published by Prospect Park Books
2359 Lincoln Avenue
Altadena, California 91001
www.prospectparkbooks.com

Distributed by Consortium Book Sales & Distribution
www.cbsd.com

Library of Congress Cataloging-in-Publication Data
Names: Orr, Jill, author.
Title: The good byline : a Riley Ellison mystery / by Jill Orr.
Other titles: Riley Ellison mystery
Description: Altadena, California : Prospect Park Books, 2017.
Identifiers: LCCN 2016031253 (print) | LCCN 2016039299 (ebook) | ISBN 9781938849916 (pbk.) | ISBN 9781938849923
Subjects: LCSH: Women journalists--Fiction. | Female friendship--Fiction. | Murder--Investigation--Fiction. | Triangles (Interpersonal relations)--Fiction. | Virginia--Fiction. | GSAFD: Mystery fiction. | Love stories.
Classification: LCC PS3615.R58846 G66 2017 (print) | LCC PS3615.R58846 (ebook) | DDC 813/.6--dc23
LC record available at https://lccn.loc.gov/2016031253

First edition, second printing

Cover design by Susan Olinsky; illustration by Nancy Nimoy
Book layout and design by Amy Inouye, Future Studio
Printed in the United States of America

To Jimmy,
for keeping the champagne on ice...
all these years

Is there room for humor in today's obituary?

"I think so. The obits section is quite misunderstood. People have a primal fear of death, but 98 percent of the obit has nothing to do with death, but with life. There are maybe two sentences in there about when or where the guy died, and with the rest, you let the person's life guide the treatment. We like to say it's the jolliest department in the paper."

—MARGALIT FOX, a *New York Times* writer, in an interview in *The Paris Review*

CHAPTER 1

Nothing says "You're going to die alone" like being asked to judge the three-legged race at the Tuttle Corner Johnnycake Festival because you're the only one without a partner. Even Mrs. Winterthorne, who had to be at least 127 years old and in a wheelchair, signed up with her nurse, Faye. Never mind that Faye was paid to be there or that she would end up with a shattered pinky toe from old Winterthorne rolling over her repeatedly for twenty-five yards, the point is that I didn't even have someone I could pay to be my partner, let alone someone who'd take a broken toe for me. The sad fact was that I was twenty-four years old and undeniably, catastrophically, alone. And the worst part was that everyone in Tuttle Corner knew why.

The day my boyfriend of seven years left me to go find himself, the good people of Tuttle unofficially changed my name from Riley Ellison to Riley Bless-Her-Heart. *"Did you hear the Sanford boy left her without an explanation? Poor Riley, bless her heart." "She'd been so sure they were headed down the aisle...bless her heart." "It's been six months and the poor dear can't seem to get over it. Bless. Her. Heart."*

People in Tuttle Corner love to bless your heart. It's code for anything from an expression of sympathy to a vicious insult, sometimes both at the same time. But most often, this is what people say when they want to call you pathetic but their strict adherence to the Southern be-polite-or-die code won't let them say that. Not to your face anyway. I knew that in my case when people blessed my heart they mostly meant it in the nice way, the *snap-out-of-it-honey* way. Which I guess was fair enough. I hadn't exactly been killing it in the having-a-life department since Ryan left. Besides, you weren't really in trouble in Tuttle Corner until people start saying that they'll pray for you.

So when I arrived at the festival alone, it took Charlotte Van Stone approximately three seconds to ask if I would judge the race. She was in a panic because Millie Hedron, Tuttle's most famous spinster and longtime contest judge, had to cancel when one of her Persian cats rolled in a patch of burrs. Apparently the shaving process had been traumatic for them both. Charlotte zeroed in on me because, as she put it, "Surely you won't be participating this year?" Then she put a hand over her enormous left breast and added, "Bless your heart."

The festival was as hot and crowded as ever, but that didn't stop the entire town from turning up. The sun beat down on the white tents and colonial flags that hung on ropes between trees. Vendors sold cornhusk dolls. My parents, Skip and Jeanie, otherwise known as the Rainbow Connection, played guitar and sang corncake-themed songs on the main stage, delighting the under-six set with their "corny" puns. And Landry's General Store (est. 1781) churned a large vat of kettle corn, which permeated the air with its sticky-sweet scent. These were the sights and sounds and smells of my childhood, as familiar and comforting as an old pair of jeans.

It was almost time for the three-legged race, so I began my walk over to the field. On the way I saw my middle school social studies teacher, Mr. Monroe, talking with a girl named Anna, who had been a few years ahead of me in school. She was holding a baby on her hip and breaking off pieces of pink cotton candy for a small girl standing next to them. I smiled and waved at Anna, who sort of half-smiled like she was trying to place me but then looked away when the baby started fussing. I turned my wave into an awkward pretense of itching my neck.

Born and raised right here in Tuttle County, I technically knew everyone in town. I could tell you who was kin to whom, which marriages had created which family trees, and who had lived in which houses three generations deep. But knowing people and having friends are two very different things. It's funny, as they can feel quite similar, and yet sometimes you don't realize how alone you are until your world falls apart and you have no one to turn to except your parents (who are contractually obligated to love you no matter what).

The truth is that I had nobody to blame but myself for my current friendless state. Seven years ago, when Ryan Sanford charmed his way into my life, I had allowed all my other friendships to fall away. I didn't mean for it to happen; he was just the kind of guy who soaked up attention like one of those cloths that can hold six times its weight in water. He took all I had, and I gave it freely because being with Ryan felt like standing in the sun. He radiated confidence and charisma, two things I lacked as a young girl. It was so easy to lose myself inside Ryan's big personality, his big plans, his big love. Until his big selfish butt decided he needed a change.

For the millionth time, I thought about the half-assed explanation Ryan gave the day he left me. He said he wanted a fresh start somewhere new (Colorado), doing something totally unexpected of an accounting major (bartending), in order to figure out who he really was (an idiot). He said he was doing me a favor and that in the end the breakup would be good for me, too. I suppose he thought I'd pick up the pieces and move on. But despite six months of pitying glances, crushing loneliness, and abject humiliation, I had not moved on. I was back working at my old summer job at the library, paralyzed by the derailment of my life. I felt stuck in a sort of purgatory—waiting for Ryan to come back to me, or not to want him back at all. So far, neither had happened.

Mrs. Van Stone handed me a list of race participants written on a long, curling piece of parchment. She was adamant that all props look as eighteenth-century as possible. The list was a patchwork of familiar names: neighbors, teachers, shop owners, former babysitters, school board members. But one name was more than just familiar; it was like a time capsule. *Jordan James.*

Jordan had been my very best friend when we were kids. We'd been the sleepovers-every-weekend, read-each-other's-minds, eat-each-other's-lollipops kind of friends that you make in early childhood. However, we'd had a divergence of interests in high school. And by a "divergence of interests" I mean she wasn't as interested in Ryan's long lashes and emerging biceps as I was.

I had heard Jordan moved back to Tuttle County after she graduated from Ole Miss and was working for the *Tuttle Times* as a reporter. I'd even thought about calling her to say hey but always chickened out. Jordan had been one of the casualties of the Ryan era. I had treated her badly, and even though we eventually got to a place where we could casually say hello, our friendship had been damaged. And I knew it was all my fault.

But seeing Jordan's name on the list at that moment

made me feel both nostalgic and hopeful. I had a sudden vision of us reconnecting and becoming friends again. I could apologize—admit that I'd been wrong and maybe she'd forgive me. I remembered her wide smile and kind eyes. I felt a jolt of excitement at the idea of Jordan and me running around Tuttle Corner again like we did when we were kids, minus the 8 p.m. bedtime. Maybe being asked to judge the contest was fate. Maybe it was a sign of good things to come instead of a sign that I was on a speeding train headed for Loserville.

I scanned the faces of the crowd but didn't see Jordan's. I followed the line across to where Jordan's partner's name was, but all that remained was a black splotch of ink. *That,* I wanted to shout at Charlotte Van Stone, *is the problem with using quills!*

The bell rang to signify that the race was about to begin. Thirty-six teams lined up on one end of the field and tied their legs (or wheels, in Mrs. Winterthorne's case) together with thick brown twine. I stood at the opposite end of the field just behind a white strip of muslin that had been staked down as a finish line.

I looked through the crowd again but saw no sign of Jordan or her mystery partner. I was disappointed. If she wasn't here then our reunion and subsequent re-best friendship would have to wait. I motioned for Charlotte Van Stone to come over.

"I see Jordan James's name is on the list, but she's not lined up."

A look of annoyance crossed Mrs. Van Stone's face, and I got the sense she was trying to furrow her heavily Botoxed brow. "No-shows just make my blood boil. It's like people think these races organize themselves or something."

"I was hoping to see her," I said, looking around again

to see if maybe she was on her way over. "Do you think she's here?"

"Well, I'm sure I don't know, Riley." Mrs. Van Stone's eyes darted to the racers. "But we can't wait on her. Go ahead and start. You snooze you lose is how I see it!"

Even though I was pretty sure they didn't have bull-horns back in the 1700s, Mrs. Van Stone shoved one into my hands and handed me a little slip of paper with the words she wanted me to say. The sting of humiliation burned my cheeks as I raised the bullhorn to my lips and announced, "Pray pardon me, neighbors! It is time for the Tuttle Corner Johnnycake Festival's annual three-legged race to begin. Huzzah!"

The race began, and it was as if I could see the whole ridiculous scene like it was in a Wes Anderson movie. The camera panned down the field as the coupled-up racers, cheeks red with effort, hopped down the field in awkward slow motion. Then the long shot of me, the lonely loser at the end of the field. Cut to the teams: full of life and happiness. Cut to me: full of emptiness and regret. Cut to them: laughing and falling onto the grass. Cut to me: writing my own obituary inside my head.

Riley Ellison, twenty-four, shelf clerk at Tuttle Corner Library, died of loneliness and shame during the annual Johnnycake Festival as a crowd of racers hopped toward her, two by two, highlighting the fact that she was a single in a world meant for doubles, a solo act among a sea of duets, an à la carte menu item in a combo-meal world.

It occurred to me in that moment that I really needed to make some changes. I didn't want to be the lonely loser at the end of the field. I wanted to be in the race. I wanted to feel the joy and pain of walking through the world with someone else. True, I wanted Ryan, but even more than that I wanted friendship, connection. I wanted to get my life back on track. And I'll admit, I wanted to show every last person in Tuttle Corner that they didn't have to bless my heart.

CHAPTER 2

In the same way one decides to start a healthy eating plan every Monday morning, I began the week determined to change my life. I texted my mom for Mrs. James's phone number, made an appointment to get my hair highlighted, and even gave in to my mother's pleas to sign up for Click.com, a dating website she swore matched up at least five of her friends. Fine. Whatever. I figured if nothing else, when I casually mentioned it to Ryan the next time we talked, it would prove to him I was moving on. And if it drove him mad with jealousy, then that was just a bonus.

So when I arrived at work Monday morning, ready to begin my new life with my new attitude, I wasn't entirely surprised to find something new at the library as well. Dr. Harbinger was already in his office with the door closed. Dr. H never closed his door and was never at work before I or Tabitha got there to let him in. To be honest, I didn't even know he still had a key.

He hadn't done any of the opening tasks, like turning on the lights or the copy machine, so I set about readying the library for business. This took me approximately three and a half minutes. The extra minute and a half was only because I stopped to clean up the sunflower-seed casings someone had left under one of the study cubicles near the new and notable section.

I was in the middle of cataloging—or rather re-cataloging—our biography section, which involved hours and hours of tedious work checking call numbers against MARC records, when Dr. H finally emerged from his office. He looked surprised to see me. "Hello, Miss Ellison!"

"Hi!" I gave him a cheery wave.

"Is it noon already?" He looked up at the clock overhead. I nodded.

"Huhm." He furrowed his brow for a long moment, then shook it off. "How was your weekend? You attended the festival, I trust?"

I nodded again. "Did you go?"

"Ah," he said with the kind of smile that is meant to comfort someone else. "No, dear. Just isn't the same without Louisa. It was always her favorite."

"I know how much she loved it."

"But I hope that you and your cohorts—the young and the restless of Tuttle Corner—stayed out late and made it a night to remember!"

"Yeah," I said vaguely. Dr. H thought I was much more social than I actually was, often asking about what I did over the weekends, then launching into some story from his wild youth. But while I liked Dr. H very much, I didn't talk to him about my personal life, such as it was. I assumed he'd heard the gossip about Ryan leaving me and would have definitely noticed that the pop-in visits from him had stopped abruptly several months ago, but it was fine by me to have it all go unsaid.

Dr. H, on the contrary, left very little unsaid. I knew all about his time in the war, and how he had served as the cook for the Sixty-eighth Infantry Division, and the time he met Paul Newman and Joanne Woodward in a café in Kansas City, and how he loved cinnamon rolls but how his

late wife never let him eat them, and every time he tried
to, she'd snatch them away from him and screech, "I'm not
going to end up married to a potbellied pig!"

Louisa passed away two years ago, and even though I
know he missed her very much, he said the silver lining was
that now he could have all the cinnamon rolls he wanted.
Dr. H could always find the silver lining, even in something
as sad as losing your wife of forty-three years to cancer.

Work passed quickly, a steady stream of people filter-
ing in and out of our little library. For a small town, Tuttle
Corner had an especially fantastic and well-used library. It
was housed in a stately plantation home circa 1821, with
large white columns and a covered porch outfitted with
rocking chairs and ceiling fans to cool our patrons who
chose to read al fresco. It was actually a privately owned
public library, bequeathed through a trust set up in 1916
by the town's then-wealthiest resident, Morris Flynn. Dis-
gusted by his family's greed, Flynn left his considerable
fortune to the library trust and specified in great detail
how the money was to be used to "advance the residents of
Tuttle County by providing a place to seek knowledge and
truth only available through the study and love of books."
It drew people in not just from Tuttle Corner, which had a
population of only twelve thousand, but from the surround-
ing county, which was a much larger geographic region
comprised of several tiny rural municipalities. We were
proud to have served more than fifty-four percent of the
county's population, according to a survey Tabitha sent out
last year.

After the midday rush (three people returning DVDs,
two on the internet-access computers, and two using our
study rooms), things were quiet, so I checked my phone to
see if my mom had texted me Jordan's mom's number yet.

She had. Not wanting to lose momentum on my new life plan, I was about to call when I heard the distinctly disappointed sound of Dr. H's voice.

"Ahem." He stared at the phone in my hand, bushy eyebrows up, lips pursed. Dr. H did not approve of cell phones at work.

"Sorry," I said, slipping my phone back into my pocket.

He shook his head. "I know it's the wave of the future, but I can't help but blame those things for the collapse of—"

"Um, Dr. H?" I cut him off. I was not up for one of his twenty-minute lectures on the dismal state of communication among Millennials. "Is everything all right?"

"Yes, of course, dear. Why do you ask?"

"No reason." I lifted a book from the pile in front of me. "I was just surprised to see you here so early this morning."

"Yes, that. Well, I was having trouble sleeping last night and finally decided to get up, get dressed, and come into work. You know what they say about the early bird and so forth."

We regularly found Dr. H asleep among the large-print section on slow days, and as a professor of library science at Cardwell College, he had a reputation for falling asleep during his own classes—once in the middle of his own lecture on preservation in the digital age. So if he came into work because he couldn't sleep, something must have been troubling him. And then there was the closed door. I'd been working here for almost a year full-time and summers before that, and Dr. H had never once closed his door.

"So," he said, "if it's all right with you, I think I'll nip out a little early today."

"Of course. I'll lock up."

With Dr. H gone for the day and less than ten minutes till closing, I decided it would be all right if I called Mrs.

James. I hoped I could call Jordan next and maybe even set up a lunch for later this week.

"Hello?" It sounded like the Mrs. James I remembered but with a little age on her.

"Hi, Mrs. James. This is Riley Ellison." I paused and waited for her reaction. I'd seen her from time to time after high school, and while she was always friendly, I never knew if she had hard feelings about how I'd treated Jordan.

At first there was no response. I started to panic that maybe she did have hard feelings. After all, I'd lied to her daughter and let her down in a major way. Granted it was years ago, but I knew the pain I'd caused had not only hurt Jordan but her parents as well.

At the end of our junior year, Jordan was nominated for a National Scholastic Press Association award, basically the Pulitzer Prize for student journalists. Jordan invited me to go with her and her parents to the awards ceremony. I'd been touched and gladly agreed. But I found out later that Ryan had gotten us tickets for the Black Eyed Peas concert on the same night. It was the stupid and selfish decision of a lovesick seventeen-year-old, but I blew off Jordan's ceremony, telling her I had the stomach flu. I couldn't even enjoy the concert, but Ryan's stupid friend Todd posted a picture of us at the show on Facebook that made it look like we were having a blast without a care in the world. I'll never forget what Jordan wrote in the comments section. *Yeah, u look super sick.* I apologized over and over and she eventually forgave me on the surface, but our friendship had never been the same since. Hopefully, that was all about to change.

But Mrs. James's pause made me worry. I wasn't good with confrontation, so I debated whether I should babble out an explanation or just hang up, when I heard what sounded like a strangled sob on the other end of the phone.

"Riley?" Mrs. James asked, her voice quiet and gravelly. I suddenly got the feeling her tone had nothing to do with high school injustices.

"Mrs. James, is everything okay? I was just calling to get Jordan's number. I know it's been a while since—"

She sniffed loudly, then her voice became fuller. "You haven't heard then?"

"No—heard what?"

"She...Jordan..." She started to explain but couldn't finish her sentence. I heard a series of rapid breaths and sniffs. I waited till they slowed and steeled myself against whatever it was that had stolen her words. In a scratchy voice that came out just above a whisper, she said, "She's gone."

"What?" I gasped, my own voice barely audible. Jordan was gone? As in *dead*? The tone of Mrs. James's voice told me that must be it. But when? How? "What *happened*?"

"That's the worst part," she said, the words darting out in staccato. "They—the sheriff—told me she did it...herself. When she didn't come in for work this morning, they checked her apartment and found her...an empty insulin bottle next to her...she was already—" She broke off into heavy sobs, and I pressed the phone close to my ear, as if this would make it easier to absorb what she was saying.

It didn't make any sense. The Jordan I knew would never have killed herself. Then again, the Jordan I knew played with Polly Pockets. The reality was that I hadn't known the grown-up Jordan at all. My last recollection of her was from the Tuttle High graduation night lock-in. She'd been on the decorating committee. I remember her saying hello as Ryan and I walked in. I told her how much I liked the balloons. She'd told me it took three tanks of helium to fill them all up. And that was probably the longest conversation I'd had with her since the tenth grade.

"I'm so sorry," I finally managed. "I had no idea...."

"Robert and I just don't understand," she said. "Everything seemed fine—better than fine, really. She had a good job at the *Times*, an adorable little place in West Bay, she just rescued another dog...and her diabetes was under control with the pump, so she'd never give herself an extra insulin shot...unless it was...because she wanted to..." It sounded almost like she was talking more to herself than to me, asking questions to which she would likely never know the answer—and probably didn't want to. I felt terrible for having inserted myself into this intimate moment when I'd abandoned my friendship with Jordan years ago. I had no right to grieve for her, and certainly not in front of her mother.

"Mrs. James, I am so incredibly sorry. I'll let you go—"

"No, no, please," she said. "I'm glad you called. I was actually thinking about you earlier today...about how you and Jordan used to..." She broke off again, but I knew what she was going to say. A memory, fresh and vivid, flooded my mind of a twelve-year-old Jordan and me sitting in my room huddled over my laptop giggling as we wrote what would be out first column together for the Tuttle Junior High newspaper. Back then I believed I was destined to become a famous obituarist like my granddad, and Jordan was going to be a Pulitzer Prize–winning investigative reporter. We came up with the idea to write an obituary section in the school paper filled with obituaries—not of people, but of things: annoying sayings, fashion trends that needed to die, even the occasional farewell to a particularly gross cafeteria offering. Our first piece, on the death of the phrase "That's hot," was a huge hit, and the Obit Girls were cemented into the history books at Tuttle Junior High.

Subsequent runs featured goodbye tributes to velour track-suits, Crocs 'n socks, Snuggies, and mystery-meat Taco Tuesdays.

Mrs. James took a breath to compose herself and said, "Do you think maybe you could help me write her obituary?"

"Oh, um," I stammered awkwardly. I couldn't possibly help with Jordan's obit. For starters, I didn't even know her anymore. And secondly, I wasn't a professional writer. I'd switched majors from journalism to English after Grand-daddy died. I vowed never to write obituaries—or anything else for a newspaper again—after I'd written my infamous op-ed piece on Granddaddy's death.

"Please, Riley?" Mrs. James pleaded. Her voice, so full of sadness and loss, crept inside my chest and tugged at me from within. "I just can't do it myself. Just the thought of sitting down to write those words."

"Wouldn't you rather have someone at the *Times* do it?"

"No." Her tone left no room for argument. "It has to be written by someone who knew the real her. I know you two weren't close recently, but you knew her. *Really* knew her. If this is to be her last—" She stopped herself, gathering strength to speak the next words. "If this is how people will remember her, it has to tell the real story of who Jordan was. Especially since...."

She could not finish her sentence. *Especially since the cause of death was suicide.* Her mother couldn't bear to let a stranger poke around in Jordan's life and stumble across whatever it was that made living unbearable enough to leave the world in that way. I understood. I understood bet-ter than anyone. And of course, Mrs. James knew I would.

"Your grandfather—" she started to say.

"My granddad taught me many things," I said quietly,

"but his craft wasn't one of them." This was a lie. My grandpa taught me everything he knew about obituary writing.

"Please," she said.

My mind flashed back to Mrs. James making Jordan and me pitchers of lemonade to sell on the corner, Mr. James raking up enormous leaf piles and letting us jump in, joking he was going to lock us in the house until we were thirty whenever the slightly older Dunn boys from next door asked if they could jump too. I remembered that Jordan was an only child, just like me. I allowed myself to imagine how my parents would feel if they lost me.

I agreed to write the obituary a half-second later.

"God is my assignment editor."

—RICHARD PEARSON,
obituaries editor, *Washington Post*

Chapter 3

I stepped outside into the humid night air, grateful that I'd chosen to walk to work that morning. The fresh air would help clear my mind, which was swirling with thoughts and memories of Jordan James. Watching movies in her basement and walking up to the pool together in the summer. The way she'd make lists of the things we would do on our sleepovers. Jordan had always been so sure of everything. She wasn't one of those friends you'd go back and forth with like, "What do you want to do today?" "I don't care. What do *you* want to do today?" Nope. Not Jordan. If you asked her a question, you got an answer. She wanted to make up a dance routine. She wanted macaroni and cheese. She wanted to play Super Smash Bros. She knew exactly what she wanted and what she didn't. Even at age ten. I couldn't believe she was dead. It seemed impossible.

I was due at my parents' house for dinner but decided to make a quick stop into Landry's on the way. My parents had gone vegan after the Rainbow Connection performed at a petting zoo in West Virginia and they shared their stage with a cow, two goats, and a chicken. Mom made a big proclamation after that about how it just isn't right to eat colleagues, and she forced Dad and me to go along with her. I knew whatever dairy-free, colleague-free fare was on the menu that night was not going to cut it for me. This was definitely a comfort food type of evening.

"Hey, Riley," Joe Landry called from the back corner of the store, where he was stacking pints of strawberries.

"Hi, Joe." I grabbed a can of Pringles (okay, two) and a bag of Granny Smith apples, which were mostly for show. As I waited for Joe to come up front, I thought about all the times Jordan and I had stood at that very counter.

The bell on the door jingled, and I turned to see Felicia Davenport and Betsy North walk in. "I can't believe it," Felicia was saying.

"I know," Betsy agreed. "Poor Debbie and Robert."

My jaw clenched. I did not want to hear Jordan's death gossiped about.

They kept their voices low, but in the quiet of the shop, their words were clearly audible. "Poor who?" Joe asked.

"Debbie and Robert James."

"What happened?"

"It's their Jordan. She's gone to be with the Lord," Felicity said in hushed, reverent tones, wiping the corner of her eye.

Joe took a step back to lean against the counter, clearly shaken. "But she was just in here this weekend, bought a fifty-pound bag of dog food." He looked from one lady to the other. "What happened?"

I felt the telltale burning in my cheeks as the three of them looked at me, as if they just noticed I was there—or rather *who* was there.

"Um." Betsy's eyes darted to me and then back to Joe. "Well, I heard the police were, um, called to her home...."

"Yes," Felicity jumped in. "They apparently found her at home. Alone." She widened her eyes at Joe to make sure the implication was clear. It took Joe about two seconds, but once he figured it out, his eyes flicked in my direction. His kind face was full of the cloying, inescapable pity that drowned me every time suicide was mentioned in Tuttle Corner.

"I see," he said.

I stood still, afraid that any participation in this unbearable conversation would lead to tears or anger. Either would add to the legend of Riley Bless-Her-Heart. But I could not stand by and let Jordan become fodder for the rumor mill. I owed her at least that much.

"You guys know she was diabetic," I blurted out. Tuttle Corner had rallied around Jordan after her diagnosis of type I like only a small town could. We organized pancake breakfasts, fun runs, and bake sales all to show support and raise money for juvenile diabetes throughout the years.

"Of course," Betsy and Felicity said in unison, like that's what they had meant the whole time. I knew they were being false, but at least it got us all off the hook.

Joe seized the opportunity. He bagged my food and said, "That all for you?"

<hr>

"We'll establish a journalism scholarship at the high school in her name," my mom said as we sat down to dinner. My mom, who doesn't do sad, had turned into a hurricane of activity upon hearing the news. Her first order of business had been to set up the Tuttle Corner meal circuit. When anyone in town had a baby, an operation, or lost a loved one, the citizens of Tuttle made a schedule to deliver hot meals and stocked their freezers with enough food to ensure that the family wouldn't have to cook for months. My mom was on the horn to Charlotte Van Stone before I'd even been able to tell her about my run-in at Landry's with the Misses Davenport and North.

My dad was another kettle of fish. He started crying when he heard the news. And not in a manly, misty-eyed sort of way. He did the full-on ugly cry.

Mom had made a Tofurky roast for dinner, which I pretended to eat, while Dad snuffled through the meal.

"It's just so shocking," Mom said in between bites.

"I know," I agreed. "It just doesn't seem like the Jordan I grew up with. She was always so in control. I mean, I know we hadn't talked lately, but can someone really change that much in just a few years?"

"Poor Debbie and Robert," Mom said, her fork suspended in midair. "I wonder if they had any idea?"

I shook my head. "Mrs. James said she thought Jordan was doing great. She seemed completely shocked."

"Well, you would be, wouldn't you? How can you ever be prepared for something like that?" Dad said, lost in memories of his own.

"Yeah, I mean, I guess..." I speared a piece of asparagus, desperately wishing my folks kept butter in the house. "But—"

"What is it, Raccoon?" Dad asked.

"Nothing. It's just that I think it's kind of strange that her parents didn't seem to know she was suffering."

My mom raised one eyebrow at me; I knew that look.

"What?" I said, shrugging my shoulders. "Don't you think you guys would know if I were depressed to the point of being suicidal?"

"God forbid," Dad said, making the sign of the cross.

"Dad, we're not Catholic. That doesn't work."

"Still," he said, and then he did it again.

"Riley, what are you getting at?" My mom was like a bloodhound. Once she caught the scent of something, she couldn't rest until she rooted it out.

"I don't know." I pushed back from the table and brought my mostly untouched plate to the sink. "I'm just saying suicide seems so incongruent with everything we know about Jordan."

"Riley." Her voice was a warning.

"What?" I said again, trying to sound all causal and innocent. I turned my back to the table under the guise of rinsing the plate. "I'm just saying...."

A few seconds later, I felt warm hands on my shoulders. "Honey." Mom spoke softly and smoothed my hair with her fingers. "Sometimes a suicide is just a suicide. It's a terrible thing. A cruel, unfair, and heartbreaking thing. But it happens."

I knew she was talking as much about Granddaddy as she was about Jordan. I'd heard this speech before. My parents had been quick to accept the "official" cause of his death as a self-inflicted gunshot wound. I had not.

It had been five years, but I still remembered every detail of the night he died. I was home from college for Labor Day weekend and had the TV on in the kitchen. My parents weren't yet back from their gig in Williamsburg, and Ryan was hunting with his dad, so I was alone eating a frozen Amy's enchilada meal when I heard Rafe Richardson on Channel 7 announce:

Albert Ellison, longtime obituary writer for the Richmond Tribune, *has been found dead from a single gunshot to the head in his home in Tuttle Corner, Virginia. He was sixty-seven years old. Ellison led a storied career writing obituaries for such celebrities as Joe DiMaggio, Princess Diana, Johnny Cash, King Hussein of Jordan, Kevin Newman, Betty Page, and Ronald Regan, among others. But he was perhaps most famous for his series on the twenty-eight schoolchildren killed in the Bridgeport school shooting in 2009. Ellison wrote a complete, individualized obituary for each child murdered that day. When some of the obits were denied due to space constraints, he famously paid out of his own pocket for a four-page spread in the* Tribune *to run them all. His body was discovered by a neighbor earlier this morning. Authorities are investigating the cause of death but do not believe foul play was involved. In other news....*

But there was no other news. Not for me. Not ever. Sheriff Joe Tackett ended up closing the case out as a suicide three days later, which was ridiculous. I pleaded with him to investigate his death as a homicide, but he wouldn't listen. He said all the evidence clearly pointed to a self-inflicted gunshot wound: gun held at close range, angled slightly upward, burn on the side of his temple, gunpowder residue on his hands. They said it was textbook. Except for two things: Granddad didn't own a gun, and he wasn't suicidal.

After Tackett shut me down, I went to Granddaddy's best friend and colleague for over forty years, Hal Flick, and begged him for help. He knew Granddad better than anyone. He had to know Granddad would never have killed himself. But Flick wouldn't discuss it. Wouldn't listen to my theory that maybe something he was working on got him killed. Wouldn't use his connections to look into it more deeply.

"Let it go, Riley," he'd said to me the last time I'd seen him. He shook his head sadly and said, "Let Albert rest in peace now."

But I didn't. I wrote a scathing op-ed about the shoddy police work by Sheriff Tackett, citing all the inconsistencies and details that made me certain my grandfather had not killed himself. Flick tried to talk me out of publishing it, said I'd regret it, but I didn't listen. And the then-editor-in-chief was all too happy to run it, knowing it would be widely read. People in small towns love it when one of their own goes off the rails. It ran in the Sunday edition of the *Times* and was the talk of the town for a solid month. But since I had little more than my own gut feeling to back up my claims of foul play, everyone, including my own parents, thought I was just a young woman overwrought with grief. They suggested I took his death personally since we were so close. Ryan was the only person who believed me, or at least didn't look at me like I was crazy. Instead he held me tight and told me to give 'em hell. It was one of the things that made our bond so strong. And his leaving so painful.

"Mom, that's not what I'm saying." I wriggled free from her grasp and ducked back toward the table to begin clearing up.

"Good," she said. "Because you've been given a great honor to help the Jameses write Jordan's final tribute."

"And I know you'll do a bang-up job!" Dad smiled at me. I rolled my eyes. I swear if you cut my father, he would bleed maple syrup.

"Why do you think she asked me?" I said, voicing the concern that had been gnawing at me ever since my conversation with Mrs. James.

"Because you're a talented writer," Dad said. "You were Dad's prodigy!"

It was impossible to get an honest answer out of my dad if it meant implying I wasn't the best in the world at something. I ignored him and looked at my mom.

"I'm sure she's just overwhelmed," she said. "And you girls were so close—remember you had that cute column together?"

"Yeah, but I hadn't seen in her years."

"Maybe that's why? Your memories of Jordan are from

a more innocent time. Before whatever happened happened, you know?"

I nodded, but that explanation didn't fully satisfy me. I had a feeling that whatever the reason Mrs. James had for wanting me to write Jordan's obit would end up coming back to my granddad. It seemed like most things in my life did.

Dear Ms. Ellison:

My name is Regina H, and I will be your personal romance concierge here at Click.com, your electronic gateway to love! On behalf of everyone at the company, I'd like to congratulate you on the smart choice to join thousands of other top-tier singles who are looking for the best way to forge lasting and meaningful relationships using today's latest technology!

I'd like to thank you for filling out the twenty-three-page questionnaire, uploading the requisite photos, and setting up the monthly auto-debit. I'm thrilled to report that your hard work has already paid off! A highly eligible Click.com member has already placed an arrow in your quiver! #thatwasfast #yougogirl

Ajay257 is a desirable prospect by any measure! A criminology professor at Cardwell College, Ajay257 enjoys hiking, biking, and spending time outdoors. He is an animal lover (prefers dogs) and recently moved to Tuttle County. He says he is looking to meet a nice girl he can spend time with. #awwww

It is in that spirit of fun and adventure that Ajay257 would like to take you on a date to King's Dominion amusement park. #howcuteisthat Please let me know if you would like to accept. I urge you to remember that in the "Additional Thoughts" section of the questionnaire, you specifically said it was time you "got off your butt and rejoined the land of the living." #hereisyourchance

I look forward to hearing from you.

Best,
Regina H, Personal Romance Concierge, Click.com

CHAPTER 4

It seemed absurd to be on a date—at an amusement park no less—one day after finding out about Jordan's death, but there I was. I've always hated amusement parks, with their nausea-inducing rides and incessant cheer, but when Ajay257 asked me out, I said yes, because that is what someone who is leaning into life would do. I told myself Jordan's death was a sign for me to live life while I had the chance. I told myself maybe I didn't really hate roller coasters. Maybe I really loved them and was just holding myself back?

Turns out, I really hated them.

Riley Ellison, twenty-four, shelf clerk at Tuttle Corner Library, perished while riding a rollercoaster aptly named the Hurler while on a blind date at the King's Dominion amusement park.

The date had started out promising. Ajay257 was true to his profile picture—cute, with olive skin, dark eyes, and hair that had been styled into place with just the right amount of gel. If there was one thing I could not abide in a man, it was too much hair gel. I watched him wait for me in front of the ticket office, and he looked nervous, which I found reassuring and even a little emboldening. It was that false sense of swagger that landed me on the Hurler. I should have known better.

"You ready?" Ajay asked. I nodded without looking at him; I kept my eyes straight ahead. As the car began its slow ascent, I couldn't help but notice it was getting harder to breathe. I took a deep breath. Yes, there was definitely a slip-through-your-lungs quality not present at lower elevations. I wondered if anyone ever asphyxiated from the air being too thin at the top of a ride?

Ellison had a previously undiagnosed condition that prevented her lungs from processing the anemic air molecules found at higher altitudes, like those at the crest of Hurler Hill. Tragically, her death could have been prevented if she would have simply been honest in her online dating profile.

"You're gonna love this," Ajay said.

I suppose it's possible he sounded so confident because on my Click.com profile I checked the box next to, "I have a need for speed." Which isn't exactly true. The truth was I had a need for air. Thick, dense air found approximately five feet, four inches off the ground. I must have had three-legged-race PTSD when I filled out that profile.

There were two teenage boys sitting behind us. Teenage boys are like wasps when it comes to sensing fear, and they zeroed in on mine. One kid said loudly to the other, "Remember when that lady fell out at the top of the second loop last year?"

"Dude, they were scraping her off the pavement for months. You can still see the stain!"

A tiny whimper escaped my throat. Ajay leaned toward me and whispered, "Don't listen to them." But he was smiling, like he thought they were funny or something. The desperate, rapidly fading swagger inside me waged one last battle and forced out a chuckle like, *Ha! This is all so fun! And funny! And who cares that we are about to plunge to our deaths?* Fear, bile, and hot dog churned in my gut.

In my quest to lean into life, I had downed a hot dog and a beer minutes before getting on the Hurler. Not the wisest choice for a sometimes vegan with a nervous stomach.

I snuck a glance at Ajay. He was definitely a cutie—very masculine looking with his five o'clock shadow and squared-off jaw. He wasn't all that tall, maybe five-ten, but he was solidly built and lean, the kind of body of someone who stays active but doesn't necessarily lift weights. And he looked younger than he did in his picture online. I tried to imagine walking into a criminology class and finding this guy as the professor. I bet he had a lot of female students asking for extra tutoring. And I'd bet any one of them would have traded places with me on that roller coaster. *If only.*

Our metal death box finally lurched its way to the top and then stopped. The evil geniuses who design these torture traps love this part: the interminable moment when you know you are about to be plunged into oblivion but you are powerless to stop it. My lungs went into overdrive, desperately processing the too-thin bird-air, in and out, in and out, in and out. If I got lucky, maybe I'd pass out and miss the whole thing.

The seconds ticked by, and I knew that if I survived, the only thing that awaited me after fifty-seven seconds of sheer torture was the humiliation of vomiting in front of Ajay257. He looked over at me, his dazzling smile not quite as wide as it had been before. He might have been catching on that I wasn't one hundred percent into this. "You okay?" he asked.

I was so not okay. I was paralyzed by fear. I couldn't even look at him, but I think I shook my head *no* just as the punk behind me leaned forward and said, "Huh? I wonder where this screw came from?" With that, the car jerked forward and we were off.

Dear Miss Ellison:

I was sorry to hear of your less than enthusiastic response to your date with Ajay257. Roller coasters can be frightening, despite the 47-inch height requirement. As you requested, I sent a communication to Ajay257 expressing your apologies for all the crying and your extended stay in the ladies room. You will be relieved to know that he didn't hear you when you screamed "I hate you" during the second loop-de-loop. He thought you said, "I hate this." I assured him that's what you meant to say! And you should know, he declined your offer to reimburse him the $39.99 for your ticket to the theme park and the $20 you offered for his dry cleaning bill. #chivalryisnotdead! Please note that I corrected your profile to select the box "I prefer to keep my feet on the ground." That should help with any further date-planning mishaps!

I am also writing with the exciting news that another Click.com member has recently put an arrow in your quiver! An avid *Star Wars* fan, BenjiC3PO enjoys cosplay, screen printing T-shirts with "bad ass" sayings, and writing fan fiction online. But those aren't the only things he is interested in. He also lists Harry Potter, *The Lord of the Rings*, and playing Magic: The Gathering under "Other Interests." BenjiC3PO has asked me to tell you that he'd like to take you to a park not so far, far, away and prepare a magical feast for you to share under the stars. #hiswordingnotmine

If you'd like to accept BenjiC3PO's offer, please let me know, and I can coordinate a mutually agreeable time.

Best,
Regina H , Personal Romance Concierge, Click.com

CHAPTER 5

So far, my plan to change my life was not going well. I'd vomited on the first date I'd had with a new guy in more than seven years, and instead of reconnecting with my old friend, I was writing her obituary. I told myself that if there was anything good to be found in the wake of Jordan's death, it was a reminder that life was fragile, fleeting, and a gift not to be wasted. Her dying the way she had both strengthened my resolve to fix my life and terrified me, because if someone like Jordan James couldn't make it in this life, what hope was there for a girl like me?

Throughout the day at work, I stole moments of down time to jot down notes and questions for the obit. I desperately wanted the finished product to reflect the feisty, take-no-prisoners girl I'd known back in school. The girl who came to our third-grade class the day after being diagnosed with diabetes and announced, "My doctor says my pancreas quit working. So now I have to get shots every day, and I can't drink soda, which is no big deal because I don't like soda that much, and I'm *not* afraid of needles."

Mrs. James had called me that morning to let me know Jordan's funeral wouldn't be until next week because they were waiting on Mr. James's mother, who was recovering from surgery and couldn't travel till then. When I asked her when she wanted the obit to run, she said, "In a town this size, the weekly newspaper isn't giving anybody breaking news, honey. It's more about having a permanent record. I'd rather you take all the time you need to make sure it feels right." I was relieved to hear her say that. I knew I had a lot of information gathering to do to illuminate the woman Jordan had become and do her memory justice.

Tabitha came into the back room as I was gathering my things to leave just before five o'clock. "Listen, if you don't have anything going on tonight, could you stay to finish up the bio section?" Tabitha knew that I didn't exactly have an active social calendar and she liked to take advantage of it when she could. I'd stayed late several times in the past few months for her because I'd figured it was better than going home to an empty house.

"I can't tonight."

She turned to me, a wry smile on her sharply angled face. "Don't tell me you actually have a date?" Tabitha loved to tease me about being single while simultaneously throwing in my face her engagement to Thad, her ultra-snobby doctor boyfriend whose family owned half the land in Tuttle Corner. *Thad told me we could move onto his father's estate once we're married. Thad says I'm the most beautiful librarian he's ever seen. Thad can do thirty push-ups with me sitting on his back!*

"Nope. No date," I said, my mind flashing back to Ajay257.

"Then stay. It'll free me up to concentrate on some of our bigger-picture issues, like the interlibrary-loan cooperation plan."

I sighed loudly. Tabitha wore me out with her I'm-more-important-than-you attitude. "Tabitha, do you remember Jordan James from high school?" I waited until she gave me a small nod. "Well, she *died* two days ago. And her mom asked me to write her obituary, so I'm a little busy."

Tabitha's mouth froze into a small "o" shape. I knew it was cheap to throw Jordan's death on her like that, but it felt good to shut her up for once.

"I didn't know you two were so close." Her voice was softer now, contrite.

"Well," I cleared my throat, "you don't know everything then, do you?"

Tabitha looked down, and guilt settled upon my shoulders. Not only had I used Jordan's death to justify not working late, but now I'd misrepresented my relationship with her to make Tabitha feel bad. Even if she was a self-important know-it-all, it still wasn't right to exploit what happened with Jordan for my own purposes.

But before I had a chance to apologize, she said, "My mom told me she'd passed away but didn't know exactly what happened. Was it her diabetes?"

For some reason, saying suicide felt like a betrayal, like I was giving too much of Jordan's private life away. I knew she'd find out what happened eventually, but I wasn't going to be the one to say it. I averted my eyes and muttered, "I'm not sure. They're still looking into it."

———•———

When I got to the *Tuttle Times* office, I was greeted by Kay Jackson, the paper's managing editor. She looked like your typical mid-market newspaper journalist: tired, stressed, and heavily caffeinated. She'd moved down to Tuttle from Delaware, and though she'd been here for four years, she was still considered the new kid by many. I had never met her before, but she seemed nice enough to me.

Kay talked quickly as she walked me back to Jordan's cubicle. "Such a shame," she said without looking back. "Good kid. Good reporter." As we walked, she pointed out the departments in one-word descriptions, which was apt, as most were one-desk departments. "Classifieds. Crime. City. Obits." These days, the obits that ran in the *Times* were almost always sent in by family or funeral homes, which made them, technically, death notices and not true obituaries. Dwindling sales and budgets forced many smaller papers to cut positions for obituary writers. But every now and then when a person with strong ties to the community died, they'd write an original or, in the case of someone famous, pick one up from the AP wire. I'd actually seen only one original in the past five years; it had been Granddaddy's.

"Not sure what I can tell you about Jordan," Kay said as we reached her cubicle. "She was a hard worker. Ambitious. Always on time, didn't complain. She was a junior reporter, which means she mostly supported the work of more senior folks, so she bounced around between departments and assisted with all kinds of pieces, from crime to lifestyle."

As I stood in the newsroom, my mind went blank. Why had I wanted to come here? I guess I thought I'd get a sense of the woman Jordan turned out to be, something I certainly needed if I was going to write about her. But what did I think I'd find at her desk? I scanned her cubicle. I saw several pictures of dogs stuck to her bulletin board with brightly colored tacks, a picture of Jordan smiling alongside her parents on what looked like a golf course, a small statue of a lighthouse made of heavy wire, and a quote from Buddha that read, "There are only two mistakes one can make along the road to truth: not going all the way, and not starting." Sitting on the edge of the desk was an engraved nameplate that read Jordan Blaise James. It was obviously not something company issued, and I wondered if it had been a gift from her parents, who were so clearly proud of their only child. I pulled open the single desk drawer and found nothing but a few pens, some sticky notes, and a blood-sugar test kit. The contents of her desk were efficient, practical, and responsible—just like their owner.

I felt Kay looking at me and tried to think of something to ask her so it didn't seem like I was wasting her time. "Um, did she have a favorite department?"

"I don't know." She thought for a second. "She seemed to like writing the human-interest pieces—you know, the feel-good stuff. Pretty common for younger reporters. She was helping research a profile we're doing on Juan Pablo Romero and seemed pretty into it."

Juan Pablo Romero was a controversial captain of industry in Tuttle County. He was the proprietor of several Mexican restaurants in the area and had recently gotten into real estate development. About six months ago, Romero shocked the community by announcing he was planning to donate a huge plot of land to the Tuttle County Parks Department. He not only planned to donate the land but pledged to build a massive recreational complex, something we desperately needed, complete with playground equipment and a running/biking trail. The cost was estimated at over eight million dollars, and Romero reportedly planned to foot the entire bill himself. It was to be called Little Juan Park, after Romero's only son.

The piece was scheduled to run next month, Kay told me. Will Holman was the senior reporter, and Jordan was assigned to help him.

Kay said, "You might want to talk with Holman. They worked together pretty closely. He might be able to help—" She cut herself off and looked at me, as if for the first time wondering who I was and what I was doing there. "What is it you're looking for again?"

"Well..." I cleared my throat to stall for time. "Her mom asked if I would write her obit-"—too embarrassed to use the abbreviation in front of someone actually in the business, I finished the word after an awkward pause—"-uary. We were good friends growing up, but I haven't seen her lately, so I just wanted to talk to some of the people she worked with to see what she was like."

Kay's eyes sharpened. She had the polygraph gaze of a seasoned reporter. "The sheriff said it was a pretty cut-and-dried suicide. You're not chasing the theory that there was foul play involved, are you?"

"No!" I said, thinking of my mother's similar accusation the night before.

"Because I've seen this before. Suicides are rough. People never want to believe their daughter/wife/husband/friend would do it. They look for alternatives."

My face was candy-apple red, I was sure of it. "I'm not looking for alternatives. I just want to get a sense of Jordan's life so I can write about it."

"What'd you say your name was again?"

Damn. "Riley." I left it at that, very much on purpose.

"Yeah, Riley, I got that part. Riley what-again?"

Here we go. I took a deep breath and said, "Ellison."

As soon as I did, Kay Jackson's entire face lit up. "You're Albert Ellison's granddaughter! You wrote that—"

"Yes, but—"

"Flick!" Kay's loud voice rang out in the mostly empty newsroom. From the corner I heard the sound of shuffling footsteps. *Double damn.*

"What?"

"You'll never guess who's here." She winked at me, the whites of her eyes sparkling against her dark skin. Having lived here for only four years, she knew enough to know my granddad had been friends with Flick, but obviously not that my family didn't speak to him anymore. My heart was beating fast now, and I could feel my pulse pound in my ears. But I didn't move.

"What is it?" the growly voice said again, and I could tell he was getting closer. I steeled myself. Flick turned the corner of the maze of cubicles, holding onto the tops of the walls for balance. He looked old.

"Hi, Flick," I said.

His eyes snapped up with an agility that I wouldn't have anticipated, given his lumbering gait. He might have been old, but Flick was clearly still sharp. "Riley."

I smiled, an automatic response. Flick did not. He looked at me, one eye squinted halfway down, as if he was staring at a big pile of manure that needed spreading. "What are you doing here?" He never was one for small talk.

Kay answered for me. "Riley was a friend of that junior reporter who killed herself. She's here to gather info for the obit."

"You're writing obits now, are you?" Flick did that old-man snort-laugh perfected by character actors in old movies.

My face flushed again. "I'm just helping out her mom," I mumbled without looking at him. I turned to Kay. "I've got to get going, but thanks for your help." I gave Flick a look that I hoped conveyed my deep and thorough dislike before turning to leave.

"Riley," Kay said. I stopped. She held out a planner, presumably Jordan's. "Maybe this'll help. And email Holman. He's a bit of an odd duck, but he'll talk to you."

"Thanks." I could feel the burn of Flick's intense stare in my peripheral vision, but I didn't look at him. I turned again to walk out.

"How's your family?" His rough voice softened slightly at the word "family."

I stopped again and turned, this time looking him squarely in his watery blue eyes. "Fine. We're all *fine.*" We stared at each other for a long moment before I turned and walked away. I left with my heart thumping against my chest wall so loud I was sure both Kay and Flick could hear it.

Seeing Flick again after all this time made fresh the pain of everything I'd lost when Granddaddy died. Flick had been like a second grandpa to me back in the day, but he abandoned me when I needed him most and I'd never forgive him for that. In the quiet of my car it dawned on me that maybe my unfinished business with Hal Flick had been the real reason I'd come to the *Times.*

I promised my parents years ago that I'd let my suspicions about Granddaddy's death go, and I had. They were worried about me, and maybe a little embarrassed after the op-ed. And so for five years, I had abandoned my research. I'd stopped interviewing his friends and co-workers, stopped making lists of people who could possibly mean that sweet old man harm. I'd done it for my parents, and for Ryan, and, if I'm being honest, for myself. It was easier and less painful to let it go. So I went back to college, came back to work at the only job I'd ever had, and made plans to spend the rest of my life as Mrs. Ryan Sanford. I convinced myself that moving on was what my granddad would have wanted for me. But I always felt Flick knew more than he let on about his best friend in the whole world's sudden "suicide." And his strange reaction to me now—his inexplicable acerbity—did nothing to convince me otherwise. I was the one who had the right to be angry, not him. He should have been glad, or at least pleasantly surprised to see me in that newsroom, but he wasn't. I felt a flicker of curiosity, but then remembered my promise to my parents and did my best to let it go.

CHAPTER 6

My hands were shaking as I fumbled for my phone. It had been four days since I'd had any communication with Ryan, and I knew I should not be initiating contact now. This was the longest we'd gone without talking or texting in maybe forever. It was one of the most dysfunctional things about our relationship—or rather about our breakup. Even though there was a part of me that hated him, we still talked all the time, still said "I love you," and still told each other every detail of our lives. In fact, there were times I could almost convince myself that we were simply in a long-distance relationship and hadn't really broken up at all. But that was part of the delusional thinking that had kept me from moving on, and I knew it needed to end. So as a part of my new life plan, I told myself I was not going to go running to Ryan every time I needed to talk. And I meant it. *Except just this once.* In that moment I really needed to hear his voice. There weren't many people in this world who could understand my complicated relationship with Hal Flick, but Ryan was one of them. So like an addict who thinks she can just have one taste, I tapped his name on my phone, still in the top slot under Favorites.

He picked up on the fifth ring. "Hey, Riles," he said. "Whass up?" His words were soft around the edges like watercolor paint. "Where you been lately?"

"Hi." I paused, wishing I hadn't called. "Have you been drinking?" I knew better, but I couldn't stop myself. A snort erupted from his throat, and then he started giggling.

Ah. Not drinking, smoking. "Whatever," I said. "I was just calling because I thought you might like to know that Jordan James died yesterday."

"Oh, man," he said, suddenly sounding richer and more lucid. "What happened?"

I gave him the quick version, then told him I'd be writing her obituary.

"That's great. I mean, obviously not about Jordan, but I think it's great you're going to write the obit. It's your calling, babe. Always has been."

His words washed over me, comforting me and melting away some of my earlier anger. I was still annoyed at how high he sounded, but I needed a friendly ear. I opened my mouth to confess how overwhelmed I was feeling after seeing Flick again when I heard the faint sound of laughter in the background. *Girl* laughter.

"Who is that?"

"Who is what?"

"Ryan, are you with someone right now?"

I heard the laugh again, this time it was louder, throaty, and devious. "Oh yeah, Ridley is here, and we're working on a—"

I punched the end button on the steering wheel so hard it made the car veer slightly to the left. White-hot anger bubbled up inside me. Ridley was there. Of course. Ridley, Ryan's new "friend" whom I'd come to think of as the bizarro-me because she was my exact opposite in every way. First of all, her name was *Ridley*. I mean, seriously? Riley/Ridley. It was laughable. Plus, she was also twenty-four years old but had white-blond hair and ice-blue eyes, was super athletic, and was, according to Ryan, "totally laid back and cool." This was all in sharp contrast to my dark hair and eyes, upper-body strength of an anemic kitten, and tendency to worry about, well, everything.

"She's such a badass," Ryan gushed to me a month ago. "Did you know she was part of the Junior Olympic snowboarding team in Sweden?" He actually asked me that! I mean, why would I know that? It's not like I followed Swedish snowboarding. And lately it seemed he tried to work her into every conversation we had. *Ridley showed me how to do a one-eighty on my board. Ridley has a tattoo of a wolf on her ankle. Ridley sprouted wings and flew to Mars where she was crowned Queen of the Badasses.* It was pathetic the way he worshiped her.

Riley Ellison, twenty-four, perished on Main Street, when her Honda Fit spontaneously caught fire upon hitting a speed of more than 120 mph. Ellison was distraught over a recent conversation with her ex-boyfriend, which caused her to lose control of her vehicle. She is survived by her parents, an unfinished obituary for an old friend, and a half-eaten block of Manchego cheese in her refrigerator.

I made myself slow down. There was no point in crashing my car over Ryan's stupid obsession with stupid Ridley. After all, if I died, how could I gloat when he came crawling back to me? Which I was still sixty-seven-percent sure he was going to do.

As I got my breathing back under control, I realized it was a mistake to have hung up on him like that. I should have played it cool and subtly dropped the hint that I too was seeing someone new. I mean, that was sort of true, wasn't it? Maybe my date with Ajay257 hadn't exactly been the stuff of romance novels, but still. I had gone out on a date with a cute, gainfully employed man. And before the roller coaster, we actually had a pretty nice time. He was funny, as I recall, and smart. Had it not been for the vomiting, who knows where it might have led?

Dear Ms. Ellison:

I am delighted (and I'll admit, a little surprised) to inform you that Ajay257 has accepted your invitation for another date! I think we can assume he didn't think you were a "complete psycho" as you suggested. #hotmessisthenewblack

Before your date, I'd like to make you aware of a service provided by Click.com. In addition to our Romance Concierge service, we offer highly trained Date Preparation Specialists. These specialists can assist you with everything from wardrobe concerns to hair-styling solutions, as well as give you personalized conversation starters and even help you find just the right wording when telling your new love interest about past relationships, money problems, past incarcerations, etc. No matter what your situation, our DPS have got you #covered! #safetynet

To give you an idea of what they can do for you, I've contacted Gemma T, from our DPS division, who had the following advice for your upcoming lunch date: Avoid choosing a thick cut of meat. You may need to spend extra time chewing, and this could lead to some unflattering moments—or the fallout from an unexpected piece of gristle. Instead, she suggested choosing a nice, flaky white fish. #noflossnecessary!

This is exactly the kind of useful and insightful information that could be yours for an additional $12.95/week. Please let me know if you are interested in upgrading your package to include your personal DPS! #opportunity!

Best,
Regina H, Personal Romance Concierge, Click.com

CHAPTER 7

When I arrived at work the next morning, Dr. H was again in his office with the door closed. I still had about half the bio section left to catalog but decided instead to get started on sorting books for the Friends of Tuttle Corner book sale coming up next week.

It was an average morning, patrons flowing in and out in a steady pattern and just enough work to keep me busy but not frantic. Just before noon, the library was empty when I heard a loud popping sound come from Dr. H's office. It sounded like a firecracker exploding. Then I heard a crashing clatter of broken glass. Terrified, I flung open the door to his office and saw Dr. Hershel Harbinger holding a pistol, looking even more dumbfounded than I was.

"I—I'm sorry, dear." He looked down at the gun in his hand as if it had just magically appeared there. "Um, I'm not quite sure what happened." He was in shock. His potted orchid lay in ruins on the ground by his desk.

"You shot your plant, that's what!" I rushed toward the paralyzed Dr. H and took the pistol from his hand. I held it with two fingers so the business end was pointed at the floor and dropped it into the small waste basket by the door. I was not comfortable around guns, even though Ryan had taken me to the range a few times. A sad excuse for a date, but not entirely uncommon in small-town America. "What the heck were you doing?"

Dr. H shuffled to his chair and sat down, his eyes glued to the flowerpot in pieces on his floor. "I, well, I was just...I wanted to see if the old thing still worked, I guess...." He put a hand to his forehead. His fingers trembled with shock.

I softened my tone. "It's okay. No one got hurt." I knelt and started to pick up some of the jagged shards on the rug.

"But my orchid—"

"We'll get you another." I peeked out front to make sure nobody had come in during the commotion. It was all clear. I walked back in and sat down across from him. He rubbed his forehead with one hand but said nothing.

"Dr. H?" I asked. "Is everything okay?" This was a stupid question. The man just assassinated an orchid by discharging a loaded weapon inside a library. Clearly, everything was not okay.

He took a deep breath in and regained some of his usual composure. "Well, no, Riley, everything isn't okay. But it will be. I can assure you of that."

"Are you in some kind of trouble? Because I'll help you if you are!"

"Dear girl." He looked at me with his warm, crinkly eyes. "You are so sweet. But I don't want you to worry about me. I can take care of myself."

I started to argue, but he cut me off. "Would you mind terribly grabbing the dust pan from the back?"

"Dr.—"

"Thank you, Riley," he said in a firm tone he almost never used with me. His eyes locked onto mine directly. "That's all."

After spending another hour in his office with the door

closed, Dr. H emerged like nothing had happened. He
made small talk, helped me with a purchase order I was
working on, walked over to Landry's, and brought back another arching white orchid, which he placed on the corner
of his desk exactly where the other had been. No one but us
would ever know it wasn't the original.

———•——•———

I was distracted the rest of the day. I had no idea what was
upsetting Dr. H, but I knew in my gut it was something
big. I didn't buy that line about wanting to see whether his
old gun worked, but because he seemed both fragile and
resolute in his desire not to talk about the incident, I didn't
press him. I just wished he'd let me help.

After he left for the day in the late afternoon, I called
my mom to see if she'd heard any gossip that might make
sense of Dr. H's odd behavior. She hadn't.

"He's probably telling you the truth, honey," she said,
her voice tinged with impatience at my inability to take
anything at face value. "Don't worry about Dr. H. He's a
grown man and can take care of himself. Now. Onto more
important stuff. You never told me about your date the
other day! Did you two make a luuuuuuuv connection?"

"Um, no."

"Is he not your type? He sounded so nice."

"He was—is—nice, but it just didn't go well."

"What does that mean, Riley?" She sounded impatient
again.

"If you must know, Mother, I cried."

"You cried?"

"Yes."

"Why?"

"Because he took me on a roller coaster."

"But you hate roller coasters."

"Hence the crying."

"Why would this man take you on a roller coaster if you hate them?"

"Because I told him I liked them."

"Why on earth would you do that?"

I sighed, a sound I patented back in my sullen high school days. "Because I wanted him to think I was cool. You know, the kind of laid-back girl who does cool, fun things." As soon as I heard myself say the words, I realized what I'd done. I was, without realizing it, trying to be more like the bizarro-me, the one Ryan was currently into as opposed to the boring version he left behind. My eyes started to well.

My mom lowered her voice and spoke softly. "Riley, you are perfect just the way you are. You should never, *ever*, feel you need to be someone else to please a man."

Her words settled onto my shoulders like a warm blanket, but I wasn't about to let her know that. One of the constants in my relationship with my mother was that she provided empathy when I needed it most, while I pretended not to need it at all. I cleared my throat and said loudly, "Anyway...I thought maybe I'd see if we could try again?"

"That's a great idea! Like a date do-over!"

"Something like that."

"Have I told you lately how proud I am of you?" I could practically see her smile through the phone. "Seven months ago, I was afraid you'd never stop crying. And now look at you. You're dating, you're writing again. You're really stepping up to the plate."

I wondered how much of her emotional reaction was pride and how much was relief. I know how worried my mom had been about me after Ryan left.

"Honey, you have to get out of bed," I remember her

pleading with me as she stood in my dark room three days after he'd left, literally pulling me out by my arms. I hadn't wanted to get up. I hadn't wanted to eat or read or go outside. I hadn't wanted to do anything. I missed a whole week of work. I can't say that I ever thought about killing myself, especially after losing Granddaddy that way, but back then, I certainly didn't feel like I had much to live for.

"I'm trying, Mom," I said. "I really am."

CHAPTER 8

Ajay257 lived in West Bay, a small bedroom community about fifteen minutes west of Tuttle Corner, but said he had some business in Tuttle the next day, and so we planned to meet on our lunch breaks. I'd chosen the Rosalee Tavern as our meeting place partly because it was one of the only places in town without the word "hut" or "shack" in the title, but also out of spite. Rosalee's had been my place with Ryan. It was where we'd celebrated all of our relationship milestones. I figured I'd casually let it slip to Ryan that I had a lunch date there, and then he could see how it felt to be replaced.

A red-lipped Rosalee greeted me with a smile. And a single menu.

"Um," I said, tucking a strand of my dark hair behind my ear, "I'm actually meeting someone today."

"*D'accord*," she said casually, with her exquisite French accent that I suspected was as much a reason for the restaurant's popularity as the food. Tuttle Corner, not known for embracing outsiders, had made an exception for Rosalee when she moved here over a decade earlier. She'd come to America as an au pair for a prominent family up in Washington, DC. No one knows the exact story, but rumor has it she'd had an affair with the dad, and when his wife found out, she insisted Rosalee leave immediately. Instead of sending her back to France, the husband moved her down here (just three short hours away from DC) and set her up with this café. Whether it was her mysterious nature, her good looks, or her blind confidence, Rosalee was immediately adopted as Tuttle's token exotic foreigner.

She suppressed a slight smile as she plucked another menu from the hostess stand and led me to a table by the window. "Enjoy, *mademoiselle.*"

The first time I came in without Ryan, Rosalee had given me a chocolate croissant on the house and said, "The best revenge is living well." Then, in the perfectly offhanded way of French women, she added, "And it never hurts to take another lover."

I wondered what she'd think when Ajay walked in. One could argue that he was definitely a more impressive prospect than Ryan. He was handsome, smart, a productive member of society—and, most importantly, actually interested in me. It may have been vengeance that had gotten me there, but as I sat in the café that day, I caught a flickering glimpse of a future in Tuttle Corner that didn't include Ryan Sanford. It was the closest thing I'd felt to excitement in a long while.

There were still a few minutes until Ajay was due to arrive. I took out my phone and checked it. No new messages. I took a sip of lemon water and debated unrolling my silverware from the napkin, but then decided it would look too eager. The last thing I needed to do was look too eager. I checked the time on my phone again. Nine and a half minutes to go. *Why did I get here so early?* I hated sitting alone at restaurants. I felt like everyone was looking at me and thinking, "Poor Riley, all alone. Bless her heart."

Since I hadn't thought to bring a book, I reached into

my bag and pulled out Jordan's planner. I flicked through the pages. Budget meetings, pitch sessions, story deadlines, interview appointments—Jordan had all the entries you'd expect a young journalist to have noted in her planner. June 21st staff meeting at 9 a.m. June 23rd parents' anniversary dinner. On June 28th, in red pen she'd written "Walk the Moon in concert at the National" with a heart next to it. Was the heart because she loved the band…or the person she was going with? Next Monday, she had a vet appointment. And the weekend after next, she was co-hosting a wedding shower for someone named Andie. This didn't look like the calendar of someone who was depressed, let alone suicidal. I made a mental note to call Andie and see if she had any clues as to what had been going on in Jordan's life.

"Riley Ellison!" An aging, honeyed voice broke through my thoughts. It was Eudora Winterthorne. If you looked up "steel magnolia" in the dictionary, you'd see Eudora's picture. She had flawless makeup and perfectly coiffed silver hair swept up into a chic chignon, and she was wearing a fuschia silk shantung blouse and white linen wide-legged trousers. She smiled as Faye rolled her up to my table. "How lovely to see you again, darling."

"Hello, Mrs. Winterthrone." I rose to kiss her cheek and gave Faye a hug while I was up.

"Sit, sit." She motioned at my chair and furrowed her perfectly penciled-in brows. "I can't stand talking to people's middles."

Obediently, I sat.

"Now, Riley," Mrs. Winterthorne began, "how are you holding up?" She'd always made it her business to know everyone else's, so I wasn't surprised by the question. Everyone in town said the only secret Eudora Winterthorne ever kept was her age.

"I'm doing fine," I said. "It's just so sad." I thought of all the things listed in Jordan's planner that she would never get to do.

"Sad?" She practically choked on the word. "Plain stupid is more like it!" Mrs. Winterthorne was known to be a little fiery, but this seemed harsh even for her.

"Well, I mean—"

"I can't understand what that boy was thinking."

"Wait, what boy?" I thought she was talking about Jordan.

"Ryan, of course!" She looked at me like I was insane.

Ryan? No one had asked me about him in months. Maybe Mrs. Winterthorne's mind was finally beginning to slip?

"Oh, I'm fine about him."

"Really?" Her eyes narrowed. "I would have thought it would have been quite a shock?"

"Well, it was at first," I said, eyeing the door for Ajay. "But, you know, life goes on!" I forced a hearty chuckle.

"Hmpf," she said, "I mean, to think he just—"

Rosalee appeared out of nowhere and interrupted her thought. "Your table, *mesdames.*"

"C'mon now, Eudora." Faye smiled at me as she tipped Mrs. Winterthorne back on her wheels to turn her round. "See you later, Riley."

"Give my best to your mother," Mrs. Winterthorne said as she was being rolled away.

As I slid Jordan's planner back into my back, I was startled to see Ajay standing in front of our table.

"Oh, hi!" I said and stood up so quickly I knocked Jordan's planner to the floor.

He bent down to pick it up. "Here you go." Our fingertips brushed together as I took it back from him. I felt a current of attraction that took me by surprise.

"What a cool place," Ajay said as we both settled into our chairs. He gave me a toothpaste-commercial-quality smile. Had I been too nervous the other day to realize just how handsome he was? The smooth brown skin, the coffee-bean eyes, and the wavy black hair. His exotic good looks made him look slightly out of place in Tuttle Corner. But in the best possible way. Out of the corner of my eye, I saw Rosalee give me an approving nod.

I felt a nervous flutter in my belly, the kind I got in sixth grade gym class when it was time for the captains to choose teams for dodgeball. "Is this your first time here?"

"Yeah," he said, "I've heard good things, though. Been meaning to try it. By the way," he said, looking up from his menu, "I'm really sorry about the roller coaster thing—"

I held up a hand to stop him. "Not your fault. I was just having a rough day."

He smiled. "Fair enough."

Rosalee came to take our order, and we sat in a small lull of silence after she left. Having gotten most of the what-do-you-do/where-did-you-grow-up questions out of the way on the last date, we were free to talk about slightly more personal things. He asked me if I'd always wanted to be a librarian.

"Well," I said, blushing, "I'm not actually a librarian."

"Oh, I thought you said—"

"I did, I mean, I do work at the library," I said quickly. "But I'm not a proper librarian. Librarians have degrees in library science, and there's no undergraduate program for that. I was an English major, so technically, I can't call myself a librarian." I looked down and fiddled with my knife, seeing Tabitha's sneering face in my mind.

"Who knew?" he said with a half-smile. "You know, you

could have just called yourself a librarian, and I'd never
have known the difference."

"But then our relationship would have been built on
lies." It was out of my mouth before I could think about
how it sounded. *Our relationship?* We'd had one failed date
and were fifteen minutes into a second, and I called what
we had a relationship? What the hell was wrong with me?
I laughed to try to cover it up. With any luck, he'd think I
was kidding.

It was hard to tell Ajay's reaction, mostly because I was
too embarrassed to look at him, but I could feel his dark
eyes on me. After a beat he said, "Well, I say if you work in
a library, you're a librarian. At least in my book." Then he
made the rim-shot noise.

I laughed, this time for real. "What about you? You said
you moved here from New Jersey?"

"Yeah, I was looking to make a change and a job opened
up teaching at Cardwell College."

"And you teach criminology?"

"Sort of." He leaned forward on his elbows. "I'm teaching a class on explosives in the criminal justice program. I
did some work for the NJPD Bomb Squad, so I was a natural fit for the position."

"Wow. I'm impressed."

"Don't be. It isn't like in the movies," he said. "People
think it's all sweating over whether to cut the blue or the
red wire. But it's mostly a lot of boring lab work. Teaching
is much scarier."

We talked through our salads, the conversation pleasant and easy. I found, to my surprise, that I was able to relax
around Ajay, despite my tendency to get nervous around
guys I find attractive. When Rosalee placed the bill on
the table, she made eye contact with Ajay first. "It was a

pleasure, *monsieur*." Then she winked and nodded at me. "*Mademoiselle*."

"A friend of yours?" he asked.

I smiled, my cheeks heating up again. I reached for the check. It had been me who suggested the date, after all.

"Not a chance." He swiped the check out from under my grasp. "What would your friend think of me if I let you pay?"

Okay. I hate admitting this, because it was a little old-fashioned and probably not very feminist of me, but I liked that he did that. It made me feel special. With Ryan, I had paid for nearly everything, because he almost always forgot his wallet.

Once we were outside on the sidewalk, Ajay said, "I'm really glad we did this again."

Standing there together directly in front of Rosalee's window, the nervous feeling in my stomach was back. In a few seconds we would say goodbye, and I wasn't sure how that was supposed to go. Do I lean in for a kiss? Stick my hand out for a cordial handshake? Neither option seemed quite right. I had been out of the dating loop for so long I wasn't sure of the etiquette. I cursed myself for not springing for the extra $12.95 for the DPS.

"Me too," I said, too nervous to look him in the eye. "And I'm sorry again about the other day. That was," a tight laugh escaped my throat, "really embarrassing."

"No worries. Everyone has off days." Then he reached out and touched my forearm. It wasn't an intimate gesture, but it wasn't wholly un-intimate either. Somewhere between *Mazel tov on your bat mitzvah* and *I like you*.

What happened next, I'll blame on the sheer terror I felt over the prospect of a goodbye kiss. There can really be no other explanation for what I said other than just needing to say something—anything—to stall for time. "Yeah, actually I'd just heard that my friend from high school had passed away, so I wasn't at my best."

As soon as I said it I was horrified. I couldn't believe I used Jordan's death like that. First, I used it to shame Tabitha, and now I was using it as an excuse for being a roller-coaster wimp. Jordan's death had nothing to do with how I behaved on our date and I knew it. I was going to hell. It was that simple.

"I'm so sorry, Riley."

"Thanks." I looked at my shoes, guilt bearing down on me. Beads of sweat gathered at my hairline—and it wasn't just because it was ninety-eight degrees outside. "It wasn't—I mean, we hadn't actually been close for a while. It was just...you know, um, sad."

"I do know." Ajay was looking at me when I finally raised my eyes off the pavement. His look was so filled with kindness and understanding, I couldn't take it anymore.

"I'm lying!" I blurted out.

Ajay's face changed from empathy to confusion in a split second.

"I'm sorry. I mean, not completely or anything. I mean, I am completely sorry—but I didn't completely lie. My friend really did pass away, that's true, but it wasn't the reason I cried on the Hurler." The words were falling out of my mouth faster than I could catch them. "I lied to you about liking roller coasters. The truth is I *hate* them. In fact, I hope I never, ever, ever have to go on one ever again. And just so you know, I hate beer too. And hot dogs. Well, I don't really *hate* hot dogs, but I don't usually eat them. My parents are vegans, and even though I'm not, a little of their craziness has rubbed off on me, and hot dogs just kind of cross the line, you know?"

Ajay's mouth hung open. He didn't know. But I kept talking, my words like a runaway train. "So the thing is, you seem really nice, and despite what it seems like, I mostly *am* an honest person, so I just couldn't let you leave here thinking that I cried on our date because my friend died. Or that I liked roller coasters...or beer...or hot dogs...."

His handsome face had contorted into a mixture of shock and something else. Was it embarrassment? Confusion? Disgust? He opened his mouth to say something but then closed it again.

I was mortified. Why couldn't I have just said "Thanks for lunch" like a normal person? I *had* to come clean. I *had* to tell him the absolute truth. I could see myself reflected in his sunglasses—two small tufts of hair above each of my ears had come loose and they looked like two tiny question marks. I looked like a crazy person. I *sounded* like a crazy person. The hot sting of tears began to collect behind my eyes. Oh God no. *No. No. No. No.* I could not cry in front of this man again! I had to get out of there fast.

"So anyway, that's all I wanted to say. Thanks for lunch!" I leaned up on my toes, kissed his cheek, and raced off like a cockroach at first light. I didn't look back to see how long Ajay stood there trying to figure out what in the hell had just happened.

Dear Miss Ellison:

I am sorry about your emotionally turbulent lunch date with Ajay257. While I'm not sure I can agree with your assessment that you are a "total loser" or a "complete spaz," please note that we all find ourselves feeling blue from time to time, and I do not think this makes you an "undatable trainwreck." #cheerupbuttercup

But since you do seem to be having a hard time right now, I wanted to make you aware of an additional service available through Click.com that might be able to help! Our Mental Readiness Service, or MRS division, specializes in helping love-seekers reign in their unruly emotions and get their heads back in the game! Being overly emotional during the beginning of a relationship can make you seem needy. And we all know the stink of desperation kills a budding romance faster than bad breath! Our MRS division can provide you with options to help soothe your insecurities through personalized daily affirmations, guided meditations, and special yoga retreats for the romantically challenged! For a mere $14.95/month, our MRS division will put your emotions through a boot camp and whip you into shape! If you are interested in adding the MRS to your current plan, please let me know! #loveisntforsissies

Best,
Regina H, Personal Romance Concierge, Click.com

CHAPTER 9

On Kay Jackson's advice, I'd called Will Holman, the reporter for whom Jordan worked, and set up a meeting for that evening after work. I waited for him on the curb in front of the *Times* building. We were supposed to meet here at 7 p.m., but I had arrived at 6:52. Early again. I took the extra few minutes to check my email. I wasn't exactly looking to see if Regina H had any news for me about Ajay, but I wasn't exactly *not* looking for that either.

"Excuse me?" I felt a tap on my left shoulder and jumped about a foot in the air.

"Sorry." A man, presumably Will Holman, stood beside me wearing a yellow T-shirt that read *A Doctor Today Keeps the Daleks Away*. "Didn't mean to scare you. Are you Riley?"

I swallowed my heart back into my chest. "Yes. Mr. Holman?"

"You can just call me Holman."

"Nice to meet you," I said, squashing the quiver in my voice, "Holman." If I sounded nervous, it's because I was. And it wasn't just that he somehow snuck up on me. It was that interviewing an award-winning investigative journalist would make anyone nervous. Especially someone who wasn't a real reporter (or even a real librarian). I had done a little research on Will Holman and learned that he had won the Worth Bingham Prize for Investigative Journalism three years ago, at the age of twenty-six, for a piece that exposed abusive group homes for children in southern Virginia. He uncovered that kids were being abused and locked into closet-size rooms for breaking arbitrary rules like not eating all their carrots. His exposé led to the state taking action against the group, including the arrest of several community leaders.

I stuck out my hand to shake his. He had one of those limp-fish handshakes. Ew.

"Nice to meet you, too," he smiled, but it didn't look like a natural position for his face. Holman was definitely an odd duck, as Kay Jackson had said. He was tall and lanky, with eyes so round it gave him the appearance of a claymation character out of a Wallace and Grommet movie. His round, wire-framed glasses did nothing to lessen the effect, nor did the fact that he appeared not to blink. Ever. He stood on the sidewalk, his circle-eyes wide open, as if he were appraising me for auction.

"Um, do you want to talk in your office? Or Coffee Zone?" I gestured to the place across the street.

"Nope," he said. "I think we should talk off the grid."

I laughed. He didn't.

"I'm serious," he said. "I don't like to have sensitive conversations in crowded places. I know a great spot we can go. No cell towers, no drones. Plus, they have the best pulled pork you'll ever eat."

Off the grid? No drones? Pulled pork? What the hell was going on here? I must have been desperate for information, because I was actually considering getting into a blue Dodge Neon and going "off the grid" with this guy.

"Um," I said, stalling for time.

"I can see why you're hesitant. But I can assure you I am not a threat to your safety."

Oddly, I believed him. *That's probably the last thought Ted Bundy's victims had, too,* I heard my mother's voice saying inside my head. I wasn't sure if it was his earnest expression or my curiosity about what was so sensitive that he had to take me off the grid to discuss it, but I got in his car.

Riley Ellison, expired at the age of twenty-four after accepting an invitation to go eat pulled pork with a man she didn't know at all. Her remains were found chopped up and frozen inside ice cubes that the perpetrator used to chill his iced tea for months after her death.

Holman regarded me before pulling out onto Whistler Avenue. "I think you have a nice face." But he didn't say this with the emphasis on "face" or even "nice." The emphasis was on "think," so it gave the whole sentence a questiony feeling, as in *I think this milk is spoiled. I think I may have run over a squirrel back there. I think you may have a melanoma.*

"Thanks," I said and looked out my window, craning my nice face away from his view.

We turned onto the highway and rode in silence for a couple of minutes. I began to question my decision. No one knew I was coming here; I didn't tell Mom and Dad. And since I pretty much had no living friends, and the only people I talked to on a regular basis were an ex-boyfriend, who lived two thousand miles away, a romance concierge who was worried about my stability, and a professor who thought I was certifiably insane, no one would miss me for days if Holman decided to hit me over the head with a shovel and dump my body in the James River. I guess

I could have texted Tabitha, but she would just have been annoyed by my impending doom, so I decided against it. But I snuck a glance at my cell phone to make sure I had full battery and a signal just in case. Check and check.

After a few silent moments, Holman said, "What do you think of my face?"

"What?"

"Objectively speaking, do you think that I have a nice face?" His eyes were glued to the road ahead, and he didn't sound the least bit uncomfortable. "I'm not asking you in a sexual way, if that's what you're worried about."

"I, um—"

"It's okay if you don't. It's all pretty clinical stuff actually. The attractiveness quotient in people can be broken down to the symmetry of facial features. Distance between pupils and the hairline, length of face, that sort of thing."

The conversation was unbearable. Who asks a question like that? "Um, yes, I guess your face is...symmetrical," I managed to stammer out.

He smiled. "Thanks. Yours is too."

"Where are we going anyway?" The trees on either side of the highway were getting thicker, and there were fewer homes and buildings off to the side.

"B's B & BBQ. Ever been?"

I hadn't. And I was getting more uncomfortable by the second. "You know," I said, making a big show of looking at my phone, "my boyfriend is expecting me home by nine, so...."

"You have a boyfriend? Do you live together? What's his name?" He fired the questions at me quickly.

"Yes. No. Ajay. Why do you ask?"

"I thought you might be making him up in order to give me the message that you're not interested in me, sexually speaking."

I really wished he would stop using the word *sexually*. But he was right, of course. I sighed. "His name is Ajay Badal, he's a professor at Cardwell College. We've only been out a couple of times, so I guess maybe he's not officially my boyfriend."

He nodded firmly. "Got it."

I changed the subject. "Kay said Jordan had been helping you on a story?"

"Yes. A piece on Juan Pablo Romero. She was a great fact-checker. Nothing got past her. I had her researching background information on him, and she was incredibly thorough. Very organized."

That was the Jordan I'd known. Her room had always been neat and orderly, bed made, desk cleared off. It was probably one of the reasons for her ability to be involved in so many organizations in school. You had to be highly structured if you were going to be the editor of the school newspaper, on the track team, and in the drama club, all while managing a chronic illness like type 1 diabetes.

Earlier in the day, I'd had a brief and fruitless conversation with Andie, Jordan's friend from college. Andie said Jordan was "as steady and driven as ever," and she was absolutely stunned when she'd heard the news. No, she didn't know if she was seeing anyone. No, she didn't think she'd been depressed. No, she hadn't spoken to her that much recently because Jordan had been so busy with work.

"Did she have many friends at the *Times*?"

Holman blinked hard, like it was punctuation. "She did not appear overly social at work. She was very focused when she was on the job." I wondered if she and Holman had been friends or just colleagues. But I couldn't think of a tactful way to ask that. Plus, I wasn't sure if we were far enough off the grid for him to answer my questions anyway.

About seven silent minutes later we pulled into a gravel parking lot. In the back of the lot was a trailer with a faded painting on the side of a black bear drinking a beer and eating a slab of ribs. The sign above read: "Bear's Beer & BBQ."

"Remember, get the pulled pork. You won't regret it," Holman said as he cut the engine.

I could not have cared less about the pulled pork. I wanted to know what was so sensitive that Holman had to drag me fifteen miles outside of town to discuss it. "Before we eat, can we talk a little more about Jordan?" I asked. "It's just that I only have a few more days to put this obit together, and—"

His hand was still on the keys hanging out of the ignition as he interrupted me. "I brought Jordan here once. And she said she had a boyfriend, too."

I was losing my patience with this guy and his weird non sequiturs. "Did you ask her what she thought of your face?" I sniped.

"Not that night. We'd been working together for months. We'd already had the face conversation. Hers was nice, too. Maybe not quite as equally proportioned as yours but close." Apparently, Holman didn't get sarcasm.

"So...?" I said, trying to edge the conversation forward.

"So what?"

"So what were you going to say? You said you brought Jordan out here and she told you she had a boyfriend...."

"That was it."

"What was it?"

"That's what I wanted to tell you. That Jordan told me she had a boyfriend."

"You brought me all the way out here, 'off the grid,' to

tell me she was seeing someone?"

"Yeah."

I shook my head. "You've got to be kidding me."

"Did you know she had a boyfriend?"

"Well, no."

"Did her parents know she had a boyfriend?"

I hesitated. "No, I guess not."

"Then it seems like I just provided you with some good information you weren't able to get from other sources." He did another hard reset of a blink. "No need to thank me. You can pay me back with a sandwich."

We ate our sandwiches (that I paid for) leaning against the hood of his Neon. Holman might have been nuttier than squirrel poop, but he was right about the pulled pork. It was delicious. About three bites in, he starting talking again.

"So I wanted to ask you about something," he said.

I felt my jaw clench. I really couldn't take any more awkward conversations with this guy. He must have noticed because he immediately said, "It's nothing sexual, if that's what you're worried about."

"Please stop telling me things are not *sexual*. I know when things are and are not sexual, okay?"

"Okay," he said evenly. "It's just that I find that symmetrical girls get bombarded with sexual advances, so I like to be clear. That's all. Just trying to keep things professional."

There was a certain sincere logic in what he said, and all of a sudden I couldn't help but laugh.

Holman started laughing, too, but after a moment said, "Wait—what are we laughing about?"

"Nothing, Holman. Eat your sandwich."

He took another bite, then with a full mouth garbled

out, "You're Albert Ellison's granddaughter, right?"

I looked at him, my silence confirming what he already knew.

"You wrote that piece after he died."

"I did."

"Bet the sheriff didn't like that."

"You win your bet."

"And then he iced you out, right? I mean, I read that he refused to reopen the case, even with all the questions your piece raised. How'd that happen?"

"Is this an interview?"

"Sorry. Occupational hazard."

"No problem," I said, hoping to steer the conversation back to Jordan. I didn't want to talk about my granddad with Holman. "It is what it is."

"Except when it isn't."

There was something about the way he said that that got my attention. I looked at him trying to get a read on what he meant. "Yes. Except when it isn't...."

Holman regarded me for what seemed a hair too long before he said, "There was something else I wanted to tell you."

"Okay."

"The story Jordan and I were working on—you know, the one about Juan Pablo Romero? We were actually going in a different direction with it."

"Meaning?"

"Meaning the paper asked us to write a piece about Romero's rise from above his tragic and troubled past into this great humanitarian. But the more we looked into Romero, the less we were convinced that he is the saint he pretends to be."

"Really?"

"And the morning that they found Jordan, I found an envelope addressed to me in her files. It contained a letter written by someone who said they wished to remain anonymous. The letter urged me to check out the taco truck at the LJP building site."

I looked blankly at him. I didn't know what any of that meant. "Okay," I said, still not understanding. "So you got an anonymous tip to check a taco truck? Was this something for the Inspecting the Eateries department?"

"You're not hearing me. Jordan opened a letter addressed to *me* when I wasn't in the office. And decided not to share it. Why do you think she'd do that?"

I felt instantly defensive of Jordan. Was Holman suggesting she had acted inappropriately? "Maybe she was trying to be helpful? I'm sure she was planning to tell you about it at some point."

He shook his head. "I doubt it. Jordan was ambitious. My guess is she thought the tip would lead to a break in our story and decided to keep it for herself."

"I don't see how you can know that," I said. Though in truth I had no idea if that was something she would have done. She had always been a go-getter; I supposed it was possible she'd try to keep that information to herself.

"I'm not angry at Jordan," Holman clarified, "but an anonymous tip to check out a taco truck on the Little Juan Park project is a big deal, especially since Juan Pablo Romero owns a fleet of them. Who knows what information that tip might have led to?"

I got a tingly feeling on the back of my neck. I wasn't sure I understood exactly what Will Holman was suggesting, but I knew we were no longer talking about information to include in her obituary.

He went on. "And why would an ambitious young

reporter kill herself after going through the effort of stealing such a potentially juicy lead? It just doesn't add up."

"Are you saying—"

"Yes," Holman cut me off. "I never thought Jordan killed herself."

"Me either." I hadn't known for sure I felt that way until the words were out of my mouth.

"Symmetrical and smart. I had a feeling about you."

"But..." I was lost in the newly formed thought circling around in my head. "...You don't think she could have been... *murdered*?" The word sounded foreign coming out of my mouth, and even more bizarre in the context of a friend.

"I think anything is possible," he said. "Romero is a powerful guy and definitely not the good guy he pretends to be. Maybe she stumbled onto something through that anonymous tip? Or maybe her death has something to do with that secret boyfriend of hers? Domestic violence accounts for nearly thirty-three percent of female homicide victims."

I looked at him, my eyes going wide. We didn't even know for sure that Jordan had a secret boyfriend. Nor did we know if Romero was a bad guy. Or if her death wasn't suicide. "This is a lot of speculation."

"I'm just saying anything is possible. That's all."

In the back of my mind, I could hear Kay Jackson's warning about chasing alternative theories. But Holman was an award-winning reporter. If he thought so too, I told my little voice, I must be on the right track.

He drove me back to my car and thanked me for the food. "Try to find out more about who Jordan was seeing, okay?"

I had the door open, one foot out. "Okay. I'll call you if—"

"Don't call me. I'm pretty sure they're bugging my phones."

"Who is 'they'?"

Holman nodded gravely. "Exactly."

"No really. Who?"

"Who indeed, Riley. Who indeed."

"Holman. I'm actually asking you who you're talking about."

In response, or maybe of no relevance at all (who could tell with him), he tapped the side of his nose and drove off.

"Most families want the stories of their loved ones told—as long as they're approached by someone who they believe will treat the story with care. I try to meet with families in person whenever possible, look through scrapbooks with them, look at the dog-eared pages of their favorite books. I want to know not just what is gone, but what remains. In the end, it inevitably ends up a cathartic experience for the family, because at a time when most people don't know what to say (so some say nothing at all), I can show up with my notebook and give them the opportunity to talk about the one thing that consumes them— stories about the person who has died."

—JIM SHEELER, Pulitzer Prize–winning
author of *The Final Salute*,
in an interview on Poynter.org

CHAPTER 10

I spent the rest of the evening looking over my shoulder for Holman's mysterious "they." If "they" were responsible for Jordan's death and were now after him, did that make me a target, too? I locked my door as soon as I got home, something I rarely did, even at night. I'd always felt safe in Tuttle Corner, but after Holman's talk of drones, bugged phones, and murderous strangers, I felt a little on edge.

My conversation with Holman played over again in my mind. On the one hand, if Jordan had been the victim of foul play, it would explain why no one in her life seemed to know she was suicidal. On the other hand, it seemed extremely unlikely that there was some big bad wolf in Tuttle County running around snuffing out junior reporters. But everything I learned about Jordan—her ambition, her stubbornness, her love for animals—none of it squared with a person who would kill herself. My mind flipped back and forth; one minute sure I was onto some undiscovered truth, the next sure I was destined for the loony bin.

The next morning before work, Mrs. James called to see if I could come by and talk with her. She said she had some stuff of Jordan's she wanted me to see. I told myself that no matter what questions I had about how she died,

I needed to focus on the job at hand. I had to stick to my role as obituary writer, *not* amateur sleuth. The truth was that the way Jordan died had no bearing on her obituary. As Granddaddy always said, obituaries are about life, not death. But if Mrs. James just happened to know if Jordan had been seeing anyone and just happened to share that information with me, then that would be okay.

I rang the Jameses' doorbell, the same one they'd had when we were kids, with the orange light on the inside of the button so you could always find it, even in the dark. As soon as I pushed it, a chorus of barking dogs rang out. I heard Mrs. James trying to quiet them as she came to the door.

"I'm sorry," she said while holding the collar of a large German shepherd who most certainly would have knocked me over had he not been properly restrained. "Come on in."

I stepped inside the house, my first time in more than seven years, and was transported back in time. They say scent is the strongest sense tied to memory, and the smell of the Jameses's house, with its combination of Chanel No. 5 and Pledge, acted like a time machine. I felt like I was in sixth grade again and ached to see Jordan bounding down the stairs to greet me.

As soon as Mrs. James let go, the dog gave me a thorough vetting. "This is Coltrane, Jordan's most recent rescue." Once he gave me his approval by way of enthusiastic tail wagging, I scratched behind his ears and patted his thick head.

"He's having a hard time without her," she said. "Was a police dog, discharged after a year and a half for being gun-shy. He's been in and out of lots of places, but I think he finally felt at home with Jordan." She stared at the dog, who turned to face her. A sad, silent understanding seemed to pass between them.

Within seconds, two other dogs, whom I recognized from Jordan's office pictures, came barreling in from the sliding door at the back of the house, tongues out, ears flapping, nails scratching against wood. They were a tornado of canine energy, unbridled exuberance on eight legs. They were the Wild West to Coltrane's Age of Enlightenment.

"Woodward, Bernstein, go to your room!" Mrs. James pointed a stern finger at the two wildlings. "Go!" They made an abrupt stop and trotted off toward the laundry room. Coltrane stayed right by Mrs. James's side the whole time. He was clearly above being cast out for bad manners.

Once the dogs had gone, she turned to me. "Let's sit in the den."

We spent the next forty-five minutes going through photo albums and scrapbooks containing Jordan's numerous awards and newspaper mentions. Everything I saw confirmed that not only had Jordan remained the same driven, confident person I remembered her being, and she'd only grown more so with age.

"Thank you for sharing this with me," I said to Mrs. James after we'd closed the last scrapbook.

Her eyes had been misting on and off during our visit, and they shone as she looked at me. "Thank you for agreeing to help me."

I paused, summoning my courage. "Um, could I ask you a couple more questions before I go?"

"Of course."

I scrambled to think of an easy question before I worked up to the harder stuff. "Um, did Jordan have a catchphrase or anything she used to say a lot?"

"A catchphrase?" She looked at me blankly. "No. No, I

don't think so."

Oh my God, why would I ask that? Who has a catchphrase? What was she—a doofus on a sitcom? *Think, Riley.* I scolded myself internally as I pretended to jot down notes on my pad.

"Did Jordan have a favorite place? Like, for example, my mother loves the teacups at Disney World. If she could, I think she'd spend all day just riding around and around and around." I smiled to lighten the mood.

"Hilton Head Island." She was definitive. "That was her happy place. We have a condo down there. She loved the sand and shelling—and the lighthouses, of course." She walked to the mantle and took hold of a large framed picture. "This was from our twenty-fifth anniversary three years ago." It was a beautiful picture of Debbie and Robert with Jordan between them. The backdrop was a tall, white metal lighthouse, sinewy and strong, rising above the thick tree line.

"It's a lovely picture."

"We chose the location of this picture because of Jordan. Everyone gets their photos taken by the Harbor Town Lighthouse—you know the red and white one?"

I knew it well. My parents and I had visited and done just that when I was fifteen.

"But Jordan preferred the lesser-known Rear Range Lighthouse. It's actually closed to the public, but since we belong to the golf club where it sits, the superintendent let us use it for these pictures." She was looking down at the photo in her hand, lost in thought. I flipped to a new page in my notepad, ready to take notes as she continued. "It's rumored to be haunted, did you know that?"

I shook my head.

She nodded. "Legend has it that in the late 1800s the

lighthouse keeper suffered a heart attack during a bad storm. His daughter, a young girl named Caroline, went looking for him after he'd been gone for hours. They say she climbed to the top of the tower during the storm wearing a long blue dress and found her father at the top, dying. Apparently, with his last breath he begged Caroline to keep the light burning, no matter what. He was a proud man, and his job was important to him. So Caroline followed her father's wishes, making several trips up and down the lighthouse to gather oil for the lamps as the wind and the rain and the sea raged around her. Hours later, though she had been successful in keeping the lighthouse functioning, her sorrow and exhaustion proved too much for her, and she died shortly after the storm cleared."

I looked up. Mrs. James's eyes were unfocused, like she was in some kind of a trance from the memory.

"For generations, people have said that on stormy nights you can see the outline of a little girl in a blue dress on the tall skeletal tower keeping watch over the island. Her ghost supposedly lives there, keeping the island safe from storms, fulfilling her father's dying wish."

Coltrane sat beside Mrs. James, his long black nose nudging her hand that hung limply at her side. She absently stroked his head. "Jordan loved that story. She said it was sad and mysterious and hopeful all at the same time." Her voice was just above a whisper. "She was such an independent woman, but a true romantic at heart."

I thought back to the wire replica of a lighthouse I'd seen at Jordan's cubicle. That must be the one she's talking about.

I looked directly into Mrs. James's pain-ravaged eyes and asked the question I'd been dying to ask since I first learned of Jordan's suicide. "Was there a note?"

She sat motionless, except for her eyes that slid over to meet mine. "There was." I thought I detected a small sense of relief in her words.

"I'm not trying to pry, but I just haven't been able to understand why...."

Tears welled in Mrs. James's eyes; she blinked and one rolled down her left cheek. She didn't wipe it away. Without a word, she turned and walked into the office, which was off the foyer down a short hallway. Coltrane stayed with me and nudged me to pet him, which I did, happy for the distraction. Within a minute, she was back. She held a folded sheet of yellow legal-pad paper out to me.

I took it without a word and opened it. I immediately recognized Jordan's handwriting, the bubbled half-cursive, half-print that she'd used since junior high. I read:

Good by. I feel I can not go on. Life is to hard for me.

That was it. Thirteen words. Half of which were misspelled. This could not be the suicide note from a well-educated perfectionist like Jordan, who meticulously managed a career, two dogs, and a complicated disease like diabetes. I was so stunned I couldn't think of anything to say.

Mrs. James read the shock on my face. "I think she must have written it after she took the insulin and before..." she paused. "As you can see, it doesn't really provide any insight."

"Thank you for showing it to me." I folded it and handed it back to her.

She took it from me, her fingers tracing the edges of the folds. This was the last thing her daughter ever wrote, and however incompatible it may have been, it was all she had left. "Riley," she started to say, but she stopped herself and shook her head.

"Yes?" I prodded her.

Another tear fell from her eye, and this time she swabbed it away, as if erasing the evidence of her heartbreak. She took a deep breath. "Nothing. I just...I just want you to know that Jordan hadn't changed that much since the time you two were close."

I nodded, not sure of what to say.

"This...her dying the way she did...well, it shocked us all. It just came out of nowhere."

I immediately thought of Holman's theory and felt goose bumps flash onto the back of my neck.

"I remember when your grandpa passed," she said, her eyes searching mine. "Did you ever get any answers?"

It broke my heart to tell her no, that we had to live with the official version of what happened to my granddad even though I knew down to my bones it wasn't right.

She lowered her eyes. "I guess I may never know what was really going on in her life...I just wish I had asked more questions. Paid more attention...."

I put my hand over hers. "This wasn't your fault." I remembered the feelings of guilt and responsibility my family struggled with after Granddaddy's death. It was torture.

After a few quiet seconds, she sat up straight and took a deep breath. "I'm sorry." She stood, a clear sign that this conversation needed to end. "I'm okay now."

When we got to the front door, I remembered Holman's directive to find out about a mystery man. "Before I go," I said, "can I ask if there was anyone special in Jordan's life?"

A ghost of a smile crossed her face. "Not that she talked to us about. She was fairly private about that stuff—and Robert always put her up on such a pedestal. He never thought anyone was good enough for her. But I know she had recently signed up for that Click.com. She didn't really like to talk about it though. I suppose she might have felt embarrassed having to use the computer to meet a man."

"But it's not embarrassing at all. It's practical! And efficient!" In retrospect, it's possible I was a little too enthusiastic in my response.

Mrs. James gave me a measured look. "Yes, well, that's what she said." She cleared her throat. "Anyway, I thought she might have started seeing someone because she hadn't been over as much as usual. We'd been watching the dogs for her a lot on weekends. Then again, she'd been traveling for work, so maybe that was it? Do you know the *Times* made her travel to DC on Memorial Day weekend to cover the national parade?"

"Really?"

"And in the end, they didn't even give her the byline," she tsked.

While Mrs. James was talking, the dog nudged my hand to pet him again. "Coltrane, off," she said, snapping her fingers. The dog immediately went back to her side, sat down, and looked at her (literally) with puppy-dog eyes. She petted his head. "Poor thing needs a lot of attention. They say dogs grieve deeply when they lose their humans." She looked at Coltrane and scratched under his chin. From the other room, I could hear Woodward and Bernstein barking and play-growling. She sighed and said with a weary smile, "Well, I'd better go."

CHAPTER 11

I still had a little bit of time until I was due at work. The day was too hot and the drive too short for the AC to even kick in, so I began to walk from the Jameses' house to the library. On a last-minute whim, I ditched into the sheriff's office. I was counting on the fact that Joe Tackett would be out sheriffing (or whatever it was he did) and not in the office. A deputy sheriff there was a friend from high school who'd also been a friend of Jordan's, and I wondered if he might have heard any rumblings about criminal activity in the area, possibly involving Juan Pablo Romero or taco trucks.

"Hey Gail, is Carl around?" Gail York worked at reception, and her father was a distant cousin of Ryan's mother.

"Sure thing, Riley. Come on back."

"Deputy Sheriff Haight?" I said when I got to the edge of his office. Carl Haight had been the quintessential hall monitor, so none of us were surprised when he went into law enforcement. And even though we used to play dress-up together in preschool, he didn't like for me to be too familiar with him when he was at work. He said it undermined his authority.

"Oh, hey Riley." He looked up from his paperwork. "Everything okay?" Carl was a nice guy, a bit officious, but genuinely concerned for the welfare of Tuttle Corner.

"Sure," I said, walking into his office like we were good friends who visited like this all the time. "I was just on my way to the library and thought I'd stop and say hello."

He arched one brow. "Really?"

I dropped into the seat across from his desk. "How's Lisa? And the baby?"

"They're real good. Now, why don't you tell me why you're really here?" He wasn't angry, but he also wasn't buying my *I just wanted to stop and chat* routine.

"Well," I said, looking over my shoulder. "Don't know if you've heard, but I've been asked to write Jordan James's obituary."

"Sad situation." Carl shook his head. "That girl was a force to be reckoned with back in school."

"She certainly was."

"Do you remember the time she had that huge 'For Sale' banner made for the school on senior prank day?"

I had forgotten about that. "Only Jordan could have done that and not gotten in trouble."

"Teachers loved her," Carl said, then added with a sad smile, "Everybody did."

"I know." I paused, working up my nerve. "It was so out of character for her to have committed suicide, right?"

"Riley." Carl sighed. "Please tell me you're not here trying to turn this into something it isn't."

"What?" I feigned shock. "Why would you say that?"

Carl raised one eyebrow again. My reputation around this department had been well established. In fact, I was surprised they didn't have a poster of me inside a red circle with a line through it.

"Even if I did know something—which I don't—I couldn't tell you," Carl said.

"I know, I know, but the thing is," I said, leaning forward, "I've been talking to a reporter she worked with who said she was onto something kind of big, something possibly to do with Juan Pablo—"

"Haight?" A thin, flint-edged voice skidded into the room. "What is *she* doing here?"

I turned my head to see Sheriff Joe Tackett standing in the doorway, one bony finger pointing at me like I was a stray cat. With fleas.

"Riley just came by to say hey," Carl said, color creeping up his neck. He kept his voice light and even, but I could tell Tackett made him nervous. Joe Tackett had been sheriff for three consecutive terms. My theory on why he kept winning elections was down to good word play: slogans like *"Tackett for Tuttle"* and *"Tuttle for Tackett."* Not exactly Keats, but it stuck with you. Last election, his opponent was George Longenecker. Poor guy never even stood a chance.

Despite his ability to win elections, Tackett had a reputation for being tough to work for. On the surface, there was nothing particularly intimidating about him. He was probably in his late forties, slight build, thinning hair, but he carried himself in such a way that people paid attention when he walked into a room. And it wasn't just because he had a badge. When he looked at you, it felt like an indictment—even when you weren't doing anything wrong. Or at least that's how it felt to me.

"Uh-huh," he said, turning to me. "Why don't I believe that?"

"In my experience, you've always had a hard time seeing the truth."

I saw a flash of anger ripple across his narrow face. "Unless you are here on business, Miss Ellison, I think you ought to go ahead and let Carl get back to work." He smiled so his upper and lower teeth were visible at the same time. It made him look like a hyena. "I know you're lonely and all, but Carl here is a busy man. And a married one, too."

My face flushed instantly. Carl's did too. Only Joe Tackett could make two innocent people feel guilty. I was so embarrassed I couldn't think of a comeback. So I just glared at him as I hitched my purse onto my shoulder. "See you later, Carl."

"In the future, Riley," Tackett said to my back as I was walking out, "don't come back here unless you're in some kind of trouble." I could practically see the smile on his lips as he said it.

"I find the mere chronology of a life really doesn't sum up that life for me. I want to get the texture and the sound and even the smell of someone—you know, get right inside the essence of that person."

—ANN WROE, obituaries editor of
The Economist, speaking on
NPR's *Morning Edition*

Chapter 12

I walked out of the sheriff's office, ruffled by my encounter with Tackett. I was thinking about all the things I should have said, all the snappy comebacks I wish I would have made. I was so preoccupied, I didn't even see the man walking into the building as I walked out and ran right into his left shoulder.

"I'm sor—"

"Riley?"

I looked up. It was Mr. Monroe, my old social studies teacher. "Oh, hi, Mr. Monroe."

"Nuh-uh." He wagged a finger at me. "Kevin, remember? I'm not your teacher anymore."

I laughed. "Sorry, *Kevin*."

"Everything okay?" He nodded toward the sheriff's office.

"Oh, yeah," I said. "I was just...um, I just went by to say hi to Carl."

"Good. Would hate to think you're in some kind of trouble with the law," he said, giving me a playful wink. Mr. Monroe had been my favorite teacher back in middle school. He was the one who actually encouraged Jordan and me to write our Obit Girl column. He was fresh out of college and full of enthusiasm, unlike so many of our other teachers. He didn't treat us like we were just kids. He made us feel smart and capable. But what we didn't realize was that teaching had been merely a gap year for him while he took the LSAT and saved money. Everyone was sad to see him leave teaching, but it had obviously been the right move, because now he was the prosecuting attorney for all of Tuttle County.

"Um," I said, tucking a strand of hair behind my ears, "did you hear about Jordan James?"

"Yes, such a shame." He shook his head. "She was a great girl."

"Yeah, she was," I agreed. "Actually, Mrs. James asked me to help put her obituary together."

A sad smile spread across his face and I knew he was remembering our column. "I'm glad," he said. "You gals were so close."

My face reddened. "Actually, we hadn't spoken in years."

"You're kidding? You two were so tight back in the day."

"Yeah, well, you know..." I trailed off.

"She was a reporter for the *Times*, right?"

The sun shone through the branches of a large Eastern red cedar tree. I put a hand up to shield my eyes. "She was." I'm not sure why, maybe it was because he was part of the criminal justice system in Tuttle Corner or because Jordan was our common ground, but I decided to take a chance. "I've actually been talking with a reporter that Jordan worked with over at the *Times*, and, well, this is going to sound kind of crazy, but he thinks—well, he and I *both* kind of think—that it's possible that Jordan's death wasn't a suicide."

Something on his face changed, his eyes maybe. He looked at me with a new expression, one that seemed awfully close to pity. "Riley," he said slowly, "I know it's natural to want to believe that the people we love wouldn't leave us on purpose."

I felt humiliation swell inside my chest. "It's not just me—it's this reporter, Will Holman, too! See, she had this meeting set up with—"

"Will Holman is...eccentric," he said carefully. "He's known for having some pretty wild conspiracy theories. His paranoia means he occasionally gets lucky uncovering stories, but I don't know if I'd throw in with him on this one."

"It's just that it seems so unlike Jordan to kill herself."

"But you said you didn't really know her anymore, didn't you?"

My cheeks felt hot. "I guess."

"And," his voice became softer, as if he wanted to cushion the effect of his words, "no one can blame you for being extra sensitive to suicides." Kevin knew my granddad and had reached out to me after I wrote the op-ed years ago. I guess he, like everyone else in town, still saw me as Riley Bless-Her-Heart.

I looked down.

"Listen," he said, "sometimes we feel the need to come up with alternatives when we don't like the reality." *Alternatives*. There was that word again. "You remember Kübler-Ross from school, right? Denial is the first stage of grief and all that?"

I nodded. Hadn't my mom said nearly the same thing to me the other night? Was it possible I'd allowed Holman's paranoia to infect my judgment? Denial did seem a far more plausible explanation than murder.

"Yeah," I agreed, "maybe you're right."

"I know I am." He put a comforting hand on my shoulder. "Unfortunately, I see a lot of this stuff in my line of work."

CHAPTER 13

W hen I got to the library, Wright and Constance Gladstone were walking up the porch steps. Constance held onto Wright's arm with one hand and carried her cloth bag full of returns with the other. I knew that inside of thirty minutes, they'd be at my checkout counter with this week's picks ready to go. They never said much more than the usual pleasantries, never asked for book recommendations or where things were located. They'd been coming to the Tuttle Corner Library for more than a quarter of a century, and they didn't need my help. Though I'd noticed in recent months, Constance's hand shook a little when she handed me her card.

"Good afternoon, Mr. and Mrs. Gladstone."

"Afternoon, Riley," Mr. Gladstone said. "Just getting in, are we?"

"I'm working till close tonight," I said, holding the door open for them. "Just let me know if I can help you find anything."

They both smiled at me, as if to say, *We know this library better than you, sweetie.* They had the kind of smiles that implied the word "sweetie."

Tabitha gave me an update on the morning before rushing out to meet Thad at the florist to start thinking about "motifs" for their upcoming wedding. She also told me Dr. H hadn't been in but had called to say he'd be working at his office at Cardwell College if we needed him.

I pulled out my phone to check if Regina H had emailed anything about Ajay257, and saw I'd missed a call from Ryan.

"Hey, Riles," Ryan's voice cooed into my voicemail. "Just calling to tell you I miss you. Sorry 'bout the other day. Love ya." He sounded fuzzy again. "Okay. That's all. Just wanted to let you know I was thinkin' 'bout chu. Love you, baby. Bye."

It was the first time since Ridley, the bizarro-me, came on the scene that I'd gotten one of those late-night messages, though there had been a handful over the months since he'd been gone. I was a mixture of angry, annoyed, delighted, and hopeful. And I hated myself for feeling so conflicted.

It was still light out when I locked up at eight. The heat of summer was a small price to pay for the extra daylight. Even working late didn't seem so bad if the sun was still shining when I was finished. It was a classic summer night in Tuttle. The kind where Ryan and I would have gone out to the lake to his family's land, him with his rod and tackle box and me with a book. We'd sit for hours in his father's fishing boat with the green peeling paint, a cooler filled with Cokes and pimento cheese sandwiches between us. There was something so comfortable about being with someone you can be silent with, no pretending to be someone you're not, no stress over goodbye kisses or saying the wrong thing. It may not be the most exciting kind of companionship, but at least it wasn't stressful. Or humiliating.

I walked past the city building, Memorial Park, and the fire station. A breeze blew by, carrying on it the sweet, sultry scent from the many harlequin glory bower trees that populated the park. As soon as the fragrance hit me, it brought an almost visceral longing for those summer nights of years past, when my life seemed anchored, fully plotted, and not the big ball of uncertainty it had become.

Everything seemed to have gone in a slow-motion downward spiral since Granddaddy's death. That op-ed turned me into an object of pity around town, and my bitterness against Flick and the system turned me off of wanting a career in journalism. I changed majors, got my degree in English, and waited for Ryan to pop a ring on my finger. But then he left, too. I was living a life I'd lost control over somehow, treading water in a self-designed purgatory.

I was just passing the sheriff's department when I looked into the parking lot and saw the familiar outline of a man. *Ajay?* What was Ajay doing talking to Joe Tackett? Even though he probably thought I was a complete lunatic, I felt it was my duty to warn him about Sheriff Tackett. I walked directly toward the pair, who was, apparently, deep in conversation.

"Riley?" Ajay said.

"Riley." Tackett rolled his eyes.

"Is everything okay?" I ignored Tackett and looked straight at Ajay.

"I'll be in touch," Tackett said, as they shook hands. Then, as he passed me on his way back inside he whispered, "Maybe you're not as lonely as I thought?"

"I hope you don't mind that I stopped," I said once Tackett was gone. "I was just so surprised to see you here. In Tuttle Corner. Again." A nervous giggle erupted from my throat.

"I do some consulting for the department," Ajay said. He was wearing sunglasses, so his expression was impossible to read.

I smoothed down the front of my skirt for something to do with my hands. "Oh, well, um, when I saw you here I thought, 'It's perfect,' because I've been meaning to call you to apologize."

A smile tugged at one corner of his mouth. He put his hands into his pockets as if to say *Go on, then.*

"I know you must think I am a total mess," I began. "And you might be right!" I fake-giggled again with all the smoothness of a Muppet. "Anyway, I just wanted to say I'm sorry for lying about the effect my friend's death had on me. And for misrepresenting my love for thrill rides. And beer. And hot dogs. And also for kind of freaking out on you the other day at lunch. And then for kissing you and running away...."

"Is that all?" Ajay asked.

I swept my bangs out of my eyes so I could look at him. "Um, well, yes. I think so."

"So you didn't stop in here to ask me out on a date?"

I froze. I felt heat flood my cheeks. "No! I do *not* ask men out on dates, I'll have you know. I mean, I guess I did suggest we have lunch the other day, but that was just more in the way of an apolo—"

His face broke out into a wide smile. *Oh.* He was kidding.

Ajay took off his sunglasses and his dark eyes met mine. "You don't have to apologize," he said. "Except for leaving before giving me a chance to respond."

"I'm sorry—"

He waved his hand. "Nah, it's nothing. I've actually been meaning to call you." I didn't know if he was telling the truth or not, but it was nice of him to say it. "I've just been busy."

"Well, I'm glad you were here so we could, um, clear

that up. From the other day, I mean."

"Me too."

We stood in the awkward silence. I wasn't sure what to say next. We weren't exactly friends, but we weren't exactly not friends either. Thankfully, before I could say anything stupid, Ajay spoke up.

"This may sound crazy, but do you want to give it another try? We could start over—clean slate and all?"

I smiled; the answer was obvious. "And this time, I promise: no more lies."

Ajay smiled back. "You've got yourself a deal."

Chapter 14

It didn't take long to get to my house in his zippy little BMW convertible. He parked his car behind mine in the driveway. We walked inside and I told him to make himself at home while I went back into the bedroom to change clothes. We planned to go out for dinner, and I wanted to put on something less librarian-y.

"I love the moldings in here," he called from the living room. "And this woodwork is gorgeous." He was right. The woodwork in the house was especially well done. The house was a Craftsman-style, with a low-pitched gabled roof and exposed beams on the inside. All of the woodwork was original and had been lovingly restored by my granddad during the years he lived here. This house was like his second son; I'd been so touched that he'd left it to me in his will. And the home reflected his personal style: no nonsense, no frills, utterly practical in every way. I'd left things mostly as he'd had them, except for buying an oversize sofa for the living room and hanging curtains in the bedrooms. My mother was always urging me to redecorate or paint, but it felt like I'd be erasing a little of him if I did. I liked that it was almost exactly as it had been when he lived here.

"Thanks," I said loudly from my small room. "In the interest of total honesty: I didn't buy it. My granddad left it to me when he passed."

I reached for the gray jeans I'd bought because I saw Selena Gomez wearing them on some magazine cover. *Forget it*, I thought. *It's too hot to try to be cool tonight.* I grabbed a cantaloupe-colored fit-'n-flare dress and threw it on, pulled my hair into a ponytail, fluffed my bangs, freshened my lip gloss, and was good to go.

I came out into the living room, slightly out of breath from rushing, to find Ajay looking at my bookshelf. It was my favorite thing in the whole house—the whole world maybe. Granddaddy had a floor-to-ceiling bookshelf built along the entire back wall of the living room, the kind with one of those rolling ladders. It was crammed with every sort of book, from Molière to John Grisham.

"Impressive," Ajay said.

"Thanks. I've been adding to my granddad's collection ever since I moved in."

Ajay raised a dark eyebrow and said, "I wasn't talking about the books."

I had nearly forgotten what a good date was like. No, not just a good date. A *great* date. And it was safe to say that Ajay and I had a great date that night. First we went over to James Madison's Fish Shack where we drank themed cocktails (which is what one must do at a place called James Madison's Fish Shack). Ajay ordered the Revolutionary Rum Runner, and I the Star Spangled Sipper, a combination of vodka, pineapple juice, lemonade, club soda, and a maraschino cherry. We split an order of cornbread-coated shrimp and a basket of potato skins.

After dinner, we left Ajay's car at the dock by the restaurant and wandered through town, taking advantage of the slightly cooler evening temperatures. It was fully dark, but the city had installed those Victorian-looking black street lamps along the path through Memorial Park a few years earlier, so we had a soft light to stroll by. Ajay told me about his childhood in a small town in Massachusetts and how he couldn't wait to leave it. His parents were both from India, and they had moved there for his mother's job as a professor of engineering at Worcester Polytechnic Institute. His father was a freelance software developer, so he could work from anywhere. His parents loved their little town, but Ajay, not so much. He was the only non-white kid at his high school, and he said that wasn't so much difficult as weird.

"Diversity in our town meant having both Catholic and Protestant kids attend the same school. They didn't know what to do with a non-practicing Hindu." He laughed. "I sort of felt like an outsider, even though I had friends and stuff. I always wanted to live in a place with more people who looked like me."

"And now you've landed in the cultural melting pot of Tuttle County!"

"Funny, right? But I went to college and lived in Jersey for almost ten years, where there were people of every kind of ethnic and cultural background you could think of, and you know what?"

"What?"

"I missed living in a small town. No one was more surprised than me—but I honestly like the slower pace of small towns."

That made me smile. "Me too. Is that why you left?"

Ajay paused and seemed to be considering what to say next. "No." It was a surprisingly curt answer from him, and I wasn't sure how to take it.

He must have sensed my reaction because he added, "It's complicated. But I left because I had to."

"That sounds ominous," I said, curious.

"It does, doesn't it?" His eyes hardened for a fraction of a second before he shook it off. "But it all worked out. I had a good opportunity here, and so far, so good."

I had the feeling that there was more to his story, but I wasn't going to interrogate him. Even full disclosure had its limits on first (or even third) dates.

"I've been talking too much," he said. "Tell me more about you. What do you do for fun?"

"Um…." I knew we were supposed to be honest, but saying *I read the obituaries from eight different papers, including two from the UK, every morning* seemed like it might be a turnoff.

"What?" he said, obviously sensing I was hesitating for a reason. "You can tell me. I won't judge, I promise."

I don't know if I was lulled into a sense of safety because of the low light or the intermittent whiffs of his cologne, but I decided I trusted him enough to open up. Just a little.

"Obituaries? Really?" he asked after I'd told him.

"Yeah."

"You like reading about dead people."

"That's really an oversimplification," I corrected. "See, an obituary—a well-written one anyway—is all about life, not death. You can learn so much about human nature by reading about people's legacies. And I'm not just talking about famous people, either. A well-done obit on Joe Schmoe from Harrisburg can be every bit as interesting as reading about Mao Tse-tung."

"Really?" He didn't look convinced. "I think it'd be sad. Reading about all those people who died."

There was so much I could say on the subject, so much I wanted to say. About how obituaries are all about what people leave behind, how their lives affected the people around them, about the power and privilege of getting to be the one who picks out which things, of all the millions of things people do in a lifetime, best encapsulate their lives. But why tell him when I could show him?

"When we get back to my house, I'll show you something that'll change your mind."

Ajay waggled his eyebrows. "Sounds interesting."

I hit him on the arm. "I said change your mind, not blow it."

"Wow." He gave a long, low whistle. "You *are* full of surprises, Miss Ellison."

I had to admit I was even surprising myself. I wasn't normally this flirtatious, or flirtatious at all, but something about this kind of perfect summer night made everything sparkle with possibility. Even me.

CHAPTER 15

We pulled into my driveway at a half past ten. I turned to face him. "I'm going to ask you inside, but since the theme of the evening is honesty, I feel like I should tell you this isn't an invitation to spend the night or anything."

"Good to know," he said, mocking my firm tone.

"I'm serious! I know that this is our third date and in some circles the third date is when...things happen. So I just wanted to be clear up front that this is not one of those circles."

We were still sitting in his car, the engine off, top down, the warm breeze all around us. "Got it," he said. "But there are things, and then there are *things*...." His dark eyes locked onto mine and he leaned forward slowly—slowly enough for me to stop him, but I didn't. The second before his lips met mine, he paused, like he was waiting for permission to come closer. Permission granted. His hand reached up for my face as he kissed me, softly but urgently. This was the way Ryan used to kiss me a long time ago. Over the course of our relationship, the kisses became lazy, and I'd almost forgotten what passion felt like. After a few seconds (minutes?), Ajay pulled back, a nice smile on his lips. "And in the interest of full disclosure, I've wanted to do that since the first second I saw you."

My heart was beating at least twice the normal rate as we got out of the car and walked toward my front door. I fumbled in my purse for the house keys, but then I remembered I hadn't locked up after he'd brought me home to change earlier. "Just come on in, and I'll get that thing I wanted to show you," I said as I turned the knob and pushed the glass-paned door open. I was going to show him my scrapbook filled with my favorite of Granddaddy's obits. It was the best way I could think of to explain why I loved to read obituaries.

But before I could reach the light switch, Ajay took my hand and turned me around. "One more," he said, his voice like molten lava. I threw my hands around his neck and kissed him like our plane was going down.

"Riley?"

I was still locked in Ajay's arms and nearly fell over as I twisted around to see a man standing inside my house.

"Ryan?"

Ryan Sanford, the love of my life, the guy I thought I'd marry and have five children with, stood in my living room wearing a hurt expression and a Dos Equis T-shirt.

"Hi." He ran a hand through his sandy blond hair. "I was just...I mean, I just got into town and thought I'd surprise you."

Ajay let go and stood beside me, completely silent.

"Well, you did!" I squeaked. I was still winded from the kiss and the shock of seeing Ryan after all this time, at this particular moment.

Ajay leaned down and said into my ear, "Do you want me to go?"

I turned around and looked up at him. I could see he was confused. Maybe hurt? Maybe angry? And I didn't blame him. "Um, I..." I ran a hand through my ponytail as I tried to think, "Ryan, this is Ajay. Ajay, this is Ryan."

The two men shook hands, and I felt like I was trapped in an episode of *The Bachelorette*.

"I'm going to go," Ajay said, putting a hand on my doorknob.

"No!" I said.

"No—I'll go," Ryan said, but he didn't take a step toward the door.

"Stop," I said forcefully. "Both of you just stay put while I think for a second." But my thoughts buzzed around my head like fireflies trapped in a jar. "Wait. No, actually, Ajay, let me walk you to your car. Ryan, stay here." I growled this instruction at him. I was furious with him for showing up unannounced and just letting himself into my house like he belonged here.

I took Ajay by the hand and walked him back out to the driveway. "I'm so sorry," I said. "That's my ex. I have no idea what he's doing here."

"I have one idea," Ajay said, the twinge of sarcasm less than subtle.

"It's not like that," I said.

"Listen," Ajay said, "I won't tell you I'm not disappointed, full disclosure and all that." He smiled. "But it's fine. You figure out things on your end, and I hope you'll call me after you do." He leaned down and kissed my cheek. I held his wrist for an extra second to keep him close.

"I will," I whispered into his neck, taking in his sexy-smelling cologne.

"I really hope so."

I turned away and watched him climb into his car. Before he drove off, he waved and flashed me one more gorgeous smile. I smiled and waved back, but my thoughts were already back inside with Ryan. I was livid with him for ruining not only the past several months of my life, but the one good date I'd had since he left. I steeled myself for battle. Half a year's worth of anger and frustration and regret boiled inside me. To hell with holding back. Ryan was going to be surprised if he thought he'd come home to find the same passive girl he'd left behind.

CHAPTER 16

I woke up the next morning from the sunlight streaming through the blinds. I could tell from the way no clouds filtered the light that it was going to be another hot one. I looked over at a shirtless Ryan sound asleep next to me. He looked thinner than the last time I'd seen him. I studied his skin—it was smooth and tan—and I searched his chest for the familiar freckles and moles; they were all still there, right where I'd left them. I knew his body as well as a pirate knew his treasure map. His stomach was flat except for a few ripples of muscle visible through the skin. I noticed a new small pink scar to the right of his belly button and took the tip of my finger and traced along it. I wondered how he'd gotten it? He stirred but didn't wake up, and I moved my hand away.

After Ajay left last night, I'd stormed inside determined to give Ryan a piece of my mind. But he was on me as soon as I got inside the door. He pushed me up against the wall and kissed me like he hadn't in years. "Riley," he said over and over again, like a prayer. "*Riley.*" He lifted my dress over my head in one swift movement, and when I saw the way he looked at me, like I was paradise found, any fight I had left in me was gone. I had spent months and months and months wanting this, and all of the sudden he was here and wanted it too. I pushed all thoughts of Ajay from my mind. It was like he never existed. Ryan was here now, here again.

We'd talked for a long time after, and he told me he'd decided to come back to Tuttle Corner for good and work for his dad. He was planning to make one last trip to Colorado after the Fourth of July and get his stuff, but then he'd be back to stay. It was exactly what I'd been hoping for since he left. He kissed me all over and told me he missed me like wildfire. He must have said "I love you" a thousand times that night, but I never got tired of hearing it. The entire night was like a dream.

By the time Ryan woke up, I'd already showered and gotten dressed. I was putting on my earrings when his croaky morning voice pleaded for me to come back to bed.

"I can't," I said, moving out of his reach. "I have to go. And you should too. Barb and Hank will be worried."

"They'll know where I am."

I felt a bit sheepish at that, like the whole world just knew I'd be sitting waiting for Ryan to come back to me. But then again, I guess I was right to wait because here he was! I'll admit it felt good to know I'd been right all along: Ryan still loved me.

"Last night was something else." He looked very proud of himself.

"Sure was." I giggled. "I guess that's what waiting seven months will do for a girl."

"I missed you, Riles. You don't even know how much I missed you."

I felt like the Grinch at the end of the book when his heart grows three sizes. I had cried a gallon of tears over this man because I always felt that we belonged together. And now I knew he did too. I could finally exhale. "Me too."

I looked at him through the mirror over my dresser and smiled.

My paisley sheets came halfway up on his belly, leaving his smooth chest exposed. His hair was longer than usual, and it looked sexy all rumpled from sleep. He held a long, muscular arm out to me. "Come back to bed." It was 8:37. I had to leave by no later than 8:50 to get to work on time. I took a half-step toward him and let him pull me the rest of the way. "God, I missed your body, babe." He nuzzled into my neck and kissed all the way up toward my ears. "The girls in Colorado are much harder. You're sooooo soft...."

Wait—*what?* I froze. Did he honestly just compare my body to "the girls in Colorado"? How many girls had there been? And what was he saying by calling me "soft"? Was that a euphemism for fat? I pulled away and shoved his chest back with both hands.

Ryan looked confused. "What?"

"*The girls in Colorado?*"

"Don't be like that, I just meant—"

"I know what you meant."

"Riley," he whined, "c'mon. It's been a long time since we broke up. And it's not like you haven't been with other people."

"I haven't!" Ryan was the only guy I'd ever been with. Period.

"I saw you last night with your tongue halfway down Mr. BMW's throat!"

Oh. That. My cheeks burned. "That was just a kiss. My first kiss since you left, by the way. That was it, Ryan. The only one—the only *anything* since you've been gone." I took a deep breath and turned away from him.

I heard him rustle out of the sheets, and then I felt his hands around my waist. "I'm sorry." He kissed the curve of my neck from behind. "I had no idea."

It was impossible to tell what I was feeling at that moment. I was both proud and ashamed that I'd kept myself on a shelf all this time waiting for him to come home. And I was angry that he hadn't, even though I knew it wasn't realistic to expect him not to have been with other women. We were broken up, after all. But still. Having it thrown in my face like that hurt more than I cared to admit.

"Riles," he said again, twisting my shoulders so I was facing him. I kept my eyes cast down. "I'm really sorry. I didn't mean to upset you. I love that you waited for me. I love it so much." He kissed my forehead, then added, "I don't deserve you."

"Obituaries are absolutely about life. In many ways it's not about what's gone but what remains, and the lessons left behind. One of my favorite questions to ask is "What did you learn from the person who died?" In many ways, that's what I want to know as a reader. What can I learn from this life that will impact my own life? In a way, many of the other questions I ask are leading up to that one."

—JIM SHEELER, in an
interview on Poynter.org

Chapter 17

I stepped outside into the morning air already thick with late-June heat. The temperature was in the upper eighties and the relative humidity above ninety percent. These were the days that sweat stuck to you like a second skin. Back in high school, Ryan called these "three-shower days" because no matter how many times you rinsed off, the minute you stepped outside again that clammy, spongy feeling came back.

I walked to work slowly in an effort to prevent the inevitable full body sweat that even the smallest amount of physical effort would initiate. This also gave me time to process the insanity that was the last twenty-four hours of my life. I passed Memorial Park, where just last night Ajay and I had walked, talking, laughing, and sharing small bits of ourselves. It seemed like a lifetime ago. I'd felt a genuine connection with Ajay, my mind (and other parts of my body) contemplating possibilities I hadn't ever considered with anyone but Ryan. And then Ryan appeared. It was as if he somehow knew I was on the verge of moving on. I honestly don't know what would have happened with Ajay had Ryan not been standing inside my house. There was no denying we had real chemistry. And he was interesting and smart and cute and he smelled so good....

I neared the path that led to the library and wrenched my thoughts back into place. Ryan was back now. As much as I liked Ajay, he was not Ryan. He was not the man I'd spent my entire adult life loving. He was not the man I'd been waiting to come back to me for almost a year. I'd just have to tell Ajay257 goodbye. I'd call him later and tell him that I was sorry, but I was getting back together with the love of my life. Okay, maybe I'd leave out the "love of my life" verbiage, but the sentiment would be the same. It wouldn't be an easy conversation, especially after that kiss, but it was wrong to let it go any further.

That kiss. My belly flipped when I thought about it. His touch was gentle and sweet—but also confident and fiery. The scruff of his five o'clock shadow against my cheek, the way he put his hand up under my ear around the side of my neck...*no*. I stopped myself again. One kiss, no matter how delicious, was not going to derail my life now that I finally had it back on track. With a confidence born of knowing I was doing the right thing, I texted Ajay that I'd be available later that day and asked if he could meet for coffee. I said we needed to talk.

"Morning, Dr. H!" I called through the once-again closed door.

"Riley?" His voice sounded strained.

"Yeah, sorry I'm a few minutes late."

"No problem. Um, I'm a little...indisposed at the moment." He sounded weird.

"Is everything all right?" I heard a whooshing sound and then a clatter. "Do you need something?"

"Well, yes, dear. Actually, a little help would be nice."

I opened the door to his office. Dr. H stood in the corner of the room on top of his desk chair with both hands handcuffed to the sprinkler-system pipe above his head.

"Oh good night!" I rushed over to him. "Are you okay? What *happened*?"

Dr. H's face was a little red, and he was breathing faster than usual, but other than that he seemed all right. "I'm fine. I had a little visit from some gentlemen who wanted a favor," he said. "They were disappointed when I wouldn't grant it."

I wasn't having any luck freeing him from the cuffs. "I'm gonna have to call the police," I said. I grabbed the desk phone and dialed 911 without waiting for his permission.

He started to argue but then stopped. "I don't suppose I can just say it was an accident?"

"Not if you expect them to believe you."

"Fiddlesticks," he muttered under his breath. Dr. H is the only person I know who would say *fiddlesticks* after being strung up by his wrists to a pipe on the ceiling.

"Who did this to you?" I said once I'd hung up with the dispatcher.

"They didn't leave their cards."

"Don't be cute."

We heard the sirens in the background. It was another advantage of living in a small town; the police were never far away.

"I'll tell you after I get down, dear. I promise." He winked at me. "But just so you know, I'm not going to tell the sheriff a thing."

It took about eleven seconds for Carl Haight to unlock the cuffs and get Dr. H down. But it took another half an hour for the paramedics to check him out and grudgingly allow him to skip going to the hospital.

After the medics left, Carl took the report. "You were doing a magic trick?"

"Yes."

"A magic trick where you cuffed yourself to a metal pipe above your own head?"

"That's right."

"And why were you doing this?"

He chuckled in his cheery-old-man way. "Well, I used to be something of a magician, and I wanted to see if I still had it. It was silly of me, looking back." Dr. H pulled a hang-dog face.

"So how is the trick supposed to work?" Carl asked. The subtext: *Not buying it, old man.*

"You're too young to remember Houdini, but he was famous for these sorts of tricks. Ideally, one dislocates one's shoulder, and then you twist a little this way and that and... presto!" Dr. H clapped his hands together loudly. "You're free!"

"Uh-huh."

"Carl?" I interrupted. "I mean, Deputy Haight?"

"Yes, Miss Ellison?"

"Since this was clearly, um, just a magic trick gone wrong, would it be okay for me to open the library now?"

There was a small crowd peering in the front windows. I could see Meryl Gradinger standing outside with Betsy North, both on their cell phones burning up the Tuttle Corner gossip network. I wasn't so much anxious to let them in as I was to get Dr. H off the hook. Whatever had happened, he wasn't about to fess up.

"Yes, ma'am," Carl said. He turned back to Dr. H. "So this is really the story you want me to go with, Doc?"

He nodded firmly. "Yes. And do say hello to your lovely grandmother for me, Carl. Tell her she still owes me a pecan pie."

CHAPTER 18

It was a while before things slowed down enough for Dr. H to talk to me without the gossip-hungry ears of Tuttle's library patrons listening in. Having sirens and flashing lights at our little library had brought in people in droves. We told everyone the magician story. I doubted anyone much believed it.

Dr. H called me into his office just before eleven. "Thank you for your help earlier, Riley." His eyes crinkled with warmth. "And for backing me up. I didn't want to involve the sheriff's office in this matter. I think things will work out better for me—and for the library—if I don't."

I nodded like I understood, even though I had no clue what he was talking about.

Dr. H settled into his desk chair and absently rubbed his shoulder. He motioned for me to take the chair opposite him.

"A while back, I was approached by a man calling himself Twain. Mark Twain. Given that this man spoke with a thick Spanish accent, I figured this was an alias." He winked. "Twain told me his boss, a man who wished to remain anonymous, would like to partner with our library to develop a bookmobile program to reach underserved communities around the area. As you can imagine, I was delighted. A bookmobile has long been on the Friends of Tuttle Corner Library's wish list."

Dr. H spoke slowly, his thick Virginia accent stretching one-syllable words to two and two-syllable words to three, sometimes four. "Mark Twain" had five. "Mah-ark Ta-way-in."

"In my sixty-some years on this planet, I've learned to listen to the little voice inside my head. And on that day my little voice was shouting at me that this was a bad idea. There was something fishy about Twain and his unnamed boss. So I politely declined the gentleman's offer, and that was that."

I was gripped; I waited for him to go on.

"That first visit from Twain was about two weeks ago, you see, and I had rather hoped the matter was settled. But then about a week ago, Twain showed up with two more associates. These men he introduced as Charles Dickens and F. Scott Fitzgerald. They wanted to clarify that their boss would like to pay all costs associated with the project—and that we wouldn't have to do anything but allow the bookmobile to be parked in our lot when it wasn't out delivering books. Once again, I thanked them for their generosity but politely declined. Twain was not happy. As he left, he said, 'You're making a bad call. Hope it doesn't'—and this part he enunciated very clearly—'*blow up* in your face.'"

Chills spread around my whole body as he said the words.

"This, as I'm sure you've guessed, is the reason I haven't been quite myself lately. And the reason for the little mishap with the gun the other day. I've been worried, apparently with good cause. This morning, the literary thugs came back and repeated their offer, which was now more of a demand. When I once again refused, Fitzgerald said he wanted to be real sure I knew where the sprinkler system was in case of a fire. And that's when they handcuffed me to the pipe."

I didn't know what to say. I was stunned. Someone was shaking down Dr. Hershel Harbinger? It was insane. I asked the obvious question. "Why not tell the sheriff?"

"Ah," Dr. H said. "Well, Twain warned me that they have a source inside the sheriff's department and that if I contacted them, he'd know. I believed him."

"Who *are* these people? And why on earth would they be so insistent on donating a bookmobile?"

"I'm not sure." He frowned. "But I think it's clear whoever they are, they're up to no good."

"What are we going to do?"

"*We* aren't going to do anything, little miss," he said, his tone suddenly becoming firm. "I have this under control, and *I* will deal with it. I do not want you involved with these people in any way."

"But—"

"That is non-negotiable, you hear?"

Just then the bell chimed, alerting us that a patron had entered. Dr. H nodded his head toward the door for me to go back out front. The conversation, at least for now, was over.

CHAPTER 19

I ran home after my shift at the library to change before making the fifteen-minute drive to West Bay to break up with Ajay257. Will Holman called as soon as I walked in the door. "So, you find anything else out?"

I held the phone on my shoulder as I shimmied out of my pencil skirt and into a pair of cut-off shorts. "About what?"

"Jordan and her mystery man. Obviously."

My conversation with Holman and our unsubstantiated theories about Jordan's death seemed like remnants from another life. Between the drama with Ajay and Ryan and now Dr. H, I hadn't had time to give it a moment's thought. Did I really think Jordan had been murdered? It seemed a little dramatic. I thought back to my conversation with Kevin Monroe and the look of pity on his face. The same look Carl Haight had given me. The same look my own mother had given me. *Poor Riley, bless her heart, she just can't accept that anyone would commit suicide.* Maybe that was true? First I doubted Granddaddy's suicide, now Jordan's. In both cases, the authorities believed it. The family believed it. The only one on my side was an oddball reporter with a penchant for conspiracy theories.

I sighed. "I don't even know if there was a mystery man.

I think I was just having a hard time thinking of her committing suicide."

"You're saying you think she killed herself now?"

I didn't know what to say. Part of me did, and part of me didn't. Most of me was just sad and sorry for her family. "I guess so. That's what the sheriff's office thinks."

Holman sighed. "And I suppose you think the sheriff is always right."

"That's not what I'm saying."

"Would it interest you to know that I found Jordan's most recent credit card statement, and there was a purchase from Victoria's Secret for $67.32?"

"Not really."

"Even though Victoria's Secret is generally accepted in our society as the place to buy reasonably priced, often risqué lingerie? This would support the claim that she had a mystery boyfriend she was trying to entice with her sexuality—"

"Holman!" I cut him off. "Victoria's Secret sells everyday stuff too. Just because she shopped there doesn't mean she had a boyfriend."

"Under items sold, the receipt lists an item called Very Sexy Chantilly Lace Babydoll. I'm not an expert on women's lingerie, but that doesn't sound like an everyday item to me."

I had to admit he was right. But still. Buying lingerie did not mean Jordan had a boyfriend. And having a boyfriend did not mean she hadn't killed herself.

"I just think between the Chantilly Lace Babydoll and her cageyness about whether or not she was seeing someone, the mystery-guy angle is worth pursuing."

"What do you mean 'pursuing'?"

"I would have thought that was obvious. I think we

should work the story."

"*We?* I'm not a reporter. I'm not even a journalist! I'm only helping her parents with the obituary because of old times...and probably because of who my granddad is—or was. Anyway, I don't *work* stories." I realized I was shouting, my voice echoing through my empty house.

"Shame. You'd make a good reporter. You have your grandfather's instincts, you know?"

A combination of guilt and flattery, with a hint of the same excitement I felt during my first conversation with Holman, took root. "Fine," I huffed, as I looked at my reflection in the mirror and dabbed on a little more blush. "I talked to Jordan's mom the other day and found out a couple of things."

I could practically see Holman's self-satisfied smile as he waited for me to elaborate.

"Apparently she was on Click.com. Her mom said she thought maybe there was a guy, but she wasn't sure."

"See, was that so hard? What else?"

"*What else?* You're lucky there was anything at all."

"Focus. Did she say anything else?"

"I don't know...her mom said she'd recently adopted a new dog and that she'd been traveling for work—"

"Hold up—traveling for work?"

"Yes, she said Jordan had taken a few work trips."

"She didn't travel for work." Holman was definitive.

I got an uneasy feeling deep in my gut. "She didn't?"

"Nope."

"Mrs. James said she'd been gone to DC over Memorial Day weekend to cover the national parade."

"Not true," he said. "We don't have the budget to send people to DC to cover parades. We always use an AP story."

"Hmmm." That was a little weird. Why would Jordan

lie to her mom?

"If memory serves, she took two vacation days over Memorial Day weekend, Sunday and Monday. Normally the junior staffers have to work holidays, but she begged for the time off. Said it was her parents' twenty-fifth anniversary and that they were going to Hilton Head."

"Wait," I said, remembering the picture Jordan's mom showed me. "Her parents' twenty-fifth was three years ago."

"More evidence of a mystery here, wouldn't you say?" Holman said.

"Maybe she went out of town with some girlfriends?"

"Then why lie about it? She lied to her parents saying she had to work; she lied at work saying she was with her parents. That doesn't sound like someone going on a girls' weekend. That sounds like someone going to a lot of trouble to cover something up."

Deep in my gut, I agreed with him. I wasn't sure what it all meant, but it seemed off. "There's one other thing," I said slowly, not sure if what I was about to say was a good idea; Holman didn't need any help in the conspiracy-theory department. "She left a note."

"She did? Did you see it? Do the police know about it?"

"Yes, yes, and yes. It was short. Full of grammatical errors. She said life was too hard but spelled 'too' with one 'o.'"

"No way," Holman said. "She was better than the copy editors at finding mistakes."

"Her mom thought maybe she wrote the note after she took the insulin."

"I don't buy it. She must have been trying to send a message."

"What do you mean?"

"To let us know she didn't kill herself willingly. Think about it. It fits."

"I don't know." I sank back onto my couch, dizzy with all this new information. "Doesn't that seem a little too Agatha Christie?"

"We need to figure out who she was going on trips with and why she was lying about it. Can you look into that?" I heard papers rustling over the line. "I'll keep looking into the anonymous tip and the Romero angle. My gut tells me there's something there, too."

I glanced at the huge clock I had mounted over the mantle. I had to leave to meet Ajay in ten minutes. "Okay. Fine. I have to go, Holman."

"Good. Call me back when you have something."

"What about your phone being tapped—are you not worried about that anymore?" I said, half-joking.

"Oh, right. Forgot to tell you: I was thinking maybe we should have code names."

"What?"

"Code names. You know, just in case someone is listening in. It would be better if they didn't know your name."

I had no idea how to react to such a suggestion.

"Do you have a nickname?" he asked.

"Um." The only nickname I had was Dad's, but the thought of being called Raccoon by Will Holman made the name even less appealing. I mean, Ryan called me "sugar" and "sweetie" and things like that, but those were hardly appropriate aliases. So I said the only thing I could think of. "Back in middle school, people called Jordan and me the Obit Girls."

"Obit Girl. Great. That is how I will refer to you from now on."

"Okay. Whatever."

"What will you call me?"

Insane, I thought. "Um, I'm not sure. Let me think on it."

"Okay," he sounded slightly disappointed. "If you need inspiration, I can tell you I have every episode of *Dr. Who* ever made on DVD, I am an avid player of *Clash of Clans* online, and I have a near-photographic memory of flags, including—"

I interrupted him. "Okay, great! That'll give me some good food for thought—but I have to go now or else I'll be late."

"Okay. Right. Over and out, Obit Girl."

"Goodbye, Holman."

Dear Regina H:

I am writing to inquire if it is possible for one Click.com member to see who another Click.com member has gone out with? Please advise.

Thank you,
Riley Ellison

Dear Miss Ellison:

I am so sorry you find yourself in a situation in which you feel compelled to "check up on" the activities of another Click.com member. If you don't mind me asking, is it Ajay257? I know the two of you got off to a difficult start, but I had rather hoped you'd been able to work through the challenges of the roller coaster and your labile emotional state. Did something else happen? Did you not order the whitefish? #hindsightis2020

Unfortunately, I am not able to provide you directly with information related to another member's account. However, Click.com does offer an added-value service called the Safe Protocol Initiative (SPI for short) available for download directly to your computer! Our patent-pending SPI software will allow you to track the activities of the Click.com members you are linked with through the arrow and quiver system. This proprietary technology was developed when we were alerted to the significant volume of Click.com members who were using the site for less than romantic purposes. One gentleman had delivered 133 arrows after he'd gotten married to another member.

And that member sued Click.com for emotional distress. The case was settled out of court for an undisclosed amount. #nochristmasbonusesthatyear!

But we believe in transparency and integrity here at Click.com, and those values can be yours for a one-time fee of $29.95. Do let me know if I can sign you up for our SPI program. And please keep me posted on your relationship with Ajay257. I'm keeping my fingers crossed! #ihaveafeelingaboutyoutwo

Best,
Regina H, Personal Romance Concierge, Click.com

CHAPTER 20

I went ahead and ordered the SPI program because I couldn't see any other way of finding out who Jordan had met through Click. Since she obviously didn't talk to anyone about her love life, it seemed like my only option. It only took a couple of minutes to download the software, which gave me just enough time to do it before I had to leave to meet Ajay. I figured that was the least I could do for him—making him wait on me to break up with him was just adding insult to injury. I quickly followed the instructions to look up Jordan's account, but it was blocked. Their software only tracked the arrows and quivers of people you were already linked with on the site, and since I didn't know Jordan's username or password, I couldn't access her account. I tried to think of a few usernames she might have chosen, but as Mr. Monroe pointed out, I didn't really know her, so I didn't have any luck. There went $29.95 down the drain.

Just before shutting down, I decided to take a quick peek at who else Ajay257 had been in contact with. You know, just to make me feel better about breaking up with him. I was sure there were tons of people interested in a guy like Ajay, and I thought it might make me feel less guilty about ending things.

Dang! Ajay had received more than 110 arrows! I'd

only gotten like twenty. Of course, I hadn't been a member as long as he had. I started scrolling through the profile names of the women who were about to get the good news that Ajay was back on the market. Stylin'Suze, AngelKitty97, HotnessAberdeen, Profgirl, HattieG, Milf73, SexyBikerBabe—gosh, there were just so many of them! I couldn't believe it. Ajay was truly a hot commodity.

And I was glad to see how in demand he was because it made me feel better about letting him go. He'd easily be able to find happiness with Latinalover69 or someone else. A pang of something tugged at me—jealousy maybe? I squashed the feeling. I had Ryan back, and that was all I'd wanted for so long, wasn't it? So what if Ajay was nice and cute and successful? Maybe under other circumstances, I could see myself with him, but not now. Not with Ryan back in my life.

I was about to close my laptop when I saw a link to the arrows he had sent out. There were only two: the one he sent to me and one to a WoodwardBernstein93. I suddenly felt like I had the wind knocked out of me. *Woodward-Bernstein93.* Jordan. It had to be Jordan. She, like me, was born in 1993. And Woodward and Bernstein were her dogs' names. It *had* to be her. And here she was in Ajay's quiver? My pulse started to race, and my mind was a jumble of emotions that hadn't even had time to distill into thoughts. With a trembling hand, I clicked on the username, and a window popped up showing that he had initiated contact with her in May. It showed she responded a couple of days later, though I couldn't read the contents of their communications. It showed that Ajay257 and WoodwardBernstein93 had made a date for May 12th. And another on May 19th.

The tingly feeling on my skin progressed into a leaden feeling deep in my chest. *Ajay and Jordan?* It didn't seem possible. How could he have not mentioned dating a girl from Tuttle Corner who died, especially after I told him I had a friend who died recently? Tuttle Corner was a pretty small town. He'd have to have guessed that I would have known her. Had he kept his relationship with Jordan a secret from me on purpose?

I was grasping to make sense of this new information. I looked at the clock. It was 4:37. I needed to go, or else I'd be late. I grabbed my purse and headed out to the car, this time locking the door behind me as I left.

———

"You already found the mystery man?" Holman said when I called him from the car. "Well done!"

"Listen—I may not even be right."

"But your boyfriend, the professor, also dated Jordan?"

"Maybe. But he's not my boyfriend. I'm on my way to break up with him right now."

"Don't!" Holman shouted.

"Don't what?" I said, as I cranked the air conditioning to full blast. A thin film of sweat covered my entire body.

"Don't break up with him! Are you crazy?"

"Are you?" I said. "I can't go out with him now. He dated Jordan! It's too weird."

"You can't cut ties with our only suspect, Riley. You have to keep seeing him."

"Suspect?"

"Yes," he said, sounding as close to impatient as I'd ever heard him.

"You think Ajay had something to do with Jordan's death? No way. Ajay would never—"

"Listen, right now we are just collecting data. We don't know who did what to whom. But since we are working from the hypothesis that Jordan's death was not a suicide, that makes everyone in her life a suspect. Especially a boyfriend she wanted to keep secret."

"Don't you think that's a little paranoid?"

"I'm in the business of being paranoid. It's the reason I'm good at my job."

I didn't know what to think. I felt as though I'd been plunked down in the middle of a bad spy movie.

"I'm going to check out a possible connection between Ajay and Romero. You try to get him to admit to knowing Jordan. But don't be too obvious. We don't want to tip him off that we're onto him."

"What am I supposed to do? Pretend to be his girlfriend and snoop around for information?"

"Exactly."

I was sure that my tone of voice indicated I was being sarcastic, but Holman must have missed it. "I can't do that."

"Sure you can."

"Holman!" I would be at the coffee shop in just a few minutes. I had no idea how I was supposed to pull this off. I was approaching full-out panic mode.

"Riley, calm down. You can do this. You're a pro."

"No, I'm a librarian, and not even a real one!"

"You'll be fine. All you have to do is see if you can get him to admit to dating Jordan. If he doesn't, then you will know he's hiding it for some reason."

"And what if he *is* hiding it?"

"Then that's another piece of data we've collected. We will need a lot more in order to figure this out, but it would be a start. In my experience, people lie for a reason."

I sighed loudly, hoping to convey how thoroughly I did not want to do this.

Holman was unsympathetic. "You'll be fine. Call me after."

I parked just across from the coffee shop and saw Ajay's BMW parked out front. Even though every nerve in my body was on high alert, I took a deep breath and opened the car door. I'd never been much of an actor, but I told myself I'd better get ready, because it was showtime.

———

"I'm so glad you called," Ajay said after we'd gotten our drinks. "But when you said we had to talk, I was a little nervous."

I felt a pang of guilt. I wasn't sure if it was for lying to Ajay or to Ryan, but either way, I wasn't used to faking things. "Bad choice of words, I guess," I said, and a jumpy giggle bubbled up. "I'm, um, really sorry about last night."

"It's okay. I understand. We all have a past." He smiled.

A past—yes, that was my opening. "Yeah," I said, fiddling with the lid on my latte. "Speaking of pasts, do you have any exes I should know about?" *Great, Riley. Not exactly subtle.*

"Uh," he said, "no, not really."

"Oh." Maybe Holman's paranoia was getting to me, but it didn't seem likely. Ajay was a good-looking, successful, smart guy in his early thirties. I was supposed to believe he'd never had a serious girlfriend before? Doubtful.

"I've been trying to meet someone but haven't had any luck until recently." He reached across the table and took my hand.

I jumped. How could he sit here and lie to my face like this? I saw his quiver! I saw how many arrows he had! Plus, I knew for a fact he'd gone out with Jordan at least twice.

He pulled back. "I'm sorry—are you okay?"

"Yes! I mean, yes." I forced my voice to sound calmer. "Why do you ask?"

"Does this have something to do with your ex?" He sounded concerned, and I felt bad for about two seconds until I remembered he was hiding something.

"No." I made myself reach for his hand despite every cell in my body screaming against it. "He's...old news. I just know how hard it can be sometimes to move forward. And before we, um, get any closer, I just wanted to make sure there aren't any surprises out there." I scrutinized his face for any hint of deceit.

"No surprises here."

An awkward silence settled around us. I decided to try another angle. "So, have you ever been to Hilton Head?"

"Yeah, a couple times," he said. "You?"

"Totally. I love it there," I said, thinking about whether or not he was the mystery man Jordan had taken to Hilton Head Island. "Have you been recently?"

"Nope." His brow furrowed, but the corner of his lip tugged up. "Riley, are you okay? You seem a little on edge."

My eyes snapped up to meet his. "Uh..." I needed to give him a reason for my weird behavior. Since I couldn't tell him the truth, I said, "I'm sorry. I've just been thinking about my friend who died. You know, that girl I told you about?"

"Oh, that's right. It's so hard to lose a friend like that."

"Awful." It was the first truthful thing I'd said since I walked in. "We hadn't been in touch lately, but still. She was my age, and we'd grown up together. It's just so sad to think she's gone. Her parents are a mess."

"I can't even imagine."

I was thinking about telling him I was writing her obituary when my cell vibrated. I turned it over to peek at who it was and saw Holman's name. I swiped the message open. *AJAY IS MARRIED. HE'S LYING TO YOU. BE CAREFUL.*

CHAPTER 21

After reading Holman's text, I faked a stomachache. It was all I could think to do. I said, "I have to *go*, like immediately." Ajay seemed a little confused, but I think he believed me. I'm sure I looked freaked out, pale, nervous, sweaty—exactly the way you would look if you were about to have an attack of diarrhea on a date.

"What do you mean he's married?" I yelled at Holman once I was safely in my car.

"Dr. Ajay Badal married Isabella Aggarwal six years ago in the state of New Jersey on April 11th." Holman paused to let the information sink in. "I found no record of divorce or annulment."

The hair on my arms stood on end. I had hoped Holman was mistaken but now had a sinking feeling he wasn't. Ajay had been pretty evasive about his past, not to mention a little too good to be true.

"What the hell is he doing on Click.com?"

"Good question," Holman said. "We need to collect more data. But if I had to make a guess, I'd guess he is cheating on his spouse."

"Really, Sherlock?" I snapped. Then I immediately felt badly. This wasn't Holman's fault. I softened my tone. "I'm sorry. But I think it's kind of obvious he's cheating." I thought back to last night and that kiss.

"There are lots of reasons why people have affairs, and we will just have to keep looking for Ajay's. But I'm bothered by the coincidences here."

"What do you mean?"

"First, Ajay finds Jordan via Click.com. Then he finds you. Jordan was investigating Romero at the time they dated. Now, you are investigating Romero. When you combine that with the fact that he recently moved here from New Jersey, where Romero is rumored to have family involved in organized crime, the fact that he is married, on a dating website, and hiding the fact that he knew Jordan—it paints a bad picture."

I think deep down I agreed with him, but I didn't want to. I didn't want Ajay to be involved in Jordan's death, or married, for that matter. I waged a weak argument. "But why me?"

"When did Ajay first contact you for a date?"

"It was the day after—" Oh, crap. It was the day after Jordan died. The day after her mother asked me to write her obit. The same day I called Kay Jackson and asked if I could come to the *Times* to learn more about Jordan's life.

"It was after you were looking into Jordan's death, wasn't it?"

I nodded, too numb to speak, forgetting that Holman couldn't see me through the phone. "And we were the only two women he ever contacted through Click as far as I could see."

"We have a lot more work to do, Riley," Holman said, but I was only half-listening. "You need to set up another date with Ajay and gather more information, okay? We can talk later about specifics, but I am going to need you to be strong."

"Okay," I said. The shock I felt when I first found out Ajay was married was now being replaced by anger, a far more useful emotion. I was pissed off that Ajay was lying to me, that he lied to Jordan, that he fooled me into believing he was someone else—someone who cared about me.

Holman said he was going to try to find a way into Jordan's electronic files to see her notes on the Romero story. I was nearly to my parents' house, so I told him I'd call him the next day.

"Sure. But one more thing," Holman asked. "Who is Sherlock?"

"What?"

"Is it me?"

I thought of what his face must look like on the other end of the phone, blank, not a trace of anger or offense, just those wide-set eyes covered by wire-rimmed glasses, waiting patiently for an answer. Clearly, Holman wasn't much for sarcasm. Despite his professional success, there was something childlike about him, and I found myself not wanting to hurt his feelings.

"Yes!" I said, and then followed up with, "um, remember how I was supposed to think of your code name?"

"Yes."

"Well, I decided on Sherlock."

He was quiet on the line for a brief moment. "I guess I am a little like a young Sherlock Holmes." I could picture him trying to suppress a smile.

"Um-hmm," I said, relieved I hadn't hurt his feelings. "I've got to go now, Holman."

"Don't you mean *Sherlock*?"

"Right. Goodbye, Sherlock."

"Goodbye, Obit Girl."

Chapter 22

My parents always liked to have me over for dinner before they left town, and they were leaving the next day for their annual Star-Spangled Tour across upper Virginia. They had a whole set of songs for kids about the Revolutionary War, including, "Don't Tread on Memaw," involving a stuffed long-tailed cat and a room full of rocking chairs; "Give Me Licorice or Give Me Death"; and "Yankee Doodle Candy." They'd be gone five days with stops in Loudoun, Fairfax, Prince William, and Stafford counties, mostly at the public libraries. They were big with the under-six set, and late June/early July was a busy time of year for the Rainbow Connection.

Mom made orange lentil and kale soup, which was my favorite of her (vegan) recipes. We settled around our usual places at the table. There was something comforting in the ritual, and I definitely needed a little extra comfort after the day I'd had.

"How's the obituary coming along?" Mom asked as we dug into our soup.

"I'm working on it." I knew I had plenty of work left to do, but it felt impossible to write a fitting obit while I had suspicions about how Jordan had died.

"I know it'll be real special, Raccoon," Dad said, giving

me an encouraging smile.

"Thanks." I didn't want to talk about Jordan anymore. Since there was no way I was going to bring up that I was working on trying to prove that she might not have killed herself or the mess with Ajay, I changed the subject. "Did you guys know Ryan's back in town?"

A look passed between Mom and Dad. A weird look.

"What?"

"Nothing, honey. That's nice. Have you seen him?" Mom asked, suddenly very interested in her soup spoon. My parents knew where Ryan and I stood. I'd never tried to hide my feelings from them. They knew how devastated I'd been when he left and about my hopes for a reconciliation. And while I knew it bothered my mom, I think my dad wanted us back together as much as I did.

"Yeah. Why are you acting funny?"

"We're not!" Dad said, plastering a huge, cheesy smile on his face that might have been indistinguishable from his normal cheesy smile to anyone but his only daughter. "How is ol' Ryan doing these days?" I thought I heard an edge in his voice. Dad never had an edge.

"He's fine," I said slowly. "Didn't Barb and Hank mention he was coming to town?" My mom played bridge with Ryan's mom every other week. I figured Barb would have at least brought it up.

Mom said, "Oh, um, gee, I don't remember if she did." It was clear where I got my bad-lying skills.

"Guys, please." I clanked down my spoon. "Tell me what's going on."

"Nothing—it's just, um, have you and he had a chance to catch up on things?" Dad asked, his voice higher than usual.

"Yeah, he came by last night." Now it was my turn to be

evasive. I didn't exactly want to admit to my parents what had gone down on Salem Street last night. There was a limit to how much I shared with my parents.

"And what did he have to say?" Mom's voice went up at the end of her question, like she was trying to sound extra casual. God, if this is what I sounded like when I lied, I'd better get it together before my next date with Ajay.

"Nothing really. We just hung out."

Dad cleared his throat again. Another meaningful look passed between them. Then he blurted out, "We have to tell her, Jeannie."

"Skip," she warned.

"Tell me what?"

My dad opened his mouth to speak, but my mom cut in. "It's not our place."

"Well, he clearly isn't going to tell her, or else he would have last night." Dad was dangerously close to raising his voice. I honestly cannot remember the last time he raised his voice, except to belt out a song.

"Someone better tell me something." I leaned back from the table. "You guys are scaring me."

Mom looked at Dad for another long moment. Some sort of silent communication passed between them, and she let out a big sigh. "Fine," she said wearily. "Riley, honey, Ryan has...well, the thing is that Ryan has recently—or I guess not so recently—but recently enough, I guess...um, Ryan has...."

Ryan has been diagnosed with a brain tumor? Ryan has enlisted in the military? Ryan has been named ambassador to Peru? "Spit it out!" I cried, my patience at its end.

It was my dad who finally came out with it. "Honey, Ryan is going to be a daddy."

Chapter 23

I don't even remember the drive over to his house. The
first thing I can recall is walking into the Sanfords'
house in the middle of their dinner and dragging Ryan
out by the collar. And then I remember hitting him. Mul-
tiple times. And then I remember tears. Mad, hot, angry
tears. And then later, the softer, slower tears of heartbreak.

"It was an accident, I swear!" He knitted his hands together on top of his head, his eyes wild with guilt and fear.
He obviously had hoped I wouldn't find out.

"An accident is when you knock over a Coke, Ryan!
Making a baby isn't an accident. I'm pretty sure you know
how it all works!"

"She said she was on the pill. I'm such an idiot. I should
have used a condom anyway."

Hearing him talk about having sex with Ridley—no, not
just having sex with her, but *impregnating* her—made me
want to peel my skin off. How could he have done this to
me? How could he have come into my house, into my *bed*
last night, and made love to me like everything was fine
when all the time he knew he was having a baby with another woman?

"You lied to me!" That was maybe the worst part. Okay,
maybe not the *worst* part, but it was close. Ryan had let me

down in so many ways over the past year, but I had always thought he was being honest with me. It was a deluded sense of propriety, but I felt like as long as he was telling me everything that he was doing—smoking weed, hanging out with Ridley, whatever—our bond remained solid. But I had been wrong. He'd been lying to me for months now. God, I felt so stupid.

"I know," he said, pacing in front of me on his driveway. "I know. I should have told you last night, but I just missed you so much and wanted some time with you without all this stuff getting in the way."

"'This stuff'? Ryan, you're going to have a baby. *A baby!* With someone else. You don't get to omit that piece of information."

"I know," he looked at me through red-rimmed eyes. "I know. But you gotta know it's always been you, Riles. I've always loved you. She was just...she was just supposed to be my rebound girl. I always knew I'd come back to you. You knew it too, didn't you?" He tried to grab hold of my shoulders, but I wrenched away from him.

"I waited for you," I said through stifled sobs, "and you ruined everything."

"I know." He started to cry too. "But we can work through this. Say we can get through this."

"Get through what? You're going to have a baby with a woman who lives two thousand miles from here." Saying the words out loud made the whole thing seem even more surreal.

"Actually," Ryan said slowly. The look he gave me from under his lashes warned me I wasn't going to like what he was about to say.

"What?"

"The thing is...Ridley doesn't have any family in the

States 'cause she's from Sweden, you know. And she doesn't want to go back there...so we've, um, decided to move her here. To Tuttle Corner. So Mom and Dad can help out with the baby."

Ridley. Tuttle. Baby. With every word, I felt more and more irrelevant.

"But me and her—we're not together anymore!" He added hastily, "It's over between us."

"Except you're going to have a baby together."

"Yeah, except for that."

I looked at Ryan standing in front of me in his UVA T-shirt, madras shorts, and Tevas. He looked like an overgrown kid with his teary eyes and hopeless expression. For a second I almost felt sorry for him. He was going to be someone's father in a few short months. He had a lot of growing up to do before then.

"Please." He grabbed my hand. "I can't do this without you." Tears shone in his eyes, and I could see the desperation he felt etched onto his face.

I squeezed his hand, then let it drop. In a voice barely above a whisper, I said, "But you already have."

"The death beat is supposed to be the worst job in the newsroom. For those of us who understand, it's journalism's best-kept secret—a place of raw emotion and endless wisdom, a place where you find lessons of life more brilliant than anything you'll ever find from the traditionally designated 'noteworthy' people who usually appear in the rest of the newspaper."

—JIM SHEELER, *Obit*

CHAPTER 24

I woke up the next morning feeling hung over, even though I hadn't had a drop to drink the night before. I was still wrung out from Ryan's bombshell. I could not believe that he was bringing the bizarro-me back to Tuttle Corner and was going to have a baby with her. Perhaps even more unbelievable than that was the fact that he thought we could still have a future together. I'm not sure what he thought—that we'd get married and raise bizarro-baby together in the house on Salem Street?

Okay. That was mean. I'm sure the baby won't be bizarre. It's half Ryan, so it'll be at least half smart and funny and charming (when it isn't being an idiot). And who am I kidding? With "badass" Ridley as the mom, its other half will probably be athletic, laid-back, and double-jointed. It's probably a good thing I'm not involved, because any offspring of mine might inherit my terrible sense of judgment and misguided loyalty.

Between Ryan and the news about Ajay, I wanted to stay in my pajamas, eat junk food, and listen to Kelly Clarkson songs all day, but I had an obituary to write. And it actually made for a decent distraction, going through my notes on Jordan, sketching out a draft, and trying to piece together the woman she had become. I created a virtual whiteboard with the various aspects of Jordan's life and personality that I wanted to include in the final version. I had a section on early life, school years, college, and working life. I divided it further into interests/passions, friends, love life, family life, and professional goals. I also created a completely separate page entitled Death, on which I listed some of the working theories Holman and I had hypothesized. That page had two sections: secret boyfriend and taco trucks.

By the time I went to meet Holman, I actually felt like I'd made some progress. He met me at the front doors and led me back to his tiny office. On the way, I noticed that Jordan's cubicle had been cleaned out, all traces of her removed as if she'd never worked there.

Holman sat on a large silver exercise ball behind his desk. "It's ergonomic. Supports correct spinal alignment," he said when he noticed my quizzical expression. I wondered if he realized he bobbed up and down slightly when he spoke. The movement made me think of the game Whac-A-Mole. *Whac-A-Holman.* I giggled.

He laughed too. "It's fun. Want to try?"

"No, that's okay." I looked around his tiny, cramped office. It was barely bigger than a cubicle and filled with Dr. Who paraphernalia, but at least it had a door. "What'd you find out about Romero?"

"I'll get to that. First, I found out some interesting information about your boyfriend," Holman said.

"He is not my boyfriend."

"He is as long as we need more information from him," Holman said, his face as serious as a heart attack. I didn't argue. "Did you know he does independent consulting in addition to teaching at Cardwell?"

"Yeah, so?"

"You knew?"

"Yeah, I guess. I think he said he works with the Tuttle County sheriff's department or something like that, to keep current in the field."

"Did he tell you he was working as a consultant for one Mr. Juan Pablo Romero?" Holman said in very dramatic fashion.

"*What?*" I felt like the air had been squeezed out of my chest.

"Yeah, Ajay Badal is listed on the roster of consultants for Little Juan Park."

"He never mentioned that." My brain felt like it was buzzing. I shouldn't have been surprised, given all the information I'd learned about Ajay in the past couple of days, but I think I was still clinging to the hope that all of this was just some misunderstanding. Obviously, it wasn't.

"This proves a three-way connection between Jordan, Ajay, and Romero. I have a feeling the mystery of how she died lies inside that triangle."

"But how?"

"Glad you asked." Holman reached into a file folder and pulled out a piece of paper. It was the anonymous letter Jordan had opened. "I think we start here."

Just then, there was a knock on his half-open door. "Come in," Holman said as he placed the note under the manila file folder on his desk.

"You're back." It was Hal Flick.

I sat up straighter, struggling to quell the butterflies in my stomach that appeared the moment I heard his voice. "I see your superior powers of observation are still intact."

"What can I do for you, Flick?" Holman said, his voice neither overly friendly nor antagonistic.

Flick wrenched his gaze from me and looked at Holman.

"I was just wondering what business you had with Riley."

"None-of-your-business business," I spit out before I realized I sounded like a three-year-old with a stutter.

"We're running a paper here, and last I heard you weren't a reporter." Flick's gruff voice made the accusation seem even harsher.

"You don't know anything about me. You gave up your right to know me five years ago when you gave up on my granddad." I hated myself for the way my voice cracked.

Flick's eyes softened, and for a moment I thought I might get the apology or, better yet, the explanation I'd waited for all these years. But after a second, the hard expression was back. He ignored me and looked to Holman. "She shouldn't be involved in our investigations."

"Actually, she has quite a knack for—"

"She's not qualified," Flick said through gritted teeth.

His tone made my blood boil. How dare he come in here and try to tell me what to do? I lifted my chin and said casually, "Actually, Holman says I have Granddaddy's sensibility—his good instincts and all that."

Flick snorted, as if to dismiss any talent I might have. "Be a professional, Holman. She may be cute, but that doesn't mean she should be your Lois Lane."

"I'll take it under advisement," Holman said. His tone was still even, but I sensed a trace of annoyance. I wondered what the relationship was between them. Co-workers? Friends? Professional rivals? Flick had been a good reporter in his day but had never gotten a Worth Bingham Prize. I wondered if he was jealous of Holman. The thought filled me with satisfaction.

"If you'll excuse us," I said, beginning to close the door on him. "We have to get back to work."

Flick glared at both of us for a good long moment

before turning to leave. Once he was gone, I pushed the door shut and took a deep breath.

"Want to talk about it?" Holman asked.

"Nope."

"You sure?"

"Yup."

"And are you sure you want to work on this story with me? Flick has a point, you're not a trained investigative reporter."

I wasn't sure if it was sitting in a newspaper office or seeing Flick or something else entirely, but I felt my grandfather's presence in that moment urging me on. It was as if he was there, driving my resolve to dig in. I took another deep breath and said, "Tell me more about Romero."

"He is an interesting guy, actually," Holman said, bouncing lightly on his ball. "A bit of an enigma. He was born in Mexico City, but his parents moved the family to the States—New Jersey—when he was just six. His father's older brother, Mateo, was already living there. Uncle Mateo was a small-time kingpin up there, and rumor has it that Juan Pablo ran for him back when he was in high school. But as soon as Juan Pablo Senior got wind that his son was working for his big, bad older brother, he up and moved the whole family down to Tuttle County, where he figured they'd be far enough away from the uncle's influence." Holman took a long sip from his water bottle before continuing.

"So, Juan Pablo Senior moves the family down here and opens up the original Romero's, the one on Fifth in West Bay. About three years later, video surveillance tapes show him walking to his car from the restaurant after closing one night. He was held up at gunpoint by someone in a horse-head mask. He tried to make a run for it and ended up shot three times in the back. Bled out on the sidewalk about ten yards from his own restaurant."

"Geez."

"Juan Pablo Junior found him. Went looking for his dad when he didn't come home that night. The man in the mask was never caught." Holman flipped to a new page in his file.

"So next thing you know, Juan Pablo Junior drops out of college. He reconnects with his uncle up in Jersey and gets involved with drugs for a couple of years. He got caught in 1993 with a kilo of cocaine and three unregistered guns in his car on I-95. He was never convicted because the officer who stopped him performed an illegal search. Lawyer got him off, no problem. But according to Romero, that scare was the come-to-Jesus he needed, and after that he cleaned up, moved back to Virginia, and went to work for his mother in the family restaurant.

"Over the past twenty years, he's done incredibly well, despite everyone's low expectations. He opened five Romero's locations in Virginia and another fourteen between DC, Delaware, and Maryland. Obviously, the restaurants have been hugely successful. Then about six years ago, he hopped onto the food-truck craze with the Tacos Los Locos trucks, and that business exploded. He has trucks running from Virginia all the way up and down the East Coast."

"Wow," I said. "I had no idea."

"It's an impressive outfit. Romero Junior got out early into the market with his trucks and has serious brand loyalty. But the problem has always been that no matter how successful he gets, he can't shake the reputation of being a gangster. People who know him say he hates that. They say he has a complex about it."

"And what about Little Juan Park? Is this just a way for him to ingratiate himself with the community? To prove he's not the black sheep of Tuttle County?" I asked, now sitting up and leaning forward.

"Seems like it," Holman said. "He's married now. Has a kid. Juan Pablo the third. And if you talk to his neighbors and friends, which we did in the course of putting the profile together, they all say he's a great dad and is always at all the games and tournaments and school parties. Then again, if they were scared he was going to have them shot in the head, they would say that, wouldn't they?"

"Yeah, I guess."

"What? You don't sound convinced."

"Well, it just seems to me that if he were such a bad guy, there'd be someone willing to talk. Someone out there who'd be willing to inform on him."

Holman nodded. "Maybe that was the source of Jordan's anonymous tip?" He handled the letter, rolling it between his long fingers. "We don't have any hard evidence, but my gut tells me Romero is still in business with Uncle Mateo."

"I just remembered something." A cold chill spread up my back. "Ajay said he left Jersey because he *had* to."

"That seems menacing."

"That's what I said. He was evasive about it but said he found another opportunity down here."

Holman's eyes narrowed. "What if that opportunity was working for Romero?" The question was rhetorical, and I didn't answer. "Riley, you need to figure out what Ajay is doing for Romero. He's a professor with expertise in explosives. It doesn't make sense that he'd consult on a park building project."

I remembered how dark Ajay's face looked when he talked about leaving Jersey. Obviously something bad had happened to make him leave. And he'd seemed so reluctant to talk about it, like he was hiding something.

"Agreed," I said, "but how am I supposed to do that?"

Holman shrugged. "Use your feminine wiles."

"My feminine *what-now?*"

"Your sexuality. I know you don't like it when I say that word."

I sighed loudly. "How am I supposed to use my...my whatever-you-call-it to get him to tell me about his work?"

"You're very symmetrical. You'll figure something out."

CHAPTER 25

D r. H did not come into work the next morning. I
called him at home, and he said he had some things
to figure out and assured me he was fine. I had my
doubts about that, but as it happened, I was fairly not-fine
myself. I texted Ajay and told him I was feeling better and
asked if he wanted to go to dinner that night. He said he'd
pick me up at eight. I had no idea how I was going to keep
my cool in front of him knowing he was married and working for Romero. The thought of being alone with him—a
married man with possible ties to organized crime—made
my stomach feel like it was churning cement.

Mr. and Mrs. Gladstone had been waiting at the doors
when I opened and were now standing at the checkout line
with their latest book selections.

"Is everything all right, dear?" Mrs. Gladstone asked as
I scanned her books. "You seem a little preoccupied this
morning."

What an insightful lady! I felt a rush of affection for
her. I was touched that she knew me so well after all our
seemingly mundane exchanges that she could tell just by
looking at me that I was off. Sometimes you never know
how much of a connection you are making with another human being just through the course of normal interactions.

"I am a little bit, actually," I said and smiled at her. "How could you tell?"

"Your derrière's hanging out, that's how!" Mr. Gladstone said, and then gave me an enthusiastic thumbs-up.

I looked down. Sure enough, my white skirt with the bold flower print had gotten tucked up into my panties, exposing my left cheek. I must have been so preoccupied when I got dressed that morning that I hadn't noticed.

"Ohmygod," I blurted out. "I am so sorry! I have no idea how that happened." I grabbed the skirt out and smoothed it down.

"No need to take the Lord's name in vain, dear," Mrs. Gladstone admonished. "Besides, lots of people your age do that kind of thing as a fashion statement. Who is it again—that singer? Wears the skimpy outfits?"

"Um, Miley Cyrus?"

"No, you know the one—"

"Nicki Minaj?"

"She also wears the cones on her front?"

"Madonna?"

"Yes, Madonna! She walks around with her backside hanging out all the time!" She was trying to make me feel better, and it was really very kind of her, though I wondered exactly how old Mrs. Gladstone thought I (or Madonna) was.

"Well, I liked it," Mr. Gladstone said definitively. "It's not every day I get to see a young—"

"Wright Wesley Gladstone."

"What?" he said innocently, then laughed a wheezy, old man's laugh until Mrs. Gladstone gave him a look that stopped him.

My blush deepened. I pushed the newly checked-out stack of books back across the checkout desk to them and smoothed my skirt down again. "Thanks for your patronage," I said, which may have been an oddly formal thing to say to two octogenarians who had just seen my left butt cheek.

"Thanks for the peep show, sweetie," Mr. Gladstone said, like he was thanking me for a nice roast chicken. Mrs. Gladstone whacked him with her sack of books, and they walked out of the library at exactly 9:20 a.m.

I had a feeling it was going to be a long day.

———•—•———

I was right. Tabitha finally left for the day at 4 p.m., and Dr. H hadn't come in, so by closing time I was alone. I shut down the computers and was walking toward the back to the children's area to turn off the lights when I heard the doorbell chime. It was 7:57 p.m. Ajay was supposed to pick me up at my house just after eight, so I needed to leave right on time. I walked back up toward the front of the library intending to ask whomever it was if they could please come back in the morning. But when I got to the front of the library, there wasn't anyone there. Our chime doesn't go off unless someone crosses the threshold of the doorway, so I knew someone had walked in. I wondered if they'd come in and perhaps realized what time it was and left again? But then the chime would have gone off twice. One chime meant there was someone here. There had to be.

I got a whooshy feeling in my stomach, the one you get when your body is telling you something isn't right.

"Hello?" I called out. "Anyone there?" My voice echoed against the large, empty cavern of the entry hall, and the hollow sound only made me feel more freaked out.

"Dr. H?" I said. Again, no response. "Tab?"

I stood stock-still for at least thirty seconds, listening hard to the silence. Nothing. Surely if someone was in here they would make some kind of noise—a rustle, a breath, a creak in the floor. But I didn't hear anything, so I figured I was safe enough to go into the backroom, get my purse, and get the hell out of there.

With my heart pounding into my throat, I set the alarm, locked the doors, and jogged toward my car in the parking lot. I was in such a rush that I didn't even see the man standing right in front of me until I ran directly into his chest.

"Hey there!" It was Ajay. He put his hands on my shoulders and said, "Excited to see me?"

My blood pressure, already at warp-speed, sped up, and I felt dizzy with panic. I started breathing fast—too fast—in and out, and in and out, but I wasn't getting any air.

"Are you okay, Riley?" His smile changed to a look of concern.

"Yeah!" I said. *Breathe. Breathe. Breathe.* "I'm fine!"

"You sure? You look a little..." I could tell he wanted to say *like you did on that roller coaster,* but instead he said, "tense."

I tried to slow my breathing down to normal speed and forced myself to laugh, which came out more like a cough. "I'm fine! Really! I'm just surprised to see you here, that's all."

Riley Ellison, "librarian," died in the parking lot of the Tuttle Corner Library at the age of twenty-four from complications of a panic attack brought on by a phantom doorbell chime and the buff chest of the man she was pretending to date. The stress of trying to elicit information from said date proved too much for Ms. Ellison. She is survived by her reputation for being a complete spaz.

"I finished up with work a little early and thought I'd come pick you up here," Ajay said. His face broke into a half-smile that would have been incredibly cute were he not a married lying scoundrel. "I couldn't wait to see you."

He leaned in for a kiss. I jerked my head to the side at the last second in a reflexive moment of panic, and his lips landed inside my ear. He pulled back and looked surprised, then embarrassed. "Oh, sorry."

"My boss doesn't like me to, um, fraternize with the patrons on library property."

I could tell I'd hurt his feelings, but he played it cool. "Yeah, totally. I understand."

We stood there awkwardly for another few moments until I remembered the phantom chime from before. "Did you just get here?"

"Yeah, I came from the sheriff's office."

"Did you come inside just now?"

"No, why?"

"No reason." I tried to laugh but again ended up sounding like I had bronchitis.

"If you're still not feeling well, we can resched—"

"No!" I practically shouted. "I'm fine. Let's just go to dinner! Are you hungry? I'm hungry. I'm starved actually." I was talking way faster than normal, and my voice sounded stilted and weird. I was the worst undercover reporter of all time.

He regarded me, knitted his eyebrows together, then shook his head as if to clear the thought *This chick is insane* from his brain like an Etch-a-Sketch.

He reached for my hand. "Why don't we take my car?"

CHAPTER 26

Don't ever let them take you to a second location. *Don't ever let them take you to a second location.* This thought played through my mind on a loop as we drove out of the library parking lot.

"Are you sure you feel like doing this?" Ajay asked as we turned onto I-95.

I wiped at my forehead, which had started to sweat a little. "I'm fine! It just, you know, takes a while to come down after work."

"Things get pretty intense at the library, do they?"

"Oh, you'd be surprised," I said as the image of poor Dr. H handcuffed to that pipe flashed before my eyes.

"Well," Ajay's eyes briefly darted from the road to me, "you're all mine now. So you can just relax."

Yes, Ajay, I can just relax because I'm with you. A married man who has lied to me about a number of things, including ties to a possible gangster who may have had something to do with my childhood best friend's death. "So, where're we heading?"

"I'm taking you to one of my favorite places, over in West Bay," he said. "It's nothing fancy, but I think you'll love it."

I decided I'd use the time in the car to see if I could get

him to talk. "So how was your day?"

"Good." He smiled at the road ahead.

"Yeah? Why was it so good?"

"Because I looked forward to seeing you all day."

My cheeks reddened. I thought, *If this man were not a big, fat liar, I'd be dying at how sweet he is.* But I made myself focus. I could not be deterred by sweetness.

"You said you were at the sheriff's office today?"

"Yeah, I'm helping them with some Continuing Ed while school is out for summer."

That didn't explain why he was listed as a consultant for Romero. I'd need to dig deeper. "That's cool."

I tried to think of what Holman would say. He'd tell me to use my sexuality. I couldn't believe it had come down to taking Holman's stupid advice, but against my better judgment, I reached up and covertly unbuttoned the top button on my Peter Pan collar. I was now showing slightly more skin than an Amish lady. I doubted my collarbone would throw Ajay into a lust-induced confession, so I unbuttoned the next one too.

"Are you too warm?" Ajay asked. "I can turn up the air conditioning."

"Oh, no, that's okay," I said. "I'm just, you know, getting more comfortable." Just then, I felt my phone vibrate inside my purse. It was Holman calling. I pressed the end button.

"You can take that if you need to."

"No, it's okay. So, you were saying you work with the sheriff?"

"Yeah," Ajay said. "Interesting guy."

"That's one word for him."

"I take it you're not a fan?"

"No."

"Sounds like there's a story there."

"Let's just say we haven't always seen eye to eye," I said and left it at that. I was on a mission. I needed to get Ajay talking about Jordan and Romero, not stupid Joe Tackett. Once again, I heard Holman's voice inside my head. Since my exposed clavicle obviously wasn't getting the job done, I tried to think of other ways to be sexy. Sexiness wasn't exactly in my wheelhouse.

In the book *Twilight*, Bella was always chewing on her lip, and that seemed to drive Edward mad with lust. I knew it wasn't much, but it was all I could think to do. I curled the corner of my bottom lip into my mouth and bit down.

No reaction. Ajay's eyes were on the road.

I angled myself toward him and tucked in my lip a little further. I felt Ajay's eyes on me. Maybe it was working? He gave me a look that could have been unbridled passion. Or it could have been unbridled bewilderment, but either way, the lip-chewing was garnering some sort of response. I kept it up.

"We should be there soon," Ajay said. He flicked on the turn signal and veered off the exit to the left. "You seem pretty hungry."

We were now stopped at a light. He turned to me. "Riley," he said, his voice slightly strained.

"Yesth?"

His gaze was intense. He seemed like he was bursting to tell me something. Could Holman have been right? Had my sexuality cast a spell over him? Was he just going to come out with it all right here and now? *I work for Romero. I dated Jordan. I know how she died....*

The light changed, and the spell was broken. He started driving, and before he could say anything, the car thunked over a pothole.

"Ow!" The force of the bump caused me to bite down

and pierce the tender skin of my lower lip. Warm, salty blood rushed to the surface.

"Oh, gosh," Ajay used his right hand to get a packet of tissues from the glove compartment. "Here. You okay?"

I dabbed the blood, but wished I had something to mop up my pride. I was botching this whole undercover thing way worse than I expected. And I hadn't expected much. Holman had put his faith in the wrong girl. Jordan had been the reporter, not me. I felt my lip starting to swell. *Great*, I thought, *because there's nothing sexier than a fat lip, right?*

I was about to make up an excuse and ask Ajay to take me home when I felt the car come to a stop. If I thought the evening couldn't get any worse, I was wrong. I looked out the car window, and my stomach lurched with fear. We were sitting in front of Romero's restaurant.

———

"You sure you're okay?" Ajay asked once we were seated inside the large, brightly colored room. "Do you want some ice for your lip?"

"I'm fine!" I insisted, completely unconvincingly. My leg bounced up and down under the table. I felt like I just drank a case of Red Bull.

"I can't believe you've never been here," Ajay said after I admitted that this was my first visit to the West Bay Romero's location. "They have great tableside guacamole here. And good margaritas, too."

"I think I've been to the one in Richmond before," I said, but I could tell I sounded distracted, agitated. I debated whether or not to excuse myself and call Holman. I wasn't sure what significance, if any, Ajay bringing me to Romero's had. But it felt creepy. I looked across the table and wondered if Ajay knew that I was after his secrets. If I called Holman, he'd probably just tell me to find a way to get information from him. I had no idea how I was supposed to do that, but I decided I'd try a little longer. If things went south, I could always text Holman to come get me.

"Want to split?"

"Huh?" I had been lost in my thoughts and didn't hear what Ajay had said.

"A peach margarita—want to share? They're pretty big."

I could not share a margarita with a married man. It was just not appropriate. My mind flashed back to our passionate kiss, and the words "not appropriate" took on a whole new meaning. I wiped the thought from my mind and pasted on a fake smile. "I think I'll just have my own, if that's okay."

The server came over and took our drink order. I ordered the top shelf on the rocks; Ajay got the peach. I looked around the restaurant. In many ways, it was your typical Mexican restaurant, painted in warm oranges and yellows, ornate iron lanterns hanging from the ceilings, a large bar with neon signs for Dos Equis and Pacifico. And it looked identical to the one I'd eaten at in Richmond. But to me, the whole place had taken on a sinister feel. Every person working looked suspicious, every customer a potential criminal.

The server came back with our drinks within a minute. Ajay held his glass up. "To us," he said.

"Cheers." I clinked his glass without looking him in the eye, then took a long, greedy sip. The cold glass felt good in my hands, a life preserver of sorts. I took another, longer sip. I had never been a big drinker, but my nerves were on overload, and I decided I really needed this margarita.

I did not, however, need the next two.

CHAPTER 27

I woke to the sound of pounding on my door at 6:15 the next morning. Or was it inside my head? I was having a dream that a tiny man was sitting on top of my head playing that Ring the Bell carnival game on my skull. *Pound-ding! Pound-ding! Pound-ding!* Eventually, though, the noise penetrated my consciousness to the point that I couldn't ignore it any longer. Someone was at my house and very eager to speak to me.

I grabbed my turquoise robe and pulled it on as I shuffled to the door, opening my eyes as little as possible on the way. The light was excruciating.

"Riley?" A panicked voice shouted on the other side. "Are you in there? Open up!"

It was Dr. H and Tabitha. What in the world were they doing at my house? Together? At 6 a.m.?

I opened the door.

"Oh, thank heavens!" Dr. H nearly collapsed with relief when he saw me.

"Riley!" For the first time ever, Tabitha actually looked happy to see me.

"Hey," my voice sounded croaky. "What's going on?"

"I'm sorry, dear, but may we come inside?"

I stepped back to let them in.

"Sorry for this intrusion at such an early hour," Dr. H said once they were inside, "but you didn't answer your phone, and we were so worried about you."

"Worried about me?"

"Yes, dear," Dr. H said. "There's been an *incident* at the library. No one was hurt," he added quickly.

"No people, anyway," Tabitha murmured under her breath.

"Okaaaay," I said.

Dr. H threw Tabitha a dark look and then said to me, "Someone blew up your car, Riley."

At first I thought I had heard him wrong. I looked to Tabitha who nodded gravely. *What?* Someone blew up my *car?* I was so stunned, I think all I said was, "What...who... wha?"

"Why'd you leave your car in the parking lot last night anyway?" Tabitha said. She had a way of making everything seem like an accusation. It was like she was suggesting that getting one's car blown up was a natural side effect of leaving it in a parking lot overnight.

"I got a call from the sheriff's department about an hour ago," Dr. H cut in, "and when I heard it was your car, well...." He stopped talking and looked at me. There were tears shining in his eyes. "Well, you can imagine how worried I was."

I reached out and gave him a hug. What a sweet man. I could tell he'd been truly worried. He sniffed a few times, and I reached over and gave him a tissue from the credenza. Tabitha, always uncomfortable with any show of emotion, pretended to check her phone.

"Anyway," he continued once he'd pulled himself together, "the police are calling it vandalism, but I think the three of us know who is behind this." He was clearly referring to the library thugs.

I was still in shock. My car had been destroyed? My car—my sweet, happy, environmentally responsible car—had been the victim of a violent crime? This didn't make any sense.

"But why would those people want to hurt my car?" I lowered myself down onto the couch.

"I think they were trying to send a message," Tabitha said, knowingly.

"But what is the message?"

"I'm not sure, but it seems too coincidental with their threats of blowing things up and all," she said.

A kernel of doubt bloomed in the corner of my brain. What if the car bombing had nothing to do with the library? What if this was about me looking into Jordan's death. What if that was the message: *Stay off the case or else.*

"Are you okay?" Dr. H touched his own lip, while looking at mine. It must still have been swollen.

"Oh, yeah. I, uh, ran into a door." He blinked at me and looked like he was about to ask a question when I cut him off. "I don't suppose you told the police anything about those men who came to see you?"

"No."

"They have a mole," Tabitha said, her tone implying I was stupid for even asking.

"Yeah, but this is—"

"Riley," Dr. H said in his most earnest tone, "if you would like to me to tell the police what I know in order for them to find and prosecute the people who did this to your car, I will gladly do so." He held my gaze for a few extra seconds to make sure I knew he was serious.

I thought about it. If there really was a mole inside the sheriff's department and it got back to Twain's boss that

Dr. H had informed on him, things could get bad for Dr. H and for the library. Obviously, these people were not messing around.

"No," I said, "it's fine. I'm sure I can claim it on insurance just as well under vandalism." I attempted a smile in the hopes of getting Dr. H to do the same. He had dark circles under his eyes. The stress of the past few weeks was showing on his face.

"I don't know who'd believe vandals blew up a Honda Fit, but whatever," Tabitha said.

I gave her a look that said *shut it.*

"Okay, dear," Dr. H said, rising to leave. "Insurance should sort you out in no time. And until then, well, you have a bicycle, I trust?" He opened the door, but before walking out he turned to me. "I'm just so relieved you're all right." His voice broke again. I gave him another tight squeeze, as Tabitha pretended to be super interested in the cracking mortar on my brick walkway.

After they left, I bolted the door, trundled back into my bedroom, and flopped onto my bed. My car had been the victim of a violent crime, I was dating a married man, and I was now more hung over than I could ever remember feeling in my whole life. When I decided to change my life less than a week ago, this was not really the direction I had in mind.

I picked up the phone to call my parents and tell them what happened, but I saw that I had one text from Ajay and three from Holman. I clicked on Ajay's first.

Hope ur feeling ok this morning.

A wave of nausea rippled through me. I tried to sift through my muddled brain for memories of what happened after that first margarita. I remembered asking him about his classes and telling him about my brief experience as a teaching assistant in Intro to English during my senior year at UVA. I remembered ordering a cheese quesadilla, which garnered a look of disgust from the server. And I remembered talking to him about Ryan. *Oh no.*

A blurry memory of me telling Ajay everything about Ryan and Ridley swam in my head. I concentrated, trying to will myself to remember. I could see Ajay's face, his eyes filled with pity. And then I got a flash of being in the bathroom talking to a woman I'd never seen before. She was consoling me. Although I couldn't exactly remember, I had the distinct impression I'd been crying.

I picked up my phone to scroll through the texts I'd sent last night hoping there'd be a clue in there somewhere. But before I could read them, another rash of pounding began on my door. My breathing stilled. What if it was the people who torched my car looking to finish the job? I grabbed the most menacing object in arm's reach, which was a quiz bowl trophy from my sophomore year in high school, and tiptoed toward the front door.

"Riley! Are you in there?" It was Holman. He rushed inside as soon as I opened the door. "Thank goodness! You scared me to death!"

"I'm fine."

"You sure?"

"Yes." I locked the door behind him. "How'd you hear about my car?"

"Your car?" He pointed to the trophy in my hand. "What's that?"

"Quiz bowl trophy. My car got blown up. Isn't that why you're here?"

"Your car got blown up, and you won a quiz bowl tournament?"

I sighed and padded over to the sofa. I slumped onto

the couch. Holman remained standing. "Dr. H just came by to tell me someone blew up my car in the library parking lot last night."

"*What?*"

"What were you worried about?"

"Your text from last night."

"Um," I said, kneading my temples, "last night is a little fuzzy."

Holman frowned. "Riley, did you drink alcohol with Ajay?"

My mouth said nothing, but my sallow skin and blood-shot eyes said *duh*.

"It's unprofessional to drink on the job, you know."

"Good thing this isn't my job," I said, fighting the urge to chuck my trophy at his head.

"You really need to decide if you are in or out. Either you want to help me find out what happened to Jordan, or you don't."

The pounding in my head was gaining strength. "You know," I said, "I'm getting a little sick of you treating me like I work for you or something. I'm a librarian, sort of, *not* a reporter. So if you don't like the way I do things, you can just work this story all by yourself!"

Holman stared at me for a moment, then turned away and walked into the kitchen. A minute later he came back with a tall glass of orange juice and a box of Ritz crackers.

"Eat," he said. "Then we'll talk."

I was too tired to argue, so I obeyed and silently munched on the crackers and drank my juice while Holman stared at me with his unblinking eyes. It was unsettling, but the more I hung around him, the more used to it I got.

"Have some of your brain cells rehydrated yet?" Holman asked once I'd finished the juice.

"Yes, thank you."

"Good," he said. "First, I am sorry about your car."

"Thank you."

"Second, I am not sorry for pushing you to be a better reporter. You have some innate talent, but you need training."

I thought about arguing but just didn't have the energy for it.

"Now, tell me what happened last night."

"Ajay took me to Romero's."

"I got that much from your text."

"Umm," I started slowly. "I think I was able to get Ajay to talk about his work a little."

"Did you use your sexuality?"

My cheeks flooded with warmth. "Yeah, I guess."

"What happened to your lip?"

My cheeks grew hot. "Collateral damage."

"Did he say anything about Jordan? Or Romero?"

"Um—"

"What does 'um' mean?"

I rubbed my head. "It means I can't remember."

"Because the alcohol killed your brain cells?"

"Yes, Holman, because the alcohol killed my brain cells."

He spared me a lecture about drinking, which I really appreciated. I took the opportunity to look at my phone. I could see why Holman had been worried enough to come over this morning.

11:24 p.m.: *Think Ajay is hide somethinn – hes weird whn i ask bout his life. Def secretive. But cute and nice. Ok. Room spinnnnng. over n out, Sherlck.*

"I wish I could remember." I closed my eyes, trying to recall something useful.

"Riley, I think we have to consider the possibility that

your car getting blown up may have had something to do with this investigation. Vandalism seems unlikely; another thing that is just too coincidental."

Part of me agreed with him, but another part thought it could easily have to do with the threats on Dr. H and the library. Holman didn't know about that, and I was sworn to secrecy. I needed some quiet time to think all this through. Maybe once I had a minute to myself I would remember more of what happened last night?

I nodded. "I've got to go to the sheriff's office," I said, standing up to signal it was time for him to go.

CHAPTER 28

The rest of the morning was a blur of activity. It's amazing how inconvenient it is to have someone blow up your car. In addition to the obvious fact that I had to walk into town to get to the sheriff's office, I spent nearly two hours there filing a report and answering questions.

Fortunately, Joe Tackett was out on a call when I arrived, and I didn't have to deal with him. Unfortunately, Ryan's cousin Gail was manning the front desk, which meant that shortly after I got there, Ryan came bursting in like a wild animal.

"Riley! Are you okay? Are you hurt?"

"Shhhhh," I said and dragged him over to a bench near the front of the office. I was still furious with him, but I could see he was genuinely scared for me. "I'm fine. My car is another story."

"What *happened?*"

It occurred to me at that moment that I hadn't told Ryan a single thing that had been going on in my life over the past week. He didn't know anything about my suspicions about Jordan's death, working with Holman, Ajay being married and a possible/maybe/hopefully not gangster, or Dr. H being attacked. And the Tuttle County sheriff's office was certainly not the place to start explaining, especially if there was a double agent here.

"It was probably just a teenage prank," I said, taking my voice down to a whisper.

"Kids making car bombs in Tuttle?" he scoffed.

Just then Gail said, "Riley, Carl needs to see you in his office."

It irritated me how Ryan walked back to Carl's office with me as if he still occupied that place in my life—the adviser, the confidant, the protector. But I was too tired to argue with him to stay put.

"I'm just finalizing this report here," Carl said. He looked down at his screen and ran a finger along it scanning for something. "Tell me why you left your car in the library lot overnight? Had your battery died or something?"

"Um, no, as I mentioned previously," I stammered, deliberately not looking at Ryan, "my date picked me up from work, and when he dropped me off later that night, I was, um, not exactly in the best condition to drive. So he just took me home." My eyes flicked to Ryan. "And then he left. Last night. After dropping me at the door." I don't know why I felt compelled to clarify that Ajay had not spent the night, but I did.

Carl had sat back down and was typing my statement into his form. I could feel Ryan's eyes on me the whole time. After a couple of seconds, Carl hit the enter key with a decisive punch. "Okay, Riley," he said, "you're free to go. We'll call you if we get any information on who did this, but it looks like a simple case of vandalism. Could've been some teenagers from West Bay or Cyprus coming out here to raise heck. We see some of that from time to time."

I nodded, though I didn't believe that for a hot minute. We shook hands and walked out front, where Gail stopped Ryan to show him pictures of her three-year-old son, Silas.

I was already halfway down the steps of the police department when Ryan caught up to me.

"You had a date last night?"

I couldn't believe he had the nerve to sound wounded. "Yes. I did." I kept walking.

"With Mr. BMW?"

"Yeah, so?" I stopped and put my hands on my hips.

"Nothing, it's just that I thought you might have waited more than two seconds before going out and getting drunk with some douchebag."

"He's not a douchebag," I said loudly. A couple of people looked over at us. I lowered my voice. "If anyone's a douchebag, Ryan, it's you. You get another girl pregnant, and you're still trying to tell me who I can and cannot date?"

"But I love you, Riles." He grabbed my hand.

"Riley?"

My head whipped around at the sound of Ajay's voice, and I dropped Ryan's hand like a hot stone. *Ajay*. Here. With me and Ryan. My pulse ticked up.

"Ajay!"

"Mr. BMW. Why am I not surprised?" Ryan muttered under his breath.

Ajay nodded to Ryan, a look of caution on his handsome face. Then he looked at me. "You okay?"

I was so not okay. I felt sick to my stomach.

"Riley?" another voice called out.

It was like a bad dream. Holman was now walking up the path toward us. All the men in my life, such as they were, were standing in the same spot at the same time.

Riley Ellison, twenty-four, spontaneously combusted into a puff of smoke when the three men in her life converged upon her outside the Tuttle County sheriff's office. Each man represented a different faction of Ms. Ellison's life—Ryan, the past; Holman, the present; and Ajay, the would-be future. The result of their confluence proved too much for Ms. Ellison's delicate constitution. Mostly because she was super hung over.

"Who's this?" Ryan asked, nodding toward Holman.

"Ajay, Ryan, this is Will Holman. Will, this is Ryan and Ajay," I said.

Holman shook hands with them both and I noticed the veins in his spindly arms bulged slightly when he shook Ajay's hand.

"What're you doing here?" I asked Holman.

"Just checking on you."

"Is everything okay?" Ajay asked, clearly confused.

"My car was vandalized last night."

"In the library lot?" Ajay looked astonished. If he was acting, he was doing a pretty good job.

"She calls it vandalism. I call it a car bombing," Holman said.

Ajay seemed too shocked to notice Holman's glare. "Someone blew up your car?"

"Yeah," Ryan chimed in. "*Someone* got her drunk and made her leave her car there all night."

Holman added, "Tuttle Corner is becoming a very unsafe place for young women these days, don't you think?" He followed it with another intense glare.

"I...I..." Ajay started, "I'm sorry—who did you say this guy was again?" He jerked a thumb toward Holman.

In the animal kingdom, this is the part where they'd start peeing all over each other. I had to stop this madness before it came to that.

"Guys." I snarled through my teeth. I gave Ryan a hard look first. "I'll talk to *you* later." He scowled at me and then at Ajay before turning to leave. Next, I looked at Holman and said in a slightly nicer tone, "You too. Okay?"

"Are you sure?"

I nodded my head as Ajay looked on, confused. "Yes." Then I mouthed "GO" to him when Ajay looked away.

"What *happened*?" Ajay asked once the others were gone.

"Where do I start?" I still was not clear on the events of last night. I wasn't sure exactly what I'd said or done, but I felt the need to apologize. "First, I'm sorry about last night—I don't usually drink that much."

Ajay looked down. "Yeah, I figured. Listen, I think we need to talk."

My stomach lurched. *We need to talk.* I knew what that meant. After all the stress of trying to fake-date Ajay in order to get information out of him, he was going to dump me. He, a married man who was clearly hiding something big—possibly criminal activity—was going to break up with *me.* It would have been funny if it wasn't so sad.

"Okay." I swallowed hard.

There was a sudden intensity to his posture, and he sort of leaned toward me when he spoke. "You and I have certainly gotten off to an interesting start."

A wave of shame rolled over me. My stomach churned with fear, dread, anxiety...and *tequila.* The stress of the morning, in addition to the mass quantities of alcohol, were proving too much for my GI system. My mouth started sweating, and I knew I was going to be sick. Like imminently.

"I'm so sorry, Ajay, but—" a gurgle erupted from my throat; it wouldn't be long. "I've really got to go!"

"Wait, Riley," he called, but I was already halfway down the sidewalk. I hoped I could make it past the corner so I could yak on a side street instead of right there on Main.

The only thing worse than being dumped in front of the sheriff's office would be puking right after being dumped in front of the sheriff's office.

I heard Ajay calling my name as I ran down the street, but I kept going. I turned the corner onto Beach, and as soon as I was sure I was out of sight, I threw up directly onto Mrs. Holyoak's boxwoods.

CHAPTER 29

A couple of hours later, after a shower, a nap, and a piece of dry toast, I was feeling semi-human again. Ajay had texted me like five times, but I had yet to respond. For the moment, I was going to stick to messes that I knew how to clean up. So I'd walked back to Mrs. Holyoak's, knocked on her door, and told her it was me who threw up in her bushes. I'd brought my bucket and asked if I could fill it from her spigot to wash away the mess. She was very understanding about the whole thing.

"The shock of what happened to your car would be enough to make anyone feel sick," she said, then put a hand up to the base of her throat. "I'm praying for you, honey."

After I finished at Mrs. Holyoak's, I stopped at the library. Tabitha confirmed that people were indeed talking about the incident and said the prevailing theory was that I'd been the victim of a hate crime against librarians. "Which is totally weird, because you're not even a *real* librarian."

"Yes, Tabitha," I said. "It really should have been you."

"Ladies," Dr. H called from his office, before Tabitha could respond. "I need to show you something."

We walked into his office, where he directed our attention to a picture on his large computer monitor. It was a blown-up version of a grainy photograph from a newspaper. The snap showed Juan Pablo Romero getting into his Escalade after leaving a fundraising event in Richmond to benefit the March of Dimes. Dr. H pointed to the man driving the truck; he was talking on his cell phone, clearly unaware his picture was being taken.

"That," he said, "is Twain."

A cold chill spread over my body. Twain and Romero. That connected Jordan's death with the threats on the library. I felt sick all over again.

"So?" Tabitha said.

"Twain, or Fausto Gonzalez, according to this article, works for Romero as the head of security operations for Romero's LLC. I tried to check into his background, but all I could find was that he moved here from New Jersey about three years ago and has been working for Romero ever since." Dr. H's eyes searched mine. I got the feeling he could tell this news had shaken me.

I stared at the screen. My mind flicked through all the pieces of the puzzle that were very slowly coming into focus. *Romero. Jordan. Ajay. Dr. H. LJP Park. The library. Twain. My car.* They were all connected. They had to be. I just needed to figure out how.

Tabitha exhaled impatiently. "Okay, so what does that mean?"

"If Twain works for Romero, then we can assume it is Romero who is behind this bookmobile business—"

I interrupted him. "I gotta go."

Both Tabitha and Dr. H turned toward me in surprise.

Tabitha narrowed her eyes. "Why do you look so weird?"

"Nothing!" I grabbed my purse and walked quickly toward the exit. I called over my shoulder, "I mean, no reason. I think I forgot to, uh, do something, and I really need to go do it. I'll see you later—bye!" And before they could say anything else, I was on my way home in a dead sprint.

———◦———

As soon as I walked in, I texted Holman and told him I needed his help. He was at my house in less than ten minutes. I told him everything I knew about Dr. H, the threats at the library, and Twain's connection with Romero. He listened silently, and when I finished, he leaned forward to place his forearms on his knees. "I know you've already connected this."

I didn't answer. Although he was right, I needed to hear him say it first. I'd been at the edge of this conclusion all afternoon, but I couldn't bring myself to say it out loud.

Holman had no trouble. "If Romero is behind the threats at the library, then he might also be behind the attack on your car." He paused, watching my reaction. "And if Ajay is working for Romero, he could have been the one who planted the bomb in your car. He had means, motive, and opportunity."

"We don't know if he has motive or not!" I jumped to Ajay's defense.

"C'mon...."

"I know it looks bad, but I just don't feel like he could do that." I still didn't want to believe Ajay was involved in any of this, but it was getting hard to deny.

Holman sighed. "Let's take a look at the facts. We know Ajay is an explosives expert. We know Ajay works for Romero. We know Ajay dated Jordan." Holman ticked each item off on his long, bony fingers. "We know he asked you out right after you started looking into Jordan's life and death."

"Yes, but—"

"Riley," Holman said firmly. I looked up. "I know you like him. I know he's successful and attractive, and he makes you feel good. But you can't let that distract you from what the data is telling us."

I played with the frayed hem on the bottom of my T-shirt. It was my UVA shirt that Ryan had given me when we'd both been accepted. I'd been leaning toward going to Cardwell College closer to home, but he encouraged me to go to UVA. He said it would be our first of many adventures together. I believed him. Was Ajay just another guy I wanted to believe was telling the truth?

"I don't know...."

"Listen, I'm not saying he definitely blew up your car or that he killed Jordan. We don't know the extent of his involvement yet. But I think at this point, it's obvious that he *is* involved."

"Okay." I took a deep breath, unable to deny it any longer. "You're right." I owed it to Jordan to keep a clear head about this. I'd have to accept that Ajay was not the guy I wanted him to be and open my eyes to the image of him that was becoming clearer with each new piece of information we uncovered.

Holman took out a huge manila folder and opened it on my ottoman. "I've been poring over Jordan's notes, and I came across something odd." He slid the folder over to me. "She had copies of a bunch of handwritten arrest citations in her file," he said. "None of which had anything to do with Juan Pablo Romero."

"Maybe they were for another story she was working on?"

"Doubt it. They were in the Romero file, and Jordan was very organized."

"So what does that mean?"

"I'm not sure, but I am going to try to find out. There were hundreds of them; it'll take me a while to comb through them all, but whatever it was, she didn't share it with me. Just like the anonymous tip. Jordan was obviously working her own angles."

"By the way, what does Kay Jackson plan to do about your piece on Romero?"

"She's letting me run with it for a while, but I'm not sure how long she'll let me stay on it if I can't come up with anything concrete. I just have to hope we can break this story soon."

I hoped so too, but it wasn't looking good. Holman started going through the arrest citations, while I took Jordan's notes and began to read them, trying to uncover what her working theories had been.

So far, we knew that the IRS had been trying for years to prove that Romero's restaurants were a money-laundering front for Uncle Mateo's drug trafficking up in New Jersey. We found evidence that Romero's holding company had been audited eight times in the past fifteen years. But the audits never turned up any evidence of wrongdoing.

"Either he's paying off the Feds," Holman said under his breath, "or he is actually running a legitimate business."

Uncle Mateo was another story. He'd been arrested several times in the past two decades for everything from gambling to racketeering to attempted murder, but managed to get off every time. He didn't bother hiding his deep dislike for the authorities. In almost every picture of him, Mateo was spitting at the camera, spitting at the police holding him in handcuffs, spitting at reporters. He looked the part of a gangster, too. He had a square face with mottled skin and a scar that ran from his cheekbone to his chin. His eyes were small and brown, and he had a thick, black mustache that in recent pictures had started to develop gray flecks. He looked, in a word, hard. His son, Dante, had the same hard look, further enhanced by a neck covered with swirling black and red tattoos.

Juan Pablo, on the other hand, was always dressed well and groomed impeccably. If you put pictures of all three men side by side, you'd never believe that they were family, let alone business partners. But they were. And I suppose it was that inconsistency that had intrigued the government enough to have all of them on their radar.

About two hours later, Holman and I were both tired and hungry and frustrated at the slow progress we were making. Still a touch hung over, I begged Holman to go get us a pizza. He happily obliged.

"Who was that other guy with you this morning outside the sheriff's office?" Holman asked after he downed his first two pieces of pepperoni.

"Ryan Sanford. My ex."

"The guy who moved away?"

"Yup."

"Is he back for good?"

"Yup."

"He's also very symmetrical," Holman reflected. "He looks like he could be in a Disney sitcom."

I laughed. He was exactly right. Ryan had the wholesome good looks of a guy who could be the lead in a bad teen movie. "Ironic, seeing that his current life-plot isn't exactly Disney material."

"What do you mean?"

I took a deep breath. "We were together for seven years. He left me in the middle of the night—literally—then got a girl pregnant in Colorado. She's from Sweden, and he's moving her here so they can raise the baby around family," I said in one continuous breath.

"I'm sorry."

The way Holman looked at me, pity emanating off of him in waves, triggered my defenses. "Don't feel sorry for me," I said. Months and months of *Bless her heart* and pitying looks and whispers behind my back had been piling up. Holman's condolence landed on top like a feather whose slight weight was enough to bring the whole stack crashing down. "It's Ryan and Ridley you should feel sorry for! I'm fine! I'm over it—*way* over it."

I wasn't over it, obviously, and just saying that I was sent the sting of tears behind my eyes. I willed myself to regain control. I really didn't want to cry in front of Holman. His DNA was at least eighty-six-percent robot, and I was sure he wasn't equipped to handle an emotionally unstable woman.

"So let me guess," he said, ignoring the quiver in my voice. "Ryan wants you back now, even though he is going to have a baby with the Swede."

"How'd you know?"

He shrugged. "Investigative reporter. Plus, his body language this morning was pretty territorial."

"He says they're over." I rolled my eyes. "And that he still loves me and wants us to be together. He says he wants—"

"What do you want?" Holman interrupted me.

Good reporters ask good questions. What did I want? I don't think I even knew. I had spent so long wanting Ryan it was hard to know if the pangs I felt for him now were real or just habit. I knew everything had changed the moment he told me he was having a baby with Ridley.

"Honestly, I just want for none of this to have ever

happened. I want Ryan to never have gone away to Colorado, Jordan to never have died, Ajay to never have been a suspect, Dr. H to never have been threatened—"

"Wishful thinking is unproductive."

"I know that," I said. "It's just that everything is just so complicated now. Why can't life be simple? I had a plan for my life, you know? I was going to move back here after college, marry Ryan, and start a family. We were going to be safe and happy, and everything was going to be perfect. And now, I'm working as an hourly employee at the library, fake-dating a married criminal who is about to dump me, and writing an obituary for an old friend. How did my life get so far offtrack?"

The question was a rhetorical one, but that didn't stop Holman from answering it. "It sounds to me like your life derailed when you handed over the controls to someone else—to continue with the train/track metaphor."

"What do you mean 'handed over the controls'?" A flash of anger rippled through me.

"You made Ryan responsible for your happiness. And when he let you down, you stayed down. It's a classic scenario, really."

"Oh, it's classic, is it?" Holman either did not pick up on, or decided not to acknowledge, my mounting anger.

"Yes, oftentimes people fall in love and lose themselves in their partner. When the relationship ends, they feel lost, like they don't know who they are or what they want anymore. I think that's what happened with you and Ryan. I think you gave him too much power in your life." He blinked and cocked his head to the side. He looked like a parrot. A stupid, annoying, infuriating parrot.

"So you're saying it's my fault? It's *my* fault that Ryan left me with no warning and got another girl pregnant?"

Holman's eyes widened. "No—"

"Is it my fault that Jordan died, too? Huh? Is it my fault that Ajay lied to me? That he's working with Romero? That he's married?" I stood up, shaking with rage.

"You're upset."

"Really, Sherlock?"

"I didn't mean to make you angry, Riley." Holman looked a little scared.

"Well, you did!" I turned away from him.

"Listen," he said, "Ryan hurt you in an unforgivable way. I get that. But *you* let that ruin your life. I think the sooner you accept that, the sooner you can get back in the driver's seat."

I folded my arms across my chest. Will Holman was the last person I needed to take life advice from. I was about to ask him to leave when I felt something touch the back of my elbow.

"I cut this out for you," he said. He was holding a newspaper clipping. "I thought you might like it."

I turned around and took the paper from him. It was from last Sunday's Lubbock *Avalanche Journal,* a newspaper I'd never heard of before.

> David "Big Mouth" Grouper, five-time winner of Nathan's International Hot Dog Eating Contest and past president of the Federation of Competitive Eaters, died at his home in Lubbock, TX. He was 47. Famous for his appetite for life and hot dogs, Big Mouth Grouper was a true Texan who lived by the mantra, "Bigger is better." Ironically, Big Mouth himself stood at just 5'6" tall and weighed in at "a buck thirty-four, soakin' wet," according to his brother, Norman.
>
> Grouper first gained notoriety on the

competitive eating circuit for his unique form of "chipmunking," where he would hold food inside his cheeks, causing them to swell to abnormally wide proportions. This earned him the nickname that would stick with him the rest of his days. He went on to win several Coney Island contests, as well as a host of smaller, local, and regional competitions.

But hot dogs weren't the only things Big Mouth was interested in. Over the years, Grouper was married six times to five different women and would proudly exclaim to anyone who cared to listen, "Not a-one of 'em weighed less than a deuce!"

Ironically, it was his love of super-size thrills that led to his untimely death. Big Mouth had accepted a challenge by fellow competitive eater Johann Wineski to a hot pepper eating contest. Much trash-talking and taunting had gone on between Big Mouth and Wineski via social media, whipping up expectations among the competitive eating community for the big contest that was set for the end of July. Privately, Big Mouth was said to be worried. In his last training session before his death, Big Mouth chipmunked six bhut jolokias, *believed to be the hottest chilies in the world. He eventually swallowed all of them, according to his coach, Steve Jenkins. But Big Mouth later suffered a cardiac event and did not survive. "It was a massive heart attack. The only kind Big Mouth woulda ever had," said Jenkins with teary eyes.*

I finished reading the clipping and felt calmer. I looked at Holman. "Why'd you give this to me?"

"I know you've been struggling with Jordan's obit, and when I read this one, I thought it was a really nice example of how a good obituary can illuminate a person's essence. I also thought it would make you laugh."

I was touched. "I'm sorry, Holman. I didn't mean to get so angry before. It's been a hell of a day."

"It's okay. I understand. We've done enough for tonight. And for the record," he said, "you can do better."

It took me a minute to figure out what he was referring to. Once I did, I rolled my eyes. "Better than someone else's baby-daddy, or a married would-be gangster?"

"Both."

"Thanks."

"And I am not just saying that to make you feel better. I do not just say things."

"I know you don't."

It was true. As strange as Holman was, there was something comforting about a person whose word you could trust, someone who would always tell you the truth for better or worse. There was clearly a lack of men in my life with that quality. Maybe Holman had more human DNA than I gave him credit for?

CHAPTER 30

After he left, I got in bed, exhausted but not sleepy. I wished for the millionth time that Granddaddy was alive so I could talk to him about this. He'd know what to do. He'd be able to sniff out exactly what was off about this situation, unlike me, who could smell something rotten but didn't know where it was coming from. A brief impulse to call Flick bubbled up, but I squashed it immediately. As helpful as Flick might be able to be, it wasn't worth owing him.

I laid in bed and thought about Holman and Ryan and Big Mouth Grouper—all people who wanted to leave their mark on the world, to find a sort of immortality through their legacy. Holman wanted it in print. Big Mouth, in hot dogs. Ryan, in Swedish babies. I think Jordan had been after a legacy too. I could just see her debating whether to open the suspicious letter addressed to Holman. Maybe she thought she'd stumbled onto something big enough to launch her career. It would have been just like her to dream like that. The Jordan I had known wanted fame, she wanted attention, she wanted a *big* life. There was no way she would have committed suicide when she was on the verge of something she thought was big. And I felt in my bones that that something big was the reason she was dead.

I leaned up to turn my pillow over to the cool side, when I heard a sound outside my bedroom window. I stilled. I heard the sound again. Shoes on pavement. Every nerve in my body at DEFCON 1, I grabbed my phone on the night table and tapped 911. I hovered my finger over the send button as I listened for the noise again. It came again, this time sounding like leaves being displaced. There was someone on my driveway.

I slipped out from under the covers and crept over to my closet, which thankfully I'd left open, so the creaky hinge didn't give me away. I hid on the floor behind the rack, sheltered by the bottoms of my dresses, my pulse pounding so hard I could feel it in my eardrums. If I hit send, it would take the police less than two minutes to get to my house.

Crouched down behind my clothes, I went through the options of what or who could be outside my bedroom window at ten o'clock at night, and none of the answers made me feel any better. Then three things happened at almost exactly the same moment: I heard the sound again, my phone vibrated, and I hit the send button.

"This is 911. What is your emergency?"

I looked at the phone in my hand. There was a text from Ajay: *Hi! Meeting ran long. Don't want to scare u but am outside your house. Wondering if ur still up?*

"911, are you there?"

"Um," I said to the dispatcher. What was I supposed to say? *A possible mobster who is also kind of my boyfriend is outside my house and wants to come in?* I went with, "Actually, false alarm! Sorry!" And hung up.

I crawled out of the closet and turned on my bedroom lamp. I texted back, *Sorry. Just went to sleep.*

He replied: *You're sleep texting?* ☺

Damn. What was I supposed to say? *Super tired. Can*

we talk tomorrow?

His response was immediate. *I really need to talk with you. And I have some news about your car.*

I supposed that was what kids felt like when a stranger offered them candy. I really wanted to know what he'd found out about my car, but opening my door to a man who might have tried to blow it up last night didn't seem like the wisest choice. I must have hesitated too long. I heard a knock on my door. I froze. Should I call 911 again? Should I slip out the back door and run for the neighbors? He knocked again.

"Riley, you in there?" I could tell by his voice that he was smiling, and it heightened the creep factor. In my panic-riddled brain, I knew that he was obviously here for one of two things: to kill me or to break up with me. What kind of a person smiles when he is about to kill or break up with an innocent librarian?

"Coming!" I shouted from my bedroom. I grabbed the quiz bowl trophy and hid it underneath my robe. I slipped my cell phone into my pocket and walked, against my better judgment, toward the door.

I saw through the peephole that Ajay was standing there, cute as ever in a blue golf shirt and khakis. I scrutinized his face. To be fair, he didn't look like a man about to kill or break up with someone. He had his hands in his pockets and was looking around my house and out toward the street like he was just taking in the scenery. Then, his eyes flicked to the peephole.

"Riley?"

———•———

Ajay stood on my doorstep waiting to be invited in. Like a vampire.

I opened the door, but did not back up from it to let him

by. "Hey," I started to say but was cut off by the deafening sound of sirens screaming toward my house.

Both our heads turned toward the sound. A brown and white Tuttle County sheriff's cruiser came flying, almost literally, into my driveway, cutting across the grass and skimming the zinnias that I planted around the mailbox by the curb. Carl Haight jumped out of the car, gun drawn, and yelled, "Sheriff's department! Put your hands where I can see them!"

Ajay's arms went up immediately. I put mine up too because I wasn't in the habit of arguing with people who had a gun. My quiz bowl trophy fell to the ground with a clatter. The little gold question mark hoisted by the faceless man broke off and bounced into the grass. Ajay looked at the trophy, then to me.

"Riley?" Carl called out. "You okay?"

"I'm fine," I shouted and lowered my hands.

"What the—" Ajay started to say, but then a second cruiser came barreling into my driveway, and this time, Deputy Chip Churner, one of my father's longtime friends, got out of his car.

"Sheriff's department!" he shouted. That was Chip, or Butter, as everyone called him, always a day late and a doughnut short.

"What's going on?" Ajay said, hands still in the air. It wasn't clear if he was talking to me or the officers. I didn't think the time was right for a lengthy explanation, so I didn't say anything. The bright lights flashed against the dark night, illuminating Salem Street like Times Square.

"We received a distress call from this location," Carl said in his official police-officer voice as he walked toward us. "Dr. Badal?"

"Hi, Carl," Ajay said and started to put his hands down.

Chip was advancing on my front porch. "Keep them hands up, buddy!" But he, too, changed his tune when he got close enough to see Ajay under the porch light. "Oh, it's just you, Doc. We thought there was some kind of trouble here."

"Can someone please explain what's going on?" Ajay said.

I kept up my campaign of silence. My eyes flicked to Ajay. There was no trace of guilt on his face, unlike mine, which was dripping with it.

Both deputies lowered their guns, apparently so confident that their good buddy Dr. Badal was not there to harm me. "We picked up a 911 call from this address. Must've been a mistake," Butter said. His fleshy cheeks were red, and he was panting.

Carl cut in, "No mistake. Riley called 911 at 10:09 and then hung up on the operator. It's standard procedure to dispatch a patrol car in those cases. The person making the call could have been forced to hang up under duress." Then he said to me, "That's when someone's forced under threat of violence."

"Thanks, Carl," I said through clenched teeth.

"You called 911?" Ajay looked at me.

"Well," I started to say, "I heard a noise and was just shaken up after what happened to my car...." I let myself trail off, hoping someone would say something and save me from having to elaborate.

"Shame about that," Chip said, digging into his pocket. "I remember when your mom and dad bought that for you." He shook his head sadly as he pulled out a fruit roll-up and began unwrapping it.

Ajay, Carl, and I all stared at him.

"What? This?" He held up the fruit roll-up. "My blood

sugar gets a little low from time to time, and Dr. Jarvis suggested I keep these on hand. Marge packs 'em in my pants every night before work." He ripped off a hunk and chewed it like a cow munching grass.

We all continued to stare at him.

"What?" Butter blinked. "You know about this stuff, Doc. Right?"

"I'm not that kind of doctor," Ajay said. His voice was quiet, and I knew his mind was still on me and that 911 call.

"Oh right, sure. Forgot," Butter said, and took another huge chunk off his fruit roll-up.

Ajay pulled out his phone. "Riley, I texted you at 10:08. Carl said you called 911 at 10:09."

Carl, Chip, and Ajay all looked at me, waiting for me to clear up this obvious misunderstanding. Their faces suggested that I owed them an explanation, like I was nuts to feel threatened by the *fantastic* Dr. Badal. I started to get a panicky feeling in my chest. I wasn't crazy. If these officers knew what I knew about Ajay, they wouldn't be so quick to lower their guns.

"Did you call 911 on *me*?" Ajay asked.

"I—I was just—"

"Making a false 911 call is a misdemeanor, you know," Carl said. "That's a criminal offense that is less serious than a felony but still carries a punishment."

"I know what a misdemeanor is, Carl!" I snapped. "Listen, I didn't make a false 911 call."

"So you *were* scared of me?" Ajay asked.

"You were scared of the doc?" Butter said, or at least that's what I thought he said—his mouth was pretty full. "But he's one of us."

"One of you? Please." I spun around to face Ajay. I'd had enough. "Do the deputies here know you work for one Mr.

Juan Pablo Romero?" I said this in the same dramatic fashion that Holman had told me the shocking news, hoping it would have the same damning effect.

"What?" Ajay said.

"You're listed as a consultant on his project manifest for Little Juan Park. I saw it myself."

Carl and Chip exchanged glances.

"So?"

"So...." I should have stopped myself right there, but I didn't. I wanted to prove to them that I wasn't crazy, that I had real reason to call 911. I felt suddenly desperate to prove that I wasn't some overwrought nut job. I lifted my chin and said confidently, "So, there is evidence that Romero had something to do with Jordan's death!"

Ajay's brow was deeply furrowed. "Jordan who?"

"Jordan James?" Carl asked. "Riley, we talked about this. That was a suicide. We found a note, the insulin bottle, everything."

"Someone forced her to write that note!" I shouted, as if saying it louder would make them believe me. "She never would have made that many mistakes—Carl, you knew her. She was the smartest person in our class."

"Who is Jordan James?" Ajay cut in.

"Oh, like you don't know," I hissed.

"Riley, you are acting a little insane right now." Ajay said this like he was talking to a two-year-old. "I don't know anyone named Jordan James."

"You went out with her! You put an arrow in her quiver—"

"Hey, hey," Butter put his hands up. "There's no need for that kind of talk."

"I saw your activity on Click. You went on two dates with Jordan James—while she was investigating Romero, *your boss*, and then suddenly she ends up dead? And then a week later you ask me out, while I'm investigating your boss, and then my car gets blown to bits? That's a little too coincidental."

Ajay said nothing for a moment. For a half-second, I actually thought he might come clean—just confess everything right there on the spot, but when he opened his mouth to speak, it wasn't a confession. His voice was tight with restrained anger. "I am listed as a consultant on Little Juan Park because two years ago there was a structure, a shed, on the land that collapsed and crushed a homeless man who'd been sleeping under it at the time. State law says that when a death occurs on property, the land must be inspected by a forensic geotechnical scientist before they can issue building permits."

He paused. I started to get a sick feeling in my stomach.

"I'm one of only four certified forensic geotechnical scientists in the area." He let this information sink in. Carl and Chip were quiet, rapt with the soap opera unfolding before them. I swear if Butter could have pulled a tub of popcorn out of his pants he would have. "I've never even met Juan Pablo Romero. I was contacted by his foreman and submitted my report via email three months ago. He did pay me my consultant fee, but I hardly think that makes him my boss."

I was shaken, but I dug in deeper. There was more than just the Romero connection that was off about Ajay. "And what about the fact that you're married, huh? Didn't think I knew about that, did you?"

There was a moment's hesitation. "That's what I've been trying to tell you all day—"

"Aha!" I yelled. "So it's true!" I looked over at Carl and Butter to see if they were getting all this. They looked thoroughly confused.

"I am married, Riley," Ajay said, "but only on paper. My wife left me a year and a half ago. She isn't a US citizen and would be deported if we divorced. It's complicated. I'm sorry I lied, it's just not something I usually bring up in the beginning of a relationship."

My mouth was as dry as a bucket of sand.

"And as for your theory that I dated your friend?" he said. "I don't know anyone named Jordan James. I went on two dates in May with a woman named Jordan Blaise, a reporter. We went out a couple of times for lunch, but it didn't work out. I got the impression she was still hung up on her ex."

Hearing the name Jordan Blaise was like a punch to the gut. "That's Jordan," I whispered, almost to myself.

"Jordan Blaise is Jordan James?"

"It's her mother's maiden name," I said, still struggling to piece together all that Ajay had just told me. An image of a twelve-year-old Jordan popped into my mind. She was holding an invisible microphone and saying, "This is Jordan Blaise signing off from Air Force One." She'd giggle and say how she thought that name sounded so reporter-like. I'll bet she planned on using it for her byline. And she must have been using it on Click.com, too.

Ajay sighed, his shoulders slumped, and put his hands in his pockets. "And that Jordan was your friend from high school, the one who died?"

I nodded.

"I'm sorry," he said quietly. "She seemed like a really nice woman."

"She was," I said. My mind was reeling. Everything I thought I knew about Ajay's involvement with Jordan's death was wrong. I hadn't gotten a single thing right. So much for me having my granddad's instincts.

Ajay stared at me. "Did you really think that I was some kind of...hitman for Juan Pablo Romero? That I would hurt an innocent woman? That I'd blow up your car? Is that why you've been acting so weird lately?"

I was mute in response.

"Wow. I'm such an idiot. You've only been going out with me in order to find out my connection to Jordan and Juan Pablo Romero." He laughed a mirthless laugh. "I actually thought we connected."

"Ajay," I started to say but was cut off by Mrs. Foley who was standing at the foot of my driveway in her cream housecoat and slippers.

"Butter," she called out, "can we shut down the discotheque, please?"

"Sorry." Butter hurried to his cruiser to turn off the lights.

"So can I report an all-clear here, Riley?" Carl said, once again using his official deputy voice.

"Yes."

"All right then," he said. "I'm going to go work on crowd disbursement. That means—"

"We know!" Ajay and I said in unison.

"Okay, okay," Carl said, looking hurt. "I'll file my report and be in touch if I have any further questions." He looked at me, then to Ajay. "Seems like you guys have some things to work out, so I'll just leave you to it."

Once Carl and Butter were gone, I asked him, "Do you want to come in so we can talk in private?"

"I don't think so."

"Listen," I started to say.

He held up his hand to silence me. "I gotta go."

"Ajay...."

He did not turn around. He walked back to his car still

parked in my driveway. I had been so sure that he was involved in Jordan's death, but I'd been wrong about it all. Everything I thought I'd figured out about the entire situation was wrong. And now, not only had I ruined what could have been a promising relationship with a great guy, but I didn't trust any of the theories Holman and I had so blindly decided were reasons for Jordan's death. If we were so wrong about Ajay, maybe we were wrong about everything else too?

"An obituary is often the last chance to tell a story, and it's crucial that it's factually correct. One of the great things about obituaries is that they last, that they are saved and put in scrapbooks and on refrigerators."

—JIM SHEELER, in an
interview on Poynter.org

Chapter 31

With my second cup of coffee in hand, I dragged my weary bones into work the next morning. All night long, my mind churned through the theories Holman and I had come up with, sorting them into two camps: reasonable suspicions and batshit-crazy conspiracy theories. Obviously, Ajay was not a henchman for Romero. That went into the batshit-crazy column. On the other hand, he was married and had been hiding that from me. But, to be fair, he had been trying to tell me something all day yesterday, and my heavy drinking and subsequent puking got in the way of that. So we were right to be suspicious of him—but not for the reasons we thought. That was justifiable batshit, I supposed. Then, there was our sentinel theory that Jordan's death hadn't been a suicide at all. That I still believed; I didn't think there was any chance Jordan killed herself. So that just left our theory that the anonymous tip about the taco trucks had something to do with how she died. I had a gut feeling this theory had merit. Then again, after last night I was beginning to lose faith in my gut instincts.

I cut through Memorial Park on my usual route into work and saw Kevin Monroe waving at me from the far side of the park, just beyond the courthouse steps. I waved back.

I wasn't in the mood for chitchat, but I didn't want to be rude. He'd always been really nice to me.

"Hold up!" he called and jogged over to where the path met the sidewalk. "Everything okay? I heard a couple of deputies were at your house last night." News definitely traveled fast in Tuttle Corner.

"It was just a misunderstanding," I said.

"Glad to hear it." He kept up with me as I walked toward the library. "How's it going with Jordan's obituary? Haven't seen it in the paper yet."

"I think it'll run in next week's edition," I said. "Mrs. James said no rush since they're waiting on having the funeral till her mother can come down."

"Gotcha," he said. "Well, I just wanted to make sure you were okay."

"Thanks." I had reached the path that led off the park to the library. I was about to turn and walk up it when I had a last-minute thought. "Mr.—I mean, Kevin—can I ask you something?"

"Shoot."

"I was wondering what kind of information could be gained by looking through arrest citations?" If Holman and I could just figure out what Jordan was working on, maybe we could figure out what it was that she'd stumbled across that got her in trouble.

"Gosh, it depends on what the arrest is for. But they'll all have the basics like time, date, name of the person arrested, name of the officer, location, charge—stuff like that. Why do you ask?"

"No reason, I was just doing some research."

He sighed. "Does this have anything to do with Will Holman's conspiracy theories?"

I didn't say anything; my silence implied consent.

"C'mon, Riley, do you really think someone murdered Jordan James? This is Tuttle Corner!"

"I know, but something isn't right about her death." I leveled my gaze at him to let him know I was not going to be deterred. I wasn't some confused young girl so aggrieved over my friend's death that I was acting crazy. I may have been wrong about Ajay, but I knew Jordan hadn't killed herself.

He stared back at me for a few long moments. "Okay," he said finally. "I'll help you if I can, but it has to stay off the record."

"Deal." I smiled, pleased to be taken seriously for once. "We think Jordan intercepted a letter meant for Holman that contained a tip to check out some of Juan Pablo Romero's taco trucks."

"Hmmm," Mr. Monroe said, "do you know if she followed the tip? Or what she found?"

I shook my head. "We don't. All we know so far is that she got the tip on the same night she died. Now why would a reporter as ambitious as Jordan kill herself when she had just gotten a tip on a big story?"

"Even if I agreed with you, which I'm not saying I do," Mr. Monroe said, "you'd have to convince the sheriff that the tip Jordan got was somehow linked to her death. Then they'd have to convince a judge to get the proper warrants to investigate further. I gotta be honest, Riley, I think that'd be a tough sell."

I agreed. "What if there's some way to get around all that and look into it ourselves? If we found—"

"If you did that, whatever you found wouldn't be admissible."

"But what if—"

"Listen," he said, lowering his head toward mine, "the

chances are slim that the alleged tip was related to the fact that she took her own life hours later." He paused. "But if you want, I can use some of my contacts and look into it. Would that make you feel better?"

"Yes!" I smiled. I wanted to do a fist pump and jump in the air. But I didn't, of course. I did, however, appropriately thank him and gave him my cell number to call if he had any news.

Feeling excited, I walked into the library and texted Holman for the second time since last night. Again, I got no response. I wanted to tell him about the mess with Ajay and about how Mr. Monroe agreed to help. I wished he'd hurry up and text me back already.

After setting my stuff down, I went to talk to Dr. H. I found him at his desk poring over a newspaper with his magnifying glass, the one Louisa had given him for their fortieth wedding anniversary. It had a black marble handle with a gold tassel at the end. Dr. H was proud that at the age of sixty-seven, he still didn't need reading glasses, but I'd noticed he was using the magnifying glass more than usual lately.

"Knock, knock," I said, hovering just outside his open door.

"Ah, Riley." He looked up. "Come in."

I walked in and sat in my usual spot, in the chair on the left facing his desk. He set down the magnifying glass and smiled at me. "You're doing better today, I trust?"

"Yes," I said, "but I wanted to see if you'd consider going to the sheriff about the threats you've been getting."

Dr. H exhaled, a heavy sound, like he was blowing out the weight of his troubles. "I've considered it, of course," he said, "but I am inclined to believe them when they say they have a source inside the department. I'd like to gather a little more information before taking my suspicions to Joe Tackett."

"Do you have any theories?"

"Well," he said, again picking up his magnifying glass and turning it over in his hand, "as you've probably noticed, I've been doing considerable research on what reason Twain and his boss could possibly have for wanting to donate a bookmobile to our little library."

"Yeah, I've been thinking about that too."

He nodded. "It's a strange thing for someone to be so violently passionate about getting books in the hands of underserved populations."

"Agreed."

"I've been going over the possible nefarious applications of a bookmobile, and to be honest, I haven't come up with much." Dr. H paused, then smiled. "Times like this I wish my dear Louisa was still here. She had such a deliciously suspicious mind....

"Anyway, the only thing I've been able to figure out is that it must come down to access. This Twain, and his boss, who I think we can safely figure is Juan Pablo Romero, are looking to gain access to outlying communities under the cover of books."

"But what for?"

"That," he sighed, "I don't know. But I think we have to figure it isn't for the enrichment of people's lives."

"What if this is like the park he's building? A donation to the community to make himself look good?" I asked, playing devil's advocate. I was no fan of Romero, but after being so wrong about so many things, I wanted to be sure the next time I accused somebody of something, I had grounds.

"Then why not make a big public show of it? Why

threaten?"

Just then we heard a deafening scream coming from the circulation desk. *Tabitha.* We raced out of the office and saw her, face white as chalk, crouching down behind the desk, screaming, "Get that beast out of here!"

I followed her pointed finger to the source of her panic. It was Mrs. James standing in the library holding a very excited Coltrane on a leash. He jumped and twisted and reared up when he saw me, panting heavily.

"No dogs allowed!" Tabitha screeched. "Shoo!"

Dr. H went to calm her down, while I escorted a shocked-looking Mrs. James and Coltrane back through the front doors.

"I'm so sorry," she said, trying to keep Coltrane from knocking me over with his enthusiasm. "I had no idea he would frighten her so much."

I had to laugh because I hadn't known Tabitha was so scared of dogs. I'd have to remember that for later. "Oh, she'll be fine." I bent down to rub Coltrane's ears. "Who could be scared of a big softy like you?"

"She has every reason to be scared," Mrs. James said seriously. "Coltrane is a trained attack dog. He's all tail wags and kisses if he likes you, but if not, he'll rip you to bits."

"I'm glad he likes me then."

"That's actually why I'm here, Riley," Mrs. James tugged on the leash and forced Coltrane into an obedient sit. "I want you to take him."

"What?"

"I heard about what happened to your car," she said, "and that the police were called to your house last night. I'm not sure what's going on, but I want you to take Coltrane. For protection." I could see how worried she looked, and it touched me.

"I'm fine," I said. "Really."

"I insist." She handed me the leash. "You'll feel a lot safer with him around. I'll feel a lot safer, too." She petted Coltrane's head and looked at him affectionately. "Besides, I have my hands full with the other two. And I think you remind him of Jordan." Her eyes glistened as she looked at him.

I didn't know what to say, so I just said, "Thank you." And just like that I became the owner of a furry, eighty-pound trained assassin.

"Mrs. James?" I asked before she walked away.

"Yes?"

I felt like I needed to say something about the obituary. She hadn't asked me when I'd be finished with it, but I knew she had to be wondering. "About Jordan's obituary...I know you probably want it to run soon, but I haven't gotten it quite right just yet. But I'm still working on it."

She smiled at me the same way she used to when I'd ask for a second helping of lasagna at her house. "I'm in no hurry," she said, with a wan smile. "I know you've been working hard on this. I hear things."

I froze, my face no doubt showing a look of one part surprise, one part confusion. Did Mrs. James know that I was looking into *alternatives*?

"I knew you were the best person for the job. That's why I asked you, Riley." And with that she turned to leave.

CHAPTER 32

Tabitha nearly had a nervous breakdown over Coltrane, so Dr. H told me I could have the rest of the day off, which worked out really well because in addition to being incredibly distracted, I needed to get my new pet some basic necessities, like food and a squeaky toy in the shape of a newspaper.

The problem was I had no car. Once I got Coltrane home and he sniffed every inch of my house, I called Ryan. His family owned the only farm and home supply center in Tuttle Corner. And he had a truck.

"I'm just glad you knew you could count on me," Ryan said as we drove over to his family's store.

"To give me a ride. Obviously not for anything more than that."

"Damn, baby, that's cold."

"Get used to it."

Ryan smiled like I had just said something nice. I had no idea why he was so thrilled to be driving me around to do my errands, but I wasn't going to ask. With my parents out of town, and pretty much no other friends in the world, my choices of people to call in favors from were slim. Plus, Ryan owed me. I figured an afternoon of hauling me around was a small price to pay for breaking my heart and ruining the future I'd planned on since I was a girl.

We got to his father's store, and after we chatted with him for a few minutes, Ryan loaded his truck with everything I'd need to take care of Coltrane. Ryan hooked me up with a large wire crate, raised food dishes, three fifty-pound bags of high-protein food, a doggie hairbrush, flea and tick shampoo, nail clippers, a retractable leash, and five kinds of chew toys. I protested, saying I couldn't afford all of this, but Ryan's father insisted I take it. "On the house, sweetie," Hank said. He was a man of few words, but the look in his eyes said: *Sorry my son is such a dumbass.*

I thanked him profusely and promised to have my parents call when they got back in town. On the ride home, Ryan asked, "Do you want to tell me what's really going on with you?"

"Not really, no."

"C'mon, Riley," he said. "Car bombings? 911 calls in the middle of the night? This isn't like you."

"Maybe it is like me," I said, sounding like a petulant child. "Maybe you don't know me as well as you think you do?" I crossed my arms across my chest.

"I know you better than anyone," he said. I hated that he was right. "I don't know what you're mixed up in, but I wish you'd let me help."

For a moment, I felt my hard shell of anger begin to crack. It would be so nice to tell him everything. He'd always been the person I'd confided in when things were tough, and he had a way of calming me and helping me gain perspective. I hesitated, trying to decide whether I should open up to him, and in that moment of hesitation, his phone vibrated. It was sitting on the console between us. I looked at the screen. Ridley's name flashed on the display.

"Your baby mama's calling," I sniped, my hard shell

re-forming.

Ryan sighed and pressed the silence button. "Riley—"

We had just pulled into my driveway, and before the truck even stopped, I had the door open. "Thanks for taking me today," I said in clipped tones, "and thanks for all the stuff. That was really generous of your dad."

"Ril—"

"Do you mind bringing it into the garage? Thanks!" I slammed the door and went inside.

When Ryan left, it was 2:30, and I still hadn't heard from Holman. I texted him again, and yet again, I waited for the telltale ellipses to pop up, but they didn't. I decided to call him instead. Maybe he was driving and couldn't text. But my call went straight to voicemail. *"Hello. You have reached the voice-recording device of William Holman. If you wish to receive a call back, please leave a message. If you do not leave a message, I will probably not call you back as I will assume you dialed me in error."*

I called the *Times*, but the receptionist said he hadn't come in to work yet. I must have been worried because that's the only explanation for what I did next. "Is Hal Flick around?"

"One moment please."

"This is Flick." His rough voice came across the line a few seconds later.

"It's Riley," I said without preamble. "I'm calling to see if you know where Holman is. It's been a while since I've heard from him, and I'm getting worried."

He paused before answering. "Haven't seen him since yesterday. Did you try his cell phone?"

"Obviously." I knew it was wrong to sound so irritated

when I was asking for a favor, but I couldn't help it. "No answer. He's not returning my texts either."

"He's a big boy. I'm sure he's fine."

I sighed, annoyed he wasn't being more helpful. But what had I expected?

"What are you two working on anyway?"

"Don't ask questions you already know the answers to. It insults us both."

"You should stay away from this story, Riley."

"I'll take it under advisement."

"This is not something you want to get involved with." Flick lowered his voice to a gruff but urgent whisper. "I'm serious. These people are not playing around."

"I know that," I said, "but I think finding out what happened to *my friend* is important enough to take a few risks. I guess that's where we're different."

In the silence that followed, I felt the sting of my words. After a beat he said, "Listen, there are things you don't know—"

"Yeah, like where Holman is. So I need to go and find out—bye!" I pressed end.

The encounter, like all my encounters with Flick, left me shaken. I couldn't think of another person in the world who made me as angry as Hal Flick. Why did he think he had the right to tell me what to do? He wasn't family. He wasn't even a loyal friend to Granddaddy in the end. He could have pushed the sheriff to investigate more completely, or he could have done what Holman was doing for Jordan and investigated the death himself. But he chose to do nothing. It was like the moment Granddaddy died, he ceased to exist for Flick. I would never forgive him for that.

I felt restless about Holman and Flick, so I threw a leash on Coltrane and decided to take a walk. The sun was still scorching hot even though it was almost 5 p.m. But, despite Coltrane's thick coat, he seemed happy to be sniffing his way along the sidewalks toward town. I didn't really have an agenda when I left the house, but decided as I walked through the park to wander over toward the sheriff's office. I thought if I just happened to see Ajay there, and just happened to have the opportunity to apologize to him, well, then that was purely a coincidence.

When I got there, it wasn't Ajay that I saw. It was Joe Tackett standing against a tree outside, smoking a cigarette.

"Joe."

"Riley."

I was going to walk straight past, but Coltrane pulled so hard on the leash I nearly fell over. He started barking— and I mean really barking—about a foot from Tackett.

"Jesus!" he screamed and scrambled away from Coltrane. "What's with your dog?"

"Coltrane!" I pulled hard on the leash to try to get him to stop, but he wouldn't. He wasn't trying to attack him, but there was definitely something about the Sheriff that he didn't like.

"What the hell!" Tackett was clearly upset. I didn't blame him. I could see what Mrs. James meant when she said Coltrane could be scary. With every bark his razor-sharp teeth flashed, and it didn't take much imagination to think how they'd feel slicing through skin. He barked and snarled repeatedly, despite my pleas for him to stop. It wasn't until Tackett climbed over the back edge of the bench and went back inside the building that he stopped barking. He was panting heavily and kept his eagle-gaze glued to the door.

"Shhhhh," I cooed, bending down to stroke his head. "It's okay. Joe is kind of a jerk, but he won't hurt you."

"Nicotine," a voice from behind me said. My heart flew into my throat, and I stumbled a little trying to get up from my crouching position. It was Ajay. "He was reacting to the nicotine," Ajay said, holding out the back of his hand for Coltrane to sniff. "Former police dog?"

I nodded, heart still pounding inside my chest. Ajay looked as handsome as ever; the only difference was this time he had no smile for me.

"Some dogs are trained to sniff for nicotine in addition to illegal drugs."

"He was a rescue," I said. "Given up for being gun shy. He belonged to Jordan, actually. I think he's mine now."

"Pretty dog." Ajay smiled at Coltrane and petted his head.

In the bright light of day, there was so much I wanted to say to Ajay, but I wasn't sure where to start. The thick wall of stuff between us would take more than a simple "I'm sorry" to break through. But I supposed it was a good place to start. I took a deep breath and said, "Listen, I want to apologize."

Ajay pulled his hand back from the dog and thrust both hands into the pockets of his pants. "For calling 911 on me?"

"Yes."

"And for leading me on?"

"Yes."

"And for thinking I was a criminal?"

"If I could just explain—"

"Why you thought I was capable of...what was it you thought I did, anyway?" he asked.

"I know it seems bad, and looking back I can see how maybe I jumped to a few conclusions, but Holman thought so too...and when he told me you were married, I just felt so stupid...." My argument petered out. It sounded less like justifiable batshit and more like the regular variety.

"If you had questions, you should have asked me."

"Fair enough," I said. "But I just want you to know that it wasn't all fake."

He rolled his eyes and looked away.

"It's true. I mean, I didn't start to think you were, um, involved in anything bad until after that night we ate at the fish shack when we...."

His eyes flicked toward me, and I wondered if he was thinking back to that moment of our first kiss, in his car. The heat, the passion, the promise of it. I thought maybe the smallest amount of tenderness was growing between us.

"But then you decided I was a criminal without having any proof whatsoever?"

"No—"

He put his hand up, stopping my protest. "Anyway. I came out here to let you know the ruling on your car explosion was catastrophic battery failure due to improper jump starting." When I looked at him blankly, he added, "User error with jumper cables."

"User error?" I asked, confused. "But it wasn't being used at the time. I was sleeping off a monster hangover if you remember."

"I remember." Ajay furrowed his brow. "But the lab found evidence at the scene consistent with an explosion due to an external ignition source and poor battery connectivity. In layman's terms, it looked like someone was jumping the car and hooked up the cables incorrectly, causing the battery to explode. The department is ruling it an accident."

I was shocked and more confused than ever. "But I don't understand—my car wasn't being jumped at the time!"

"According to the investigators, it was."

I didn't know what to say. I stood there with my mouth

hanging open for at least three solid seconds. "So that's it? That's what the official report is going to say?"

Ajay shrugged. "I guess so."

My voice rose in protest and a shrill, "No!" escaped from the back of my throat.

Ajay flinched.

"Someone else must have jumped it and connected it wrong on purpose! I'm sure they wanted it to look like an accident! It was probably Romero or, or—"

Ajay looked at me, an unreadable expression on his face. I had clearly lost all credibility where my hunches were concerned. I let my voice trail off, feeling a little bit like the girl who cried gangster.

"I'm just the messenger here, Riley. If you have questions, I'd suggest asking Carl or Joe."

I deserved his coldness, but it still stung. I knew he could have looked into this further for me—he was an explosives expert, after all. He just hadn't wanted to. He was obviously still angry with me. I'd have to take it up with someone whose heart I hadn't just stomped on.

I took a steadying breath and said, "Okay. Thanks."

"Just doing my job." He gave Coltrane one more pet on the head and walked inside.

"I tell my students to look for clues to the life story that's left behind. Sometimes there are poems, emails, or journals that often, in a way, write the story for you, or at least give you a map."

—JIM SHEELER, in an
interview on Poynter.org

CHAPTER 33

I cut through Memorial Park again on my way back home, agitated by what I'd just learned. Whoever blew up my car had been savvy enough to make it look like an accident. And, it seemed like they were going to get away with it. Joe Tackett hated my guts, so he'd be no help, and I had already admitted to Carl that I'd been drinking that night. I wondered if I could convince Carl to look into it? That this was all an elaborate setup?

We had just reached the edge of the park when Coltrane started pulling at the leash, carrying me in his wake and nearly ripping my arm from its socket. He was headed straight for Mr. Monroe, who was standing almost in the same place I'd seen him earlier that morning outside the courthouse.

"Don't worry, he won't hurt you!" I said in case the sight of a German shepherd running toward him might make him nervous.

By the time I caught up with Coltrane's leash, Mr. Monroe had already bent down and made nice with him. "Hey, puppy! Whose a good doggy?" he asked using a goofy dog-voice. Coltrane whined and wagged his tail and licked Kevin's face.

I was still on edge about our conversation from earlier, but there was no getting around stopping to chat—not with

Coltrane practically licking him to death. "He sure likes you."

Mr. Monroe stood. "What can I say? I'm a dog person."

Coltrane looked up at him like he was holding a T-bone steak. Mr. Monroe petted his head and patted his side, but after a few seconds, he snapped at Coltrane, who sat immediately.

"I'd say so," I said, impressed. "You need to give me some tips. I just got him from Mrs. James. He was Jordan's most recent rescue."

"Ah," Kevin nodded as he scratched behind Coltrane's ear. "Seems like a good dog. Glad he found a new home." He paused. "Listen, I have an update for you on that stuff we talked about."

"Wow—that was fast!"

"I talked to a guy I know in the sheriff's department, and he said Romero is one-hundred-percent clean. 'A model citizen' were his exact words. If Jordan got a tip about his taco trucks, maybe it was a complaint about food safety or something—but nothing sinister is going on there, I promise you."

Kevin laughed, but I felt like I could cry. I'd been wrong. *Again.* I'd listened to Holman and allowed myself to be deluded into thinking there was some evil taco chef running around Tuttle Corner killing innocent young reporters. Even I had to admit how stupid it sounded when you really thought about it.

"Okay, thanks, Kevin," I said, just wanting to get home and forget all about this day.

———

I worked on Jordan's obituary for a couple of hours, mostly just writing and rewriting the same four sentences. The truth was I hadn't had much luck coming up with anything fitting. What I had so far was a dry accounting of facts, the exact opposite of what I hoped to create. Every time I tried to write about her, the vision of how she died stopped me cold. I felt sure this was no cut-and-dried suicide, but other than Romero we had no suspects. If he was clean, like Kevin said, who could possibly have wanted to kill Jordan? It was like I had to know how she died in order to write about her life. I was completely blocked. Eventually, I gave up, telling myself I'd try again tomorrow.

Coltrane's wet nose nudged me out of my dreamless sleep at 6:02 a.m. It was a bright, clear morning. The air was muggy and held the promise of the heat that was sure to come later in the day. The sun had just poked above the horizon, the birds swooped and chirped as they gathered breakfast, and I could hear the sounds of neighbors' sprinkler systems rat-tat-tatting. I took a deep breath and drank in the morning. As early as it was, I felt completely refreshed. I'd slept better than I had in months. Coltrane's presence, whether it was because I felt safe with him around or simply because I wasn't alone for the first time in a long while, relaxed me enough to allow a glorious eight hours of sleep. And boy, was I going to need it.

The Friends of the Tuttle Corner Library book sale happened twice a year, in June and December. Citizens were encouraged to donate books for the sale throughout the year, and we'd sell them for fifty cents per hardcover and twenty-five cents for a paperback. Next to the Johnnycake Festival, the book sale was one of the biggest highlights of the year, and the June sale was today.

I was running from fiction to nonfiction to reshelf Sarah Palin's *America by Heart*, and I ran into a pair of rather toned biceps. "I'm so sorry—" I started to say, but when I realized it was Ajay, my voice faded away.

"You've been saying that a lot lately," he quipped, lowering the book he'd been looking through, Ben Mezrich's *Sex on the Moon*.

"Hi," I stammered once I could find my voice. "You're here...."

"Yeah. Just came over on a break between training sessions at the department. This book sale is the talk of the town."

"Looks like you've got a winner there." I pointed to the book in his hand.

"You've read it?"

"It's pretty wild."

"Sex on the moon would be."

I blushed. "It's not really about that. It's about this college student who was interning at NASA. He promises his girlfriend that he'll get her the moon—or moon rocks, in this case—and plans this crazy heist to steal them for her."

Ajay cocked one eyebrow up. "And does he?"

"He does," I said. "But then he goes to prison."

"You spoiled the ending."

I looked into his eyes and wanted to say something profound. Something about how I wish we could start over and maybe there could be another ending for us, but I lost my nerve. I was sure he didn't want to hear it anyway.

"Nah, you can read as much on the jacket. You should get it. I think you'd like it."

"Well, I never turn down a book recommendation by a librarian."

"She's not actually a librarian." Tabitha's saccharine voice cut the air around us. "And she really needs to get back to work." She twitched past us.

Ajay whispered, "Tabitha?"

I nodded.

"She's a real treat."

"You have no idea."

Ajay gave me a weak smile, and I thought for a fleeting moment he was going to say something else. But he didn't.

"I've got to get back to work," I said, then lowered my head because I just couldn't bear to look at him when I said the next part. "But maybe if you're free sometime—"

"I'm going to get going, too," he said, making it clear that there was no chance of him ever being free for me. Who was I kidding? Of course he'd never forgive me, let alone give me another chance. And maybe that was for the best. All I really knew about him was that he was a nice guy whose kiss made me melt into a puddle of hot goo. Surely there'd be other guys like that out there. I didn't need to go chasing one I'd already offended ten different ways.

So I said, "Take care," and left it at that.

———◦◦———

The day had been busy with people in and out of the library. Mrs. Gradin donated her collection of gluten-free cookbooks and bought several new ones on baking. Judging by the size of Mr. Gradin's belly, the gluten-free diet hadn't gone over so well in their house. Mrs. Winterthorne bought Janet Evanovich's Stephanie Plum novels, numbers one through nineteen. And Betsy North invested in a complete set of the Harry Potter books for her grandson, Nick.

I had just finished checking in Mrs. Chruner's copy of *The Alchemist,* which she said she found blasphemous, when I heard a familiar voice ask, "Is it too late to make a donation?"

"Of course not, Mr. Monroe," Tabitha said, snapping

her fingers at me. "Riley will be glad to help you with this."

"Hey," I said walking over to the makeshift sales desk. I'd seen more of Mr. Monroe in the past few days than I had in the past few years.

"Hey, yourself." He held a pile of five or six books in his hands.

With Tabitha looking on, I didn't want to risk appearing too chatty, so I got right down to business. "What have you got for us today?"

He set down the books. "Just clearing out the old bookshelves. This sale is always a good excuse to do that."

I picked up the books one by one and turned them over to make sure there weren't any visible signs of wear and tear. I figured Mr. Monroe wasn't the type to abuse his books, but you never know. People have tried to donate books with no covers, books with the spines ripped off, books that are missing the last ten pages. It's kind of sad that they think just because we're a library that we'll take any old thing.

He made small talk while I worked. "You guys been busy?"

"Yes," I said picking up a perfect copy of *Into Thin Air* by Jon Krakauer. "How about you?"

"Oh, yes. That's one thing you can count on in Tuttle County. Lots of bad guys to prosecute." He laughed. "So, how's it going with Coltrane?"

"Good," I said automatically, but as soon as I did, something niggled at the back of my brain. I didn't remember telling him Coltrane's name. In fact, I specifically remembered that I hadn't said his name when we met on the street. Ryan's Dad gave me that tip. He said a dog will always let his guard down around a person who knows his name, so don't tell anyone their name except people you trust one hundred percent. And while I'd always liked Mr. Monroe, I didn't know him well enough to know how much I trusted him.

"That's good. He seems like a great dog. Real smart."

My mind was furiously trying to figure out how Kevin would know Coltrane's name. I picked up the last book in the pile. I turned it over to check its condition, and I nearly stopped breathing. *The Ghost of Rear Range Lighthouse: The Inside Story on Hilton's Head's Most Haunted Attraction.*

I felt the color drain from my face. Mr. Monroe must have noticed it, too. "Riley? What's wrong?"

"This book...."

"Yes?" He smiled. "Have you read it?"

"Where did you get it?"

He took one look at my face, and for a split second I saw fear in his. He quickly wiped the look off his face and replaced it with a smile so fake it looked like his mouth was being drawn up at the corners by puppet strings. "What?"

"Where did you get this book?"

"Hilton Head, obviously." His laugh sounded forced, and his eyes darted toward the door.

Something was off, and he knew it. It all started to make sense. *Him knowing Coltrane's name. Jordan's favorite lighthouse. Hilton Head.* "Kevin," I said slowly, "how well did you know Jordan?"

His smile faded in an instant. "What do you mean?"

"You know what I mean."

He looked around and dropped his voice, "She was a former student just like you. Why are you asking?"

"How did you know my dog's name?"

Before he could answer, Tabitha hawked back over to where we were standing. "Riley, I really need you in the back. You can visit with Mr. Monroe another time, okay?" Her tone was more direct order than question.

"I'm going on break," I said. She started to complain that she hadn't had a break in two years, but I walked right past her. I grabbed Kevin's sleeve and dragged him out the front doors to the library. We needed to talk.

"You were seeing Jordan." I launched the accusation on pure instinct.

For a second he looked shocked. "Wha—" he started to say but then stopped himself. He paused, dropped his head, and stared at the sidewalk for what seemed like an eternity. Finally, when he lifted his eyes to look at me, they were shining. "How did you know?"

"Coltrane, for starters. He clearly knew you."

Kevin blew out a big sigh. "We'd been seeing each other since last fall, but no one knew. At first we decided to keep it under wraps because it might look weird since she was my former student. I didn't care so much, but Jordan thought her parents would have a hard time accepting it."

I could understand that. I was having a hard time accepting it. Even though there wasn't that big of an age difference, the student/teacher relationship was a pretty big mental hurdle to get over.

"I tried to get her to tell her family, but even after several months she said she wasn't ready." His eyes fixed once again on the sidewalk beneath our feet. "But we were serious—I mean, for a while it really seemed like she was the one." His voice broke off. I wondered if he had talked about Jordan with anyone since she died. "She was smart and funny and beautiful and so passionate. We traveled together on weekends, visiting her parents' place in Hilton Head, and we went to Dauphine Island and the Outer Banks. She was so adventurous—always up for something new."

But I knew Jordan had been on Click.com just a few months ago. I wondered what might have happened to this *Lolita*-turned-storybook-romance to send her back to on-line dating?

As if he read my mind, he continued, "I guess it was late spring, I told Jordan I didn't want to keep our relationship a secret anymore. I was thinking about asking her to move in with me, and I told her that if we were going to have a future together, she had better be able to be seen with me in public. She refused, said her dad would never accept us."

Mr. James had always been a bit overprotective, but Jordan was a grown woman. I had to believe that sooner or later he would have accepted her choice. It wasn't like Kevin was that much older.

He breathed in a shaky breath. "So I broke things off. I told her I didn't want to sneak around anymore. Told her to call me when she was ready to go public. She begged me not to, but I just figured she would come around. I never thought—"

"So were you two broken up when she...?"

"Not exactly. We'd just started talking again. Trying to work things out. But on the morning of the festival, she freaked and said she wasn't ready to tell her parents yet. We had a big fight." He wiped at the corner of his eye. "Later that night was when she...." He took a steadying breath. "I'll never forgive myself."

I could feel the weight of his guilt as it crushed down upon him, his shoulders slumped with grief and remorse. "I miss her so much." His face crumpled, and I worried he might start crying again.

"So you think she killed herself because of...you guys?" I asked gently.

"I ask myself that every day."

I thought for a moment. "And you definitely don't think there is any chance that her death had something to do with the story she was working on about Juan Pablo Romero?" I was having a hard time letting that theory go, despite the mounting evidence against it.

"No way." He shook his head. "Jordan was a lot more emotionally fragile than people realized."

We talked for a while longer. I still wasn't completely convinced that Jordan had committed suicide, but it was clear Kevin thought she did. I understood what he was going through—the guilt, the endless wondering what you could have done differently. He was in his own private hell, and I was probably only making it worse by complicating things. But in the back of my mind, I thought if I could just somehow prove that she hadn't killed herself, it might give him some peace.

Chapter 34

When I got home after work, Holman was waiting in my driveway. "Where have you been?" I snapped at him. There was so much that had happened since I'd last spoken to him, I hardly knew where to begin.

"You've been worried about me," he said. "That's sweet."

"I'm not worried," I lied. "I'm angry. Why did you go dark on me for twenty-four hours?"

"I'm sorry," he said, following me into my house. "I had to go up to DC to meet with a source. What is that?" He pointed a finger at Coltrane.

"It's a dog, Sherlock."

"Yeah, but whose dog?"

"Mine."

"When did you get a dog?"

"Yesterday." I was irritated at him for making me worry and didn't want to stray from the subject by explaining how Coltrane came to be here. And I was curious about what was so important that he couldn't call or text me back. "So what was up in DC?"

He stepped carefully around Coltrane, who was looking at him as if he were an archaeological curiosity. "I followed a hunch and it turns out, Uncle Mateo was arrested about seven years back for meth trafficking."

"Yeah. He's a bad guy. We knew that."

"There's more." He pulled a folded piece of paper out of his pocket and smoothed it out on my ottoman. "A colleague of mine has a connection to someone who works for the DEA up there. He gave me access to some of the reports filed during their investigation of Mateo. Their case ultimately failed because of a lack of evidence. But one of the investigators who worked the case noted in the file that one of the reasons it was hard to pin charges on Mateo was that his distribution network was really diffuse. They suspected he was selling in a bunch of rural areas."

"Okaaaaay...."

"The DEA seemed to believe he was branching out from the bigger cities and taking his product to small communities. The agent said he thought Mateo was either working for the Mexican mafia distributing meth in the US, or that he launched his own operation, staying clear of the territories held tight by other organized crime syndicates. That would explain why he went outside urban areas."

Connections were slowly materializing in my brain. "It could also explain why he wasn't caught," I added. "Rural law enforcement agencies are always so understaffed."

"That's right," Holman said, looking at me over Coltrane's head. The dog had positioned himself right in front of where Holman sat on the couch, waiting patiently to be petted. By the look on Holman's face, he was going to be waiting a while.

"And if Uncle Mateo wanted to sell drugs away from the cities," he said, "it would stand to reason that he'd involve his favorite nephew who just happens to live in rural Virginia."

As soon as Holman said that, it hit me. "Taco trucks!" I

blurted out.

"Ding-ding-ding-ding!" Holman smiled.

"Mateo has been using Juan Pablo's Tacos Los Locos trucks to run drugs from Jersey all the way down to Virginia?"

Holman nodded. "Obviously, this is all conjecture at this point. But I think it fits."

"Oh my gosh, I'll bet that's what he wants the bookmobiles for, too."

"I thought of that, but what would a bookmobile get him that he isn't already getting with his taco trucks?"

"Bookmobiles go to only the least populous areas—areas where a taco truck would look out of place. So it could reach the really rural areas without drawing suspicion. And since the library is privately owned, there'd be no oversight except from Dr. H. I'm guessing that's what those visits from the library thugs were all about. To get Dr. H on board through either bribery or intimidation."

Holman was quiet as he thought. "I'll bet this is what Jordan found out—at least in part," he said. "Whatever it was, it was big enough to kill for. And protecting millions in drug money would certainly be big enough."

"I'll bet you're right."

"I just wish she would have come to me."

I pictured Jordan alone at the office, heartbroken from her fight with Kevin—maybe feeling hopeless and alone—and then opening that letter with the tip big enough to blow the roof off the entire town. The Jordan I knew would never have called for backup. She'd want to be the star, the lead, the girl with the golden pen. That was Jordan. She aimed high, believed in herself to the fullest extent, was tenacious and bold. And she didn't look back. She didn't think things to death. I always admired her for that. But there is a thin line between confidence and recklessness.

"How do we prove it?" I asked, snapping my fingers for Coltrane to stop staring at poor Holman.

"I'm going to start by retracing Jordan's steps the night she died and do a recon mission to the taco truck at Little Juan Park."

"You mean *we* are going to do recon."

"Mmmm."

"What do you mean 'mmmm'? I'm your partner on this."

"I don't know," he said. "It could be dangerous."

"C'mon." I softened my tone, trying to catch the fly with honey. "We're a team! Sherlock and Obit Girl, remember?" I smiled big and batted my eyelashes at him.

"Your sexuality won't work on me," Holman said flatly. "As symmetrical as you are, I have laser-like focus when I'm at work. Even Princess Leia couldn't cause me to compromise my ideals."

"Princess Leia?"

He shrugged. "I have a thing for strong women. Whatever. The point is that even she—in her little gold bikini, kicking ass and taking names—could not convince me to go against my gut when I'm working." He pointed at Coltrane. "I'm kind of like your friend there. I might look all dopey and cute, but when I'm on the job, I'm a killer."

I stared at Holman, slack jawed. There was so much in what he just said I wanted to comment on, I didn't even know where to begin. *Little gold bikini? Dopey and cute? A killer?* But it would have to wait.

"What am I, a china doll?" I stood up and put my hands on my hips. "I don't care what you say, I'm going and so is he." I pointed at Coltrane. "And that is final."

———◆———

"Aren't you going to ask me what my big news was? I texted you like a million times," I said once we were in the car on the way down to LJP.

"Right," he said. "What did you find?"

I told him all about Ajay coming over, the 911 call, and how Ajay had been furious with me for suggesting he had ties to Romero. Then I told him that Ajay was never Jordan's mystery man, it was Kevin Monroe.

"Jordan Blaise, of course," Holman said. "She said she was going to use that name once she got her own byline."

"You could have mentioned that," I snapped.

"I didn't think it was relevant. Besides, how was I to know she'd use an alias for online dating?"

He had a point. "Anyway. Can you believe all that?"

He nodded, not looking nearly as shocked as I thought he should be. "Interesting. I guess it makes sense that she'd want to keep that secret from her parents. It can be hard for only children to allow their parents to see them as grown adults."

"*Interesting*? That's all you have to say about it?"

He paused. "I said the thing about her parents, too."

"I mean, aren't you going to say anything about how wrong you were that Ajay was involved? You were sure he was involved with Romero, remember?"

"No, I wasn't."

"Yes, you were! In fact, you got me convinced he was in league with Romero and had something to do with Jordan's death."

He shook his head. "No, if you recall, I said it was clear he was involved *somehow*. Now we know he casually dated Jordan a couple of times and consulted on Romero's park project. So really, if you think about it, I wasn't wrong at all. Ajay was involved, just not in a bad way."

I wanted to throttle him. A few days ago, Holman was ready to get Ajay charged with Jordan's murder, and now he was acting like I had made it all up. "Because of you, Ajay is really mad at me."

"I'd be mad too if a girl I was seeing thought I was involved in criminal activity and tried to entrap me." Since Holman didn't do sarcasm, I knew he was being completely serious.

"But you said you thought he was involved!"

"He was involved. Riley, we just went through this."

I hit his shoulder as hard as I could. How could he feel no remorse for filling my head with all these suspicions when they were so obviously unfounded? "You ruined what could have been a promising relationship, you know."

"Ow. And no, I didn't."

"Yes, you did! He liked me, Holman. He wanted to date me. Do you know how hard it is to find a decent man to date in this town?" My voice was bordering on shrill. Coltrane whined and nosed the side of my cheek.

"Riley," Holman said calmly, "that relationship was never going anywhere. You can pretend it ended because I made you suspicious of Ajay, but you and I both know you are not ready to move on. You're still tangled up with Ryan."

What? I was not tangled up with Ryan! If I was still tangled up with him, I would have agreed to his crazy plan to keep seeing him while he had bizarro-baby with Ridley. But I didn't. I cut that off. I was ready to move on. Which is exactly what I was about to tell Holman when he pulled off the highway and onto the access road toward the construction site for Little Juan Park. We'd be there in under a minute.

"You're wrong," I said. "And later when we aren't on a

stakeout I can explain to you exactly how wrong you are. But for now, I need to concentrate."

"Whatever you say." His voice dripped with self-satisfaction.

After a few silent moments, he cut the lights as we slipped onto the gravel road that provided access to trucks and other heavy vehicles at the back entrance to what would be Little Juan Park in a few more weeks. As of now, it was just a privately owned construction site. That we were about to break into.

I was equal parts electrified and terrified. I'd never done anything so dangerous in my life. It was fully dark by now, and Holman had pulled into the heavily wooded area just about behind the construction fence. We opened our doors, and Coltrane practically bolted out of the back seat. Luckily I had a hold of his leash and was able to stop him from running off. Holman pocketed the keys, came around to my side of the car, and put them on top of the right front tire. "In case we get separated."

He gave me a look that was filled with meaning. It was as if he wanted me to understand that this wasn't a game. The stakes were real, and if one of us got into trouble, it'd be up to the other to save themselves and go for help.

I nodded.

We walked silently along the edges of the bushes toward the park. It was dark and quiet, except for the crunching of twigs under our feet. The moon was full and bright, and it helped light our way as we walked down the road that ran along the back of the future park.

As we nestled into the trees, Holman took out his phone and checked the time. Then he reached into his fanny pack (yes, he had a fanny pack) and drew out a Phillips-head screwdriver. He whispered, "For the door. Just in case."

Coltrane seemed to be in his element. Focused. Alert. Scanning the dark, ears up at attention. I wondered how many other stakeouts he'd been on? How many times had he assisted in solving crimes? Looking at him now, so full of determination and purpose, I felt badly for him. Put out to pasture because of one tiny flaw.

Holman checked his watch and signaled to me by holding up one index finger. I felt confident that we were well hidden in the foliage, but I was still so nervous that my heart thundered against my chest wall. I held tight to Coltrane's leash and stroked his head—a gesture he hardly seemed to notice as he surveyed the dark around us, seeing and hearing more than Holman and I ever would.

Seconds later we heard the sound of a vehicle; I guessed a golf cart by the quiet whine coming off the motor. Holman reached out and put a hand across me, like a mom does when she stops too suddenly in the car. Coltrane's head whipped up to Holman at the gesture. I stroked his head again, assuring him that I was all right.

The golf cart got closer, and we saw a flashlight beam scan the area, sweeping left, then right in wide swaths. After a couple of minutes that felt like hours, the golf cart retreated, taking the light along with it. The night was once again dark and silent, save for the quiet panting sound of Coltrane, who was most assuredly ready to get to work.

"Follow me," Holman mouthed. We slipped out of the trees and crossed the gravel road until we were just behind the Tacos Los Locos truck. Holman, holding his screwdriver, motioned for me to stay back near the cover of trees while he tried to jimmy the door open. It was hard for me to imagine him having very good jimmying skills, but the more I got to know him, the more I was surprised by his range.

Having had no luck with the door, he moved his attention to the order window. Coltrane and I hung back, and I could just make out Holman's long, spindly arms as he tried to remove the hinges from the window. I heard a snapping sound loud enough to turn Coltrane's head but not so loud as to echo into the night. We were in. The problem was how to actually get inside. The window was at least five feet off the ground.

"C'mon. I'll give you a boost." The whites of Holman's wide eyes were visible even in the dark of the night.

"You're crazy," I whispered. "I'm not going in first!"

"It'll be fine," he said, kneeling down and cupping his hands for me to step into. "No one's in there."

"Then you do it."

"Do you really think you can lift me?"

"Can't you just pull yourself up?"

He shook his head. "I lack significant upper-body strength. I've been like this my whole life. When I was little, my mother tried to make me feel better about it by saying my strongest muscle is my brain. Of course she was speaking metaphorically, because technically it's my gluteus maximus—"

"All right!" I shout-whispered. I really did not want to veer into conversation about Holman's gluteus maximus. I sighed and looked up at the window. I wasn't happy about it, but apparently if we were going to get into that truck, it'd have to be me. With great reluctance, I handed him Coltrane's leash, and he looked at it like it was a snake. On fire.

"You want to lift him up too?" I raised my eyebrows.

"Fine." Holman took the leash and tucked it under his armpit while he again bent down to offer me a boost. Coltrane whined as I put one foot in Holman's hand and heaved myself up with my arms. It was tricky holding the window open with one hand while using the other to hoist myself up, but after a few tries, I was able to get myself through. On the other side, thankfully, I found a stainless steel counter that I used to balance myself before sneaking through the truck to unlock the door and let Holman and Coltrane in.

"Good job."

"Thanks," I said all casual-like, but on the inside I was fizzing with adrenaline. I felt as much like a badass as I ever had. And I was surprised at how much I liked it.

Inside the truck it was pitch-black, the only light coming from occasional glints of moonlight against steel. My eyes were accustomed to the dark, but even still, all I could see were shapes of counters, and refrigerators, doors, and handles.

"What are we looking for?" I turned on my flashlight.

"Anything that looks out of the ordinary."

The place wasn't big, and it didn't take long for us to make an initial pass with our eyes, opening and closing cabinet doors and drawers, looking in every space we could see. It looked exactly how you'd expect a food truck to look. I started to worry that we were wrong, that this was just another entry for the batshit-crazy column.

The more worried I got, the angrier I got. Holman was supposed to be this award-winning investigative journalist. How could he be wrong all the time? First, he'd been wrong about Ajay. Now it looked like he was wrong about the drug-dealing taco truck. His theories were based on little beyond instinct and imagination—so why was I so eager to believe him all the time? Meanwhile, Holman moved through the truck checking every dark corner but hadn't come up with anything.

"There's nothing here," I said.

"There has to be."

"I think we should just go." I gripped Coltrane's leash tighter. The disappointment of not finding a shred of evidence hit me, and fear settled in beside it. I just wanted to get out of there before we got arrested for breaking and entering. Or worse.

Holman stood with both hands on the stainless steel counter. He leaned forward, his body taught with concentration. "We're just missing it...I know there's something here."

"C'mon, let's go," I whispered.

Just then, we heard gravel crunching under tires. I immediately clicked off my flashlight, and we ducked down. It sounded like the golf cart was back. Coltrane, glued to my side, was silent. At that moment I was thankful for whatever police training he'd had that made him not bark in a situation in which most dogs would. He was still and focused, like he'd just been called up to the majors.

The sound of the golf cart got louder. Then we heard a man's voice. I couldn't make out what he was saying, but it sounded like he was speaking into a radio or a phone. The voice got closer and my stomach flipped over. Holman reached out for my hand and squeezed it. *It's going to be okay*, the squeeze said. I didn't believe it, but the gesture comforted me just enough to stop my shaking.

"I thought I saw something," the man's voice was now just outside the truck.

Coltrane stood, ears at attention. If that man came inside the truck right now, I guessed there was no way I could stop Coltrane from attacking.

"I had an all-clear at 9:45," the man said, "but then I coulda swore I saw a light over this way when I was making a pass by the perimeter."

I grabbed Holman's arm. His skin was clammy, and I wondered how worried he was despite his calm demeanor.

"Nah," the guard said. "I must've been seein' things. Dreaming up ways to make this job more exciting." He laughed. We saw a beam of light shine through the window and illuminate the tops of the truck walls. "We're all good."

We waited about five minutes after he drove off before we moved a muscle. My feet were tingling with the pins and needles that come from crouching too long. Finally able to exhale, I slumped onto my butt and leaned back against the cabinet behind me. "That nearly gave me a heart attack."

"I don't think this place has a portable AED, so it is lucky you didn't have one."

I laughed. *Holman.* I don't think I'd ever met anyone so literal.

"C'mon, let's go," I said and started to get up from my position on the floor. In order to get leverage I leaned back against the steel cabinet and planted my heels on the stainless steel floor, the kind with the tiny x's in it, but I must have slipped because the next thing I knew I felt something give way beneath my feet, and I fell back down on my bottom.

"Ouch!"

"Are you okay?"

I couldn't see what had caused it but felt the burning of steel slice through the skin just above my achilles. Coltrane started to bark. "Shhhh!" I tried to placate Coltrane, to let him know I was okay.

Holman shone the flashlight on my ankle and sure enough, dark red blood had bubbled to the surface and was starting to drip down the back of my ankle. Coltrane continued to bark. Loudly. "Shhhh," we both said, trying to get him to stop, as Holman gently lifted me up by my elbow.

We looked down to see what had cut me. It looked like my foot had slipped on some sort of false panel on the floor. The pressure from my foot must have caused the top to slide open, revealing a rectangular cache underneath. Coltrane reared up and chased his tail and barked over and over again, his snout pointing directly at the hole in the floor.

I knew we had only seconds before the guard would be back. Holman knelt down, shined the flashlight inside the compartment, and reached inside. Coltrane barked and snarled. He pulled out a plastic bag that smelled strongly of something I couldn't quite place. It wasn't unpleasant, but the odor was overpowering in such a small space. He opened the bag and I saw his jaw clench. He held it out to me. The bag contained tens of smaller zip bags filled with jagged, whitish shards of rock and powder. I wasn't exactly sure what I was looking at, but I knew it wasn't taco seasoning.

Coltrane was nearly foaming at the mouth now, his sharp teeth flashing with every piercing bark. We saw a beam of light shine through the window. The guard was back. And if he was close enough to shine the light, he could definitely hear Coltrane's bark.

"Can you walk?"

"I think so."

"I'll take Coltrane," Holman dropped one of the bags into his fanny pack and reached down and got out the others. He slid the dummy steel panel on the floor back into place and wound Coltrane's leash around his hand twice.

The man's voice was closer now, and though I couldn't make out what he was saying over the barking, I heard the urgency in his voice.

"Coltrane, off!" I said desperately, remembering how Mrs. James had silenced him that day I had been at their house. To my shock, he stopped barking.

"C'mon," Holman said. He had one hand on the leash and held the other out to me as he led me toward the back of the truck. He carefully opened the back door and helped me out. He followed quickly behind, not even bothering to close it. We hustled to Holman's car still hidden in the bushes.

It wasn't until we were safely heading down the gravel road that we heard the guard yelling at us to stop. Obviously, we didn't listen.

CHAPTER 35

"How did this happen again?" Ryan's mom, Mrs. Sanford, asked as she swabbed me for a third time
with hydrogen peroxide. She was a nurse, and even
though Ryan and I were finished, I knew I could count on
her any time of the day or night. Which proved true when
she opened her door to Holman and me at 10:38 p.m.

"We were taking Coltrane for a walk in the park, and I,
um, tripped. I must have landed on a rock." I said all of this
is one fast stream without making eye contact.

"Uh-huh," she said. I could tell she wasn't buying it.

"Riley, what were you doing walking around alone at
night?" Ryan loomed over us in the kitchen, pacing like a
nervous tiger.

Holman, who stood by silently the whole time, finally
spoke up. "She wasn't alone."

Ryan, as if noticing him for the first time, gave him an
appraising look, trying to decide if Holman was a threat or
not. "Oh yeah, I forgot she had her *dog*."

"Ryan," I hissed at him, "you're not helping."

"What's with the fanny pack, dude?"

"Leave him alone," I warned.

The two men stared at each other, Holman in his
wide-eyed, scientist way and Ryan in his decidedly more

caveman-like manner. Mrs. Sanford broke the tension. "I don't think you need stitches, but it'll be sore for a good while." She laid a fresh gauze pad over the cut and taped it into place. "Also, we should get you a tetanus shot. Come by the office tomorrow, and I'll fix you up."

"Thanks." I smiled at her and tried to convey my deep gratitude not only for fixing my cut but for not asking too many questions. The tetanus-shot comment proved she knew that cut wasn't left by any rock.

"That's quite a dog you've got there," she said, nodding to Coltrane. He sat right by my side the entire time Mrs. Sanford worked on me, like my own personal bodyguard.

I reached out and scratched behind his ear. "He's a keeper for sure."

Ryan stood, arms crossed, looking at me, Coltrane, and Holman.

I got up, holding onto the table for balance, the pain in my leg shooting through me as I did. I'd taken three Advil when I got to their house, but the pain was still strong. "Thanks again," I said, leaning forward to give Mrs. Sanford a hug. "I'll see you tomorrow."

"I don't like that as soon as you start hanging around with," Ryan jerked a thumb at Holman, "Beanpole over here, you end up in all kinds of trouble. This isn't like you."

"Sherlock," Holman said.

"Excuse me?"

"Sherlock is my nickname. Not Beanpole."

"Is this guy for real?"

I scowled at Ryan and then held a hand out to Holman to help me out. "Let's go, Will." Coltrane followed us to the door. I thanked Mrs. Sanford one more time, and we walked gingerly out to Holman's car.

"You called me Will," Holman said once we were sitting

in the car.

"That's your name, isn't it?"

Out of my peripheral vision I saw a smile creep across his face. In the dark of the car, I felt one nip at the corner of my mouth too.

———◆———

The rest of the drive back to my house, all one and a half minutes of it, we were quiet. It wasn't until we were inside and Coltrane was locked in his crate in my bedroom that we addressed the elephant in the fanny pack.

"What are you going to do with all that...*stuff*?"

Holman walked over to my large front picture windows and closed the plantation shutters. He came back to the couch, sat down beside me, and stared at the contraband now on my ottoman. "I guess take it to the police."

"What's that smell?" I asked, again noticing the strong odor coming from the bags.

"Patchouli oil. I think it's meant to mask the smell of the drugs."

"Obviously it didn't fool Coltrane. As soon as that trap door slid open, he knew exactly what it was."

The silence was broken by my phone vibrating. It was on the table near the door where I'd dropped it when we walked in. Holman got it for me and glanced at the display. "Blocked." He held it out to me.

My stomach turned over. I had a bad feeling before I even said hello.

"Is this Riley Ellison?" a man's voice asked.

"Yes." I sat up. Holman leaned in so he could hear too.

"I think you have something that belongs to me." The voice was deep, and I thought I detected a slight Spanish accent.

"Who is this?"

"Call me Twain." Chills broke out all over my body in an instant. He continued in his eerily pleasant, measured tone. "You and your tall friend took something of mine. So I've taken something of yours."

In the background I heard a stifled scream. It was a voice I'd know anywhere. Ryan's voice. A cry escaped my throat. I couldn't speak. Holman took the phone from me and put it on speaker.

"This is Will Holman. To whom am I speaking?"

"This is Mark Twain."

"I don't believe that's your real name, but if we are going to use aliases, could you please refer to me as Sherlock?"

"What?" For the first time in the conversation, the man sounded thrown off.

"That is my preferred code name: Sherlock."

In the brief silence I could hear Ryan's voice, muffled, crying out in the background. My whole body started to shake.

"Whatever you say, *Sherlock*. As I was explaining to your girlfriend, we have a little something of hers we'd like to exchange for what you two stole tonight."

Holman paused before answering. He was trying to play it cool, but I could see he was trying to figure out how to handle this. A person's life could be at stake. "Actually, Riley and I are not romantically involved. While her face is quite—"

"I don't give a shit about her face!" We heard a ripping sound and then a scream.

"Riley!" It was Ryan. Then we heard the sound of a slap to skin. I thought of Mrs. Sanford. Had they taken her too? Mr. Sandford?

"Don't hurt him!" I gasped. *"Please!"*

Holman held his hand up as if to tell me to stop talking.

"You'll never see your product again if you hurt him."

Twain laughed again and said, "I hardly think you're in any position to make demands."

"I disagree. From my calculations, I have what appears to be, oh...maybe $500,000 worth of methamphetamine that belongs to your boss. I'm guessing it's worth more to him than Riley's ex-boyfriend is to me." He immediately held out his hand to me so I knew he was only bargaining. I held my breath and waited for Twain to respond.

"Damn, Sherlock." He forced a chuckle, but the earlier cockiness in his voice was gone. Holman had him worried. "So what do you want?"

"I want to talk to Romero."

"Romero who?"

"Don't toy with me. I know all about Romero's drug trafficking out of the trucks."

The line was quiet for a bit. "I don't know what you think you know, but you're wading in awfully deep water here."

"I'll assume that's a metaphor, which is good because actually I never learned to swim."

Twain erupted with a sharp laugh. "I'll see what I can do about a meeting. But if you even think about calling in the cops—and believe me, we will know—*guapo* here is dead."

"Romero brings an unhurt Ryan to the picnic benches at Riverfront Park at 10 a.m. tomorrow, or I'm taking the stash straight to the cops. And in case you think of coming near me or Riley before then, let me assure you that we are well protected." Before I could stop him, he pressed end.

"What was that? You're going to get him killed!" I shouted.

The sound of Ryan's terror-stricken voice played over in my head. I'd never forget the fear, the desperation in his screams. What if they decided to kill him anyway? What if they hurt him or maimed him? How could I ever live with myself? Then, I thought of the bizarro-me and the baby. A fresh wave of sickness churned in my stomach, and for a minute I thought I might throw up. I clutched my stomach as I breathed harder and faster, still not getting enough air to fill my lungs.

The sound of my hyperventilation must have kicked Holman out of his panic-induced trance, and he looked at me for the first time since he hung up. "Are you okay?"

"Does...it...look...like...I'm...okay?" I gasped between heaving breaths.

"Take a big breath in," he said, miming the gesture, "then hold it at the top for five seconds. Do that three times."

I did what he said and was surprised that it actually worked. Within moments, my breathing was back under control, even if my emotions were not. "How did they find us? And why would they take Ryan?" I asked, still struggling to comprehend what had happened. Why hadn't they just come after us?

"That security guard probably radioed the break-in, and they sent someone to follow my car. And they didn't come after us directly because when reporters go missing, people ask questions. Especially two reporters working the same story at the same paper. Twain is just looking for a way to control us without causing any more suspicion about Romero."

"They're gonna kill him. What do we do?"

"Listen, we have the upper hand here. We just have to figure out how to maximize our leverage."

"How're we going to do that?"

"I have some ideas," he said, rising to leave. "I've worked with a couple of guys from the Warren County sheriff's office on other stories...."

"But they said no cops!" I said, my panic rising. "You heard him...he said they'd know...he said they'd kill Ryan if we called the sheriff!"

"Riley," Holman said, his voice low and serious. "I don't think they have any intention of letting Ryan live no matter what we do."

A fresh wave of nausea gripped me again, and the tears came instantly.

"I also think there is a high probability they are also planning to kill both of us. These people have killed to protect their secret at least once."

"So what are we going to do?"

"I'm going to take this," he gestured to the drugs, "to a safe place. This is our only bargaining chip. In the meantime, I need you to stay here, lock the doors, and wait for my call. Okay?"

I looked at him like he was crazy. "I can't just sit here."

"I will call you as soon as I can, after I check with a source I have about how to proceed."

"Who? What source?"

He shook his head. "The less you know at this point, the better, Riley." He was at the door now. "As soon as I leave, let Coltrane out of his crate and lock all the doors. Whatever you do—do NOT answer your cell phone unless it is me, okay?"

"But what if they call back? What if they change the meeting?"

"They won't."

I looked at Holman a long moment, trying to gain some much-needed reassurance from his eyes. "I wish you'd tell me your plan."

He came toward me and put a hand on each of my shoulders, a surprisingly intimate gesture for him. "I'm

doing this to keep you safe. You have to trust me. I think
I can find a way out of this, but I need a little time, okay?"

I nodded.

"Remember, don't answer the door or your phone."

I nodded again, and he left.

Chapter 36

It had been four hours since Holman left, and I hadn't slept a wink. I looked at my phone: 3:56 a.m. Coltrane, on the other hand, was sleeping comfortably on the couch, his head resting on my lap. I eased myself out from under him, his sleepy eyes opening briefly, then closing again. I moved to the kitchen to put on some coffee. I clicked on the TV and tried to watch the news but couldn't focus. What source did Holman have? Was it someone from the paper? I thought of Kay Jackson. Maybe she was his trusted source. Newspaper editors were better than lawyers when it came to protecting secrets, so it was possible Holman had gone to her for advice. Or maybe it was his DEA guy up in DC?

The coffee, to which I had added more cream and sugar than most people would deem reasonable, coursed through my veins. The caffeine heightened my already agitated state. I felt restless. No—powerless. No—scared shitless. I poured myself another cup, then forced myself to get dressed and brush my teeth. I was so nervous I couldn't even read through the obit pages like usual.

I sat back down on the couch and must have dozed off, because when I looked at my phone it was 5:28 a.m. Still no word from Holman. Coltrane was awake now and needed to go out. *Damn*. Holman had left specific instructions not to leave my house, but I had to take Coltrane out. I grabbed his leash, resolving to only walk him around my front lawn. He circled and whined with anticipation.

Coltrane was not satisfied with this abbreviated version of his morning walk and pulled at the leash toward the sidewalk. I scanned the area. No one was out on the street. No suspicious cars. No shady-looking characters. Nothing but the same familiar houses of neighbors and friends, some with lights on as people got ready for the day. The sun had just come up, bringing enough light with it so that I could see down the street in both directions. I felt pretty sure no one was watching me or waiting in the bushes to grab me.

"Fine," I said, moving Coltrane toward the sidewalk. "One block and that's it."

We had just neared Mrs. O'Flannery's house on the corner of Salem and Beach, with its black wrought-iron fence topped with fleurs-des-lis, when Coltrane's ears perked up. A trill of fear shot through my heart. I was about to turn and run back to my house when I looked up to see Kevin Monroe turning the corner on his way to work.

"Riley?" he said, sounding surprised.

"Oh, hi," I said, putting a hand over my heart to slow its rapid beating.

Kevin was already kneeling down to pet Coltrane, who lapped up the attention. "Didn't mean to scare you," he said, smiling. "I'm just heading to the office a little early."

I was tense with pent-up nerves. I tried to smile back at him, but I'd never had much of a poker face.

"Is everything okay?"

I tried to say a breezy yes, I really did. But what came out instead was a strangled gulp, followed by tears.

"Hey." He stood up and looked at me. "What's going on?"

"It's just..." I knew I should have made something up, but the stress of the past few hours had wound me as tight as a rubber band. "I'm really scared, Mr. Monroe." I wiped away the tears.

"Whatever it is, I'm sure it's gonna be okay." He took Coltrane's leash out of my hands. "Let me walk you home."

I nodded, feeling like a kid back in school, glad for his comfort. "Thanks," I said when we got to my driveway. "I'm sorry, I've just got a lot going on right now...." I let my sentence trail off.

"You know," he said, "you can talk to me about anything. I'll even help if I can."

I pulled out my cell phone. Still no word from Holman. It was almost six now. That left only four hours till the deadline. What if he'd gotten into trouble? What if he wasn't able to meet Romero at ten? My head was dizzy with the possibilities of everything that could go wrong and the sickening consequences. I heard Ryan's scream in my head, his cry for help, the fear in his voice.

"I'm not sure if you can," I said in a voice barely above a whisper.

"Try me," Kevin said, leading me to my front door.

Kevin Monroe sat in my living room and looked nearly as sick as I felt. He was quiet while I told him the whole story. When I was finished talking, he said, "So why don't you just give them back their drugs?"

"For starters, I don't even have them anymore." I handed him a cup containing the last of the coffee I'd made earlier. "And even if I did, Holman thinks they're planning to kill Ryan anyway. And probably us, too." I could hardly believe what I was saying.

Kevin let out a big sigh.

"And they warned us not to call the police," I reiterated.

"No," he shook his head. "You can't go to the cops with this. Not yet."

"Holman said he had a plan, but it's been hours, and I haven't heard from him. I'm worried something's happened to him."

"I know you put a lot of trust in Holman," Kevin said, "but I don't think he's the guy you think he is."

"What do you mean?"

"He has a reputation for being," he paused, considering what word to choose, "reckless."

"How so?"

"Jordan worked with him, and she said he had something of a superhero complex. Thinks he's smarter than everybody else and therefore takes chances that maybe he shouldn't."

It was hard for me to reconcile the Holman I knew with the one Kevin was describing. He did say he wanted to keep me safe, which I guess could fall under the category of hero-like behavior, but he'd never seemed reckless to me. Paranoid, irritating, odd? Yes. But reckless? No.

"I don't know," I said. "I've gotten to know him, and I think he's a pretty reliable guy."

Kevin sighed again, his fourth since we'd come inside. He looked and sounded much older than his thirty-two years in that moment. "Did he tell you what happened to the junior reporter who worked with him before Jordan?"

I shook my head.

"It was a young kid named Alex Wright. He was working the Blexor story with him a couple of years back."

I had a vague recollection of the controversy about Hubert Blexor, an English teacher at St. Augustine's, a

Catholic school in West Bay. He'd been accused of inappropriate conduct with several students. As I recall, it was the *Times* that broke the story. I didn't know which reporter, but it stood to reason it would have been Holman.

Kevin continued. "Alex was a recent grad, like Jordan, and Holman had him go undercover as a student in need of math tutoring in order to get close to Blexor."

"Okay."

"Journalists occasionally do undercover work, but it is highly unusual—and downright unheard of—to ask an inexperienced reporter to go into such a dangerous situation. But Holman thought it was the best way to break the story."

"What happened?"

"Well, he was right. Alex wore a wire on his fourth tutoring session with Blexor. And when Blexor put his hand on Alex's leg, Holman had enough proof to run the story."

"Okay, so surely Holman rushed in and saved him before Blexor could *do* anything, right?"

Kevin gave me a sad look. "Wrong. Holman let things 'develop' to see how much dirt he could get on Blexor. Alex, inexperienced and naïve, waited for Holman to bust in, so he didn't stop him when he moved his hand up his leg."

I felt sick.

"Alex waited for Holman as that scumbag Blexor breathed hot kisses into his ear, whispering the kinds of sick things that a person's not likely to forget. Still Holman waited."

I was quiet, trying to absorb this horrendous information. "But—why?"

"Because he cares about the story above all else," Kevin said, looking directly into my eyes. "He didn't care what happened to Alex, and he doesn't care what happens to Ryan."

His words swirled around in my head like a swarm of

bees. This was the opposite of everything I knew about Will Holman.

"Alex was so traumatized by the experience that he left town and moved back to Missouri. And he didn't even get the byline," Kevin said. "I don't think Holman can be trusted, Riley. Jordan didn't think so either."

An image of Jordan opening the tip addressed to Holman materialized before my eyes. She hadn't called Holman to share it. I'd assumed it was down to her ambition, but what if it were something else? What if she didn't tell Holman because she didn't trust him?

Kevin's voice cut across my thoughts. "But if you want, I think I might have a way to help you get out of this mess without anyone else getting hurt."

CHAPTER 37

Ten minutes later Kevin and I were speeding down the back county roads to meet his mysterious source. We drove for about twenty minutes and were approaching the outer edge of Tuttle County when I saw a huge metal warehouse on the left-hand side.

"This is where we're meeting my guy," Kevin said as he turned into the gravel parking lot.

"Looks a little shady." I took in the vast, windowless building. "Why are we meeting here again?"

Kevin pulled around to the back of the warehouse and put the car into park. He came around to my side and opened my door for me. "The thing is," he said as he closed the door behind me, "Romero has people everywhere."

It wasn't until that exact moment that I realized Kevin was one of them.

———◆———

Holman finally called at 9:13 a.m.

"Hello?" I said.

"Hey. Sorry it took me so long—"

"Hol—" I tried to warn him, but the sharp point of Twain's gun poked between my third and fourth ribs.

"Riley?"

"It's not Riley." Twain laughed into the phone, then

turned his back to me and walked away. I couldn't hear what they were saying, but I knew Holman must have been furious that I'd been stupid enough to get myself kidnapped. I struggled in vain against the restraints that bound my wrists behind my back.

"How could you?" I railed at Kevin, who sat at a nearby desk in the warehouse nervously spinning in a chair while Twain talked to Holman. "You're the reason she's dead!" I spat at him. My throat was raw and painful.

Kevin hadn't looked me in the eye since he'd helped Twain bind my arms, then my legs, together with duct tape. But they hadn't blindfolded me. I watched enough TV to know that was a bad sign. After they'd tied me up and slumped me against the wall, they walked to the far part of the warehouse to discuss something in hushed tones.

After they'd left me there, I noticed the lump lying about six feet from me. I looked closer and started to shake with fear when I realized the lump was Ryan. His arms and legs were bound like mine, and I could see dried blood crusted under his left ear. I called his name over and over, but he didn't respond. I'd nearly been out of my mind with grief until I saw his chest rise and fall slowly.

"Ryan," I whispered-shouted. Kevin had walked back to stand near Twain, who was still on the phone with Holman. "Wake up! I need you—*please* wake up." No response. I didn't know if he'd been knocked out or given drugs to make him sleep, but either way, he was solidly unconscious. I didn't allow myself to think about the possibility that he wouldn't—or couldn't—wake up. All I knew was that he was alive. At least for now.

I banged my head against the metal wall behind me, and it made a sound like thunder. The situation was completely hopeless. I looked around for any weak point of entry—a place to escape from, if by some miracle I was able to get myself free from the restraints—but there was nothing. The building was massive and built like a fortress. It looked like it used to be an airplane hanger, but now it housed taco trucks.

"Tsk, tsk, tsk," Twain drawled as he walked back over to where I was sitting on the floor. "Such a shame to hear a grown man cry." He laughed as he slid my phone back into his pocket. "Sherlock was pretty torn up about you being here, *querida*."

I gave him a hard look, ignoring his bait. "What are you going to do? Kill me? Kill all of us? Do you honestly think you could get away with that?"

Kevin walked up behind Twain. He looked nervous, agitated. "So what's the plan?"

Twain shot Kevin a deadly look, then said to me, "You'd be surprised what we can get away with. My boss has a wide circle of influence. And if he wants three people to disappear without a trace?" He snapped his fingers. "They're gone."

Kevin, not happy to be ignored, tried again. "Seriously, Gonzalez, what's the plan?"

Without warning, Twain backhanded Kevin across the face. Kevin staggered back and cried out in pain. "What the hell?" He held his cheek as blood started to drip from the corner of his lip.

"No names," Gonzalez growled at him.

Kevin looked like a deer who had just heard the clicking release of a gun safety. He was in trouble now, and he knew it. "Listen, I can fix all this," he spoke quickly, desperately. "All we need to do is threaten the kids. Riley and Ryan aren't going to say anything to anyone about this. Holman is another matter, but we can figure out—"

"I've had enough of your 'plans,'" Gonzalez barked, punching a number into his own cell phone, mine still in his back pocket. "Hey," he said into the phone. "Yeah, I'm sending Fitzgerald and Dickens to pick him up. Do you want to talk to him before—"

Bile rose into my throat at the word "before." *Before what?*

Riley Ellison, twenty-four, almost-librarian and wannabe reporter, was found dead, bound and gagged. Everyone who knew Ellison was surprised because she seemed like such a quiet girl, not prone to engage in activities that would lead to a gangland-style execution.

"Nah, I just wondered if you wanted to know—" he broke off listening to whatever instructions his boss was giving him on the other end of the phone. "Okay, okay. Yeah, fine. Okay. I'll call you when it's done." He clicked off the phone.

Gonzalez was ruffled; his boss must not be happy. Kevin cowered nearby, glowering at Gonzalez as he dabbed at the cut on his lip with the back of his hand. Since I was pretty sure I'd just overheard someone ordering my death, I figured I had nothing to lose. My only thought was to get Gonzalez talking. Maybe he'd slip up and say more than he intended to? Maybe he'd say something I could use to get us out of here alive? "So what *is* your plan, *Gonzalez*?"

His eyes narrowed, glinting with evil self-satisfaction. "Well, we can't very well pump you full of insulin like we did your little friend." He checked my face for a reaction. "Or didn't you figure that out yet?"

I felt the air leave my lungs. Of course, I knew they'd done it, but hearing him confirm it, like it was nothing, shocked me more than I expected.

Gonzalez's eyes darted to Kevin, whose face had gone white at the mention of Jordan. "She was a lot like you, you know. Feisty to the very end."

"You killed her." I directed this to Kevin. "She trusted you and you killed her." I struggled to keep the tears at bay. What point is there in crying when you have only hours (*minutes?*) to live? I decided my last few moments on earth would not be spent sad. I would go down swinging.

Kevin's eyes flicked to mine, then back down to the floor. He looked as if he might throw up. Or run away. But he did neither. He just stood there, impotent, dripping with guilt.

"Coward!" I shouted at him.

"She wasn't supposed to be involved...." Kevin said, a small blood blister forming at the corner of his mouth.

"Had to be done," Gonzalez said with no hint of remorse. "I just wish I knew who tipped her off."

Kevin closed his eyes. "I never wanted her to get hurt...."

"Nah, man, you just wanted your take," Gonzalez said in a venomous tone. "You've done pretty good working for the boss man."

Rage flooded my veins. "You killed Jordan for money?"

"She wasn't supposed to be involved! I didn't want her to find out. I was trying to prote—" As if he realized he'd said too much, he shut his mouth. He was hiding something. But before I could figure out what it was, a loud, rumbling sound erupted from the far end of the warehouse, and a black Ford Ranger drove in through the garage door. *Holman.*

"Your friend is here. Now the real fun can begin," Gonzalez said before strolling back to meet the truck, with Kevin following. I kicked and struggled against my restraints again, crying out in fear and frustration. The lump lying next to me stirred. "Ryan! Ryan—wake up," I whispered urgently.

His large, dark frame stirred. Eventually, he opened one eye and looked toward the sound of my voice. "Riles?"

"Ryan, wake up—we have to get out of here!"

He spun himself slowly, not able to get himself to sitting but able to face me. "Are you okay?"

"I'm fine. Listen to me: They're going to kill us. We've got to figure out a way to get out of here." My voice was just above a whisper now; even though Gonzalez and Kevin were at the other end of the warehouse, I didn't want to risk them seeing that Ryan was awake. I was afraid of what they'd do to him.

Ryan's eyelids fluttered, struggling to stay open. I looked at his face properly. It was a mess. He had a swollen black eye that couldn't open all the way, a bloody lip, and a broken front tooth. The sight of him so badly beaten made my stomach lurch in fear. "I'm so sorry. I never meant to get you mixed up in all this...."

"Hey, hey," he said, "this isn't your fault, honey. You didn't know they'd come after me."

"And your mom? Is she—" I couldn't even finish the sentence. The thought of any harm coming to Mrs. Sanford was unbearable.

"She's fine. I told her I was going to see you. She probably thinks I'm still at your place. These assholes grabbed me before I got to my truck."

I gasped in relief and tried to control my breathing. I needed a clear head if we were going to have a prayer of making it out alive. I took a deep breath, held it at the top like Holman taught me, and reminded myself that anger was a more useful emotion than sadness in life-or-death situations.

"It was Mr. Monroe," I said after I'd regrouped. "He's somehow working for Juan Pablo Romero—they're dealing meth, and Jordan found out. They killed her."

Ryan closed his eyes and nodded. "I overheard them talking. This is some serious shit here, Riley."

We heard a clatter and a chorus of yelling ring out from the far end of the warehouse. "Riley?"

Holman's frantic cries touched my heart. "I'm here!"

His escorts, two large men and Gonzalez, kicked and prodded him over to where Ryan and I were being held. He too had been beaten, and I could see the yellowing of a fresh bruise developing under his right eye. His glasses had a crack in the right lens. I gasped when they shoved him down, and he tumbled to the floor.

"Are you okay? Did they hurt you?" He searched my face for signs of injury.

"I'm fine. You?"

He looked at me with tears in his perfectly round eyes. "I'm so sorry...."

"Yeah, yeah, everyone's sorry," Gonzalez snapped. "You have something that belongs to us."

Holman nodded toward the large man standing to his right. "Charles Dickens has it. He wouldn't let me hold it on the way over."

"Wait!" I said, without really knowing what I was going to say next.

Holman turned to me. "It's okay, Riley." Something about the way he said this quieted me. I wondered if that magnificent bastard had a plan after all.

CHAPTER 38

Dickens went back to the truck and retrieved the large olive-green Rubbermaid container that contained his boss's meth. I could smell the patchouli oil waft into the air. Holman was looking at the container like it was his last lifeline, which in a sense, it was. Gonzalez undid the latches on either side and lifted the lid.

"What the hell is this?" he roared as he looked inside.

Holman cleared his throat before speaking. He was obviously terrified but resolved to fight through his fear. "That," he leveled his gaze on Gonzalez, "is a live video feed of your methamphetamine strapped to an explosive device with an active timer. Sitting on top of several bags of white rocks meant to approximate the size and weight of the real thing, of course."

I saw Gonzalez's jaw clench and the muscles in his neck flare. "You idiots didn't check the product?"

Dickens and the man I assumed was Fitzgerald looked at each other, then at Gonzalez. "Um, it smelled like the stuff...we just figured...."

"You don't get paid to figure," Gonzalez shouted. "I should just—"

Holman interrupted Gonzalez's fit. "I'm attempting to bribe you."

At this, Gonzalez actually laughed. "Oh, you are, are you?"

"Yes. You see, I need you to let Riley and Ryan go free, and the drugs are the only leverage I have to ensure their safety. It was really my only play. You'll note there is a timer on the bomb. It will detonate in about an hour if I don't call in the code to disarm it."

Gonzalez ran a hand through his thick, black hair. "You think you can threaten me with this amateur shit?" He stared at Holman with such venom that I feared he might shoot him right then and there.

To his credit, Holman maintained his icy gaze, though his trembling voice gave him away. "We make a simple trade," Holman said. "You let Riley and Ryan go, and you can have your drugs back."

I stared, open mouthed, at Holman. *What was he doing?*

"Or how about I blow your head off right here, right now?" He leveled his gun at Holman.

"I've got half a million in meth that says you don't."

If Holman had put on a dress and started singing "Let It Go" from the *Frozen* soundtrack, I could not have been more surprised. Will Holman was playing hardball with gangsters. And judging by the look on Gonzalez's face, he was winning.

"All you have to do is let them go," Holman continued, his voice gaining strength from Gonzalez's obvious shock. "And then I disarm the bomb and take you to the drugs. At that point, you can do whatever you like with me."

"No!" I cried.

He looked at me briefly, then back to Gonzalez. "The way I see it, your boss wants two things: his product back, and me out of the way. Killing two innocent people is only going to complicate your situation."

The warehouse was dead quiet as we watched the standoff between these two unlikely competitors. The seconds stretched on.

Ryan finally broke the silence with. "Riley and I won't say a word about any of this—"

"Ryan!" I shouted, horrified. "Holman, you can't do this! There has to be some other way."

Gonzalez lowered his gun and yelled a string of curses in Spanish so loud it reverberated against the metal walls of the warehouse. "How do I know that these two are gonna keep their mouths shut?"

Holman said calmly and quietly, "Because Ryan is about to become a father." As his words sank in, all eyes turned to me. The implication, that Holman obviously intended, was that I was carrying Ryan's baby.

"You're pregnant?" Kevin's voice was somewhere between confused and panicked.

I looked at him but said nothing. Out of the corner of my eye, I saw Holman gave Ryan an almost imperceptible nod. *Go ahead*, the nod said, *save her*. Maybe Holman really did have a hero complex?

"We will forget this ever happened," Ryan said. "We won't say a word. Ever. Just let us go. *Please*."

Gonzalez looked from Ryan to me to Holman, slowly focusing on each of us as if his eyes were a polygraph trying to determine the truth. Between the bombshell Holman just dropped and the literal ticking time bomb, the air crackled with tension.

"All you have to do is let them go." Holman kept his voice even. "Just let them go, and I give you the code and the drugs, and everyone can move on."

"Except you, Sherlock," Gonzalez said in a low growl.

Holman nodded. "Except me."

Gonzalez walked away to call the boss and get approval for this unexpected change in plans, and Fitzgerald and Dickens stood in front of us, guns in hands. Once Gonzalez was out of earshot, I whispered to Holman. "You can't do this, Will! They'll kill you for sure."

"It'll be okay." He kept his eyes straight ahead, not daring to look at me.

"Listen," Ryan said to me. "Once you and I are safe, we can call the police. We can make sure they come back for Holman before anything bad happens...."

"How can you be so selfish?" I snapped at Ryan.

"I'm not being selfish, Riles. I'm thinking of you—and the baby." His expression was deadly serious, and despite my wanting to be angry at him for choosing us over Holman, the look of papa-bear protectiveness in his eyes softened my resolve. He wasn't being selfish—or at least not entirely. He was behaving like a father who wanted to be there to see his child grow up. "Once we're free, we'll send someone back for him."

I looked from Ryan to Holman, and my eyes instantly filled with tears. "No," I said. "There has to be another way."

Holman turned to me. He smiled, but then Gonzalez walked back over. He pointed his gun directly between Holman's eyes.

"The lady is right," he said. "There *is* another way. My way."

CHAPTER 39

"Here's what's going to happen," Gonzalez said once Fitzgerald and Dickens had loaded Kevin, Ryan, Holman, and me into the back of one of the Tacos Los Locos trucks. Gonzalez sat in the passenger seat, Fitzgerald to his left in the driver's seat, and Dickens stood sentinel just behind them with a gun pointed our direction. "You're going to disarm the half-ass kitchen bomb you made, *pendejo*, and take me to my product."

"Not until Riley and Ryan are safe." His words remained on message, but the confidence in Holman's voice had faded.

"Nah," Gonzalez sneered. "See, I came up with a new plan. We're going to head over to a place of great importance to your girlfriend—" He reached under the seat and brandished a bottle filled with an amber-colored liquid and a dirty rag sticking out of the top.

Holman interrupted him. "Remember, we are not romantically involved. Despite Riley's symmetry, our relationship is not—"

"*Shut up!*" Gonzalez roared. "The only relationship you need to worry about right now is the one between you and the old people at the Tuttle Corner Library reading their newspapers and shit."

Gonzalez smiled, hyena-like, as he watched our reactions. "You think you can call the shots with me? That you can threaten *me*?" His voice rose as he watched our horrified faces absorb this reversal of fortune. "Nah, the way I figure it, if you're willing to die to save two innocent people, you ought to be willing to give back what is rightfully mine in order to save a bunch more. And even if you don't, I need to send a message over there anyway. Two birds, one bomb, you know what I'm saying?"

Shock rippled through the food truck. Gonzalez was going to throw that Molotov cocktail into the library if Holman didn't cooperate.

The truck pulled out of the warehouse and into the bright sunlight. I didn't know exactly what time it was but figured it was close to two o'clock. The library would be filled with patrons. Images of Dr. H and Tabitha swam before my eyes.

Holman's face drained of color. He had not expected this. "But if you kill us all, then you'll never get your methamphetamine back."

"See, I don't think it'll come to that. I think you'll swoop in and save the day. Why save two lives when you can save so many more?"

"Don't do this," Kevin interjected. "We can still get the product. Just let me talk to Holman—I'll get him to give up the code. I personally guarantee it."

"Your personal guarantee doesn't count for shit. And by the way, there is no more 'we,' Monroe."

Kevin froze. He'd been cut off, just like that. In the space of one second he went from one side to the other. A prince to a pauper, a general to the enemy. Now he was in exactly the same situation as Holman, Ryan, and me.

Gonzalez enjoyed seeing the realization settle over

Kevin. "I've been thinking about it, and I think you're the reason we're in this situation to begin with."

"What? No—"

"Yeah, I think you sent that tip in yourself."

"I didn't—I swear!" Kevin was as bad a liar as I was.

Gonzalez ignored him. "I didn't put it together until earlier when you were talking in there—but I think you were getting scared. You'd already gotten a ton of cash for fixing charges, but you couldn't handle it anymore. Didn't have the stomach for it. Or maybe your girl was getting too close, and you didn't want her to find out you were involved. So you sent in the tip yourself so we'd all get busted, and no one would ever know about what you were doing." Gonzalez may have been a madman, but he was smart.

Kevin looked terrified as Gonzalez explained what had undoubtedly happened. "Fausto—I swear!"

"Stop," Gonzalez roared, and Dickens stepped toward Kevin, the barrel of his gun pointed directly at his chest. "Sit."

"How do you think you're going to get away with bombing a library?" I asked, voicing the obvious, practical question. "The police will figure out who did that. There will be some shred of evidence that will lead back to you and your 'boss.' Even Romero can't kill dozens of people and get away with it."

Kevin said quietly, "Romero isn't the boss." His voice was flat, resigned, like he had nothing left to lose.

"Watch it," Twain warned.

But Kevin wasn't listening. His face was chalk-white, beads of sweat appeared around his hairline, and his eyes were unfocused as he stared at the floor in the truck. "He doesn't even know about the drugs."

"Monroe," Gonzalez snarled again in warning.

"It's all coming from Romero's uncle up in Jersey. Well, he and—"

"Shut *up!*" Gonzalez nodded to Dickens, who punched Kevin in the ribs. Hard. I screamed as Kevin doubled over, moaning in pain.

Understanding clawed at the edge of my brain. The reason the government had never been able to pin any charges on Romero was because he really was running a legitimate business—as far as he knew, anyway. It had been Mateo pulling the strings from New Jersey all along. I'd bet anything Mateo got Gonzalez the job as head of security for Tacos Los Locos. It put him in the perfect position to gain access to the trucks and plant the drugs.

And then a thought shot into my head like it had been fired from a cannon. I ignored Gonzalez and looked directly at Kevin. "It's Tackett, isn't it?"

His eyes rose to meet mine. He nodded.

I should have known. That dirty sonofabitch. It wasn't so much that they had a mole in the sheriff's department as they had the sheriff himself in their back pocket. Owning the sheriff and the county prosecutor...it's no wonder they were able to get away with such brazen criminal activity.

"Enough!" Gonzalez yelled. "You'd better give me that code right now, or else you're going to die with a lot of blood on your hands."

Holman ignored him, his hunger to tell the story stronger than his fear. He must have figured this out earlier. "It all clicked when I was going through Jordan's notes. Remember she had all those citations in her file?"

I nodded.

"She was checking arrest records against evidence logged into the sheriff's department. There was a suspicious lack of guns and drugs being reported. Jordan must have suspected something wasn't right. My guess is she told Kevin about her suspicions—after all, he was the prosecutor, not to mention her boyfriend."

Kevin picked up Holman's thread. "The irony was, she didn't even know about the taco trucks yet. I figured if I tipped you off, it'd send your investigation in another direction, away from me. I waited until I knew Mateo had product in the truck onsite at LJP and then sent you the letter. I had no idea that Jordan was going to intercept it."

"Stop. Talking." Gonzalez said through a clenched jaw.

But Kevin didn't stop. It was like he couldn't. He was unburdening himself in the way a guilty man does when he knows he is about to die. "She wasn't supposed to find out," he said to Holman. "It was supposed to be you. I didn't know Jordan would go in to work that night or that she'd open it. God, if I'd had any idea…."

"Since you obviously couldn't go to the police, you came to me," Holman said, putting the last piece of the puzzle into place.

Kevin nodded silently.

"I knew it." Gonzalez was now suddenly interested in Kevin's confession. "But your girlfriend wasn't as smart as you thought. She went out to the truck like she was Nancy fucking Drew, rolled up on us as we were loading the truck. She tried to run, but we caught her. When I saw her insulin pump, it didn't take long to figure out how to get rid of her without raising suspicion."

It was as if his words shot a hole through Kevin four inches wide. He groaned in agony, finally letting go the anguish he'd bottled up all this time.

Gonzalez ignored him and looked to Holman. "You have a decision to make." He held up the bottle. "What's it going to be? I'm sure the sheriff would have no problem declaring that Kevin Monroe, the county prosecutor, went on a murderous rampage, killing reporter Will Holman and two former students, just before blowing up the Tuttle Corner Library. Motive unknown...."

"Just give him the code, dude!" Ryan pleaded.

Holman shook his head. "I can't do that."

"We're all gonna die if you don't!"

Fitzgerald pulled the truck into the library parking lot. I saw Dr. H's gold Ford Crown Victoria, Tabitha's BMW convertible, and nearly a half dozen other cars. There was no telling how many people were inside. Or who those people were.

"You can't do this," I said to Gonzalez. "Think of all those innocent people—you can't—"

"There's about ten minutes left on here," Fitzgerald said, looking at the phone with the video feed of the bomb-strapped meth. "I thought the boss told you to get the drugs?"

Gonzalez turned on him abruptly. "The boss isn't here, is he? I'm in charge. I'm running this!" In that moment, he looked like a true madman. Holman had hatched his plan assuming Romero was in charge. He'd counted on him being a good businessman above everything else, and because of that, he wouldn't allow his meth to be destroyed. But Mateo was another animal, and Gonzalez was wilder still.

In desperation to save his failing plan, Holman said, "What do you think Tackett will do when he sees he has to clean up another one of your messes? And how will Mateo feel when he finds out that you allowed hundreds of thousands of dollars in meth to be blown to bits?"

"Give. Me. The. Code." Gonzalez pointed his gun at Holman.

"No."

"Will," I said, "maybe you should just tell him? It may be too late for us, but it isn't too late for all of them." I nodded my head toward the building.

"I can't, Riley."

"Don't be reckless here—remember what happened to Alex Wright?"

"Who?"

"Alex Wright—from the Blexor story."

"What are you talking about? I wasn't on the Blexor story."

I don't know why I was surprised. The whole story had been just another lie Kevin told me to try to turn me against Holman. There probably was no Alex Wright.

"Um, guys, maybe you could have this little argument when you're dead. Right now, we've got to figure out how to get out of here." Ryan's biting sarcasm brought us back to the moment.

"We have nothing to discuss. No code." Holman's eyes found mine and held steady there for at least two full seconds. He was trying to tell me something with that look—but I couldn't figure out what. *An apology? Goodbye? You have a little something on your face?*

My heartbeat thundered. This was really happening. This was really how I was going to die. Now that the moment was here, I had no pithy obituary ready in my head. Only fear and shock.

"Okay, Sherlock," Gonzalez said. "If this is how you want it, fine. Dickens, do the girl first, then the others. Holman last. Let him watch what he did. Put the gun in Monroe's dead hand—get the prints on there real good. Not that we're going to need much proof—but just in case Tackett has to answer any questions."

"Are you sure?" Dickens looked scared, like he knew

Gonzalez had gone off course. "Maybe we should just take them back to the warehouse and wait for the boss to—"

"I'm the only boss who matters right now."

Holman sat, expressionless, as if sitting in a van awaiting his imminent death was nothing out of the ordinary. I couldn't decide if it was bravery or Holman's unique brand of idiosyncrasy that kept him from panicking.

Ryan started crying. "I want you to know I've always loved you, Riley," he said through tears. "No matter what. It was always you. I need you to know that." He fought back a sob, and with no hands free to wipe his face, the tears and snot ran down his cheeks. I thought of the baby who would grow up, probably in Sweden, not knowing his father. It was so unfair. Ryan had nothing to do with this and was only taken hostage because of me. A torrent of guilt, shame, sadness, and anger raged inside me.

I looked at Holman, hoping to catch a glimpse of some emotion from him—sadness, fear, even a shared sense of guilt? As much as I'd involved Ryan in this mess, Will had involved me. Did he feel anything about that? His vacant expression suggested no.

Kevin seemed barely conscious, as if he was resigned to death, even welcoming it. He wasn't fighting against his restraints or trying to escape. He just lay there on his side, staring into nothing. I felt a tiny scrap of pity for him in that moment. I could tell he meant it when he said he hadn't meant to get Jordan killed.

"Will," I said urgently, "*Do something!*"

Just then we heard a knock on the window.

CHAPTER 40

Everyone froze. The knock came again. Gonzalez nodded to Fitzgerald, who was the closest. The order window was on the side of the truck directly above my head. Fitzgerald leaned over me and opened the window about four inches. He bent his head down. "Yeah?"

"Yes, I'd like a pollo chimichanga, hold the onions, please."

I couldn't see anything but knew in an instant that it was Dr. H's voice. I started to scream his name, but Fitzgerald kicked me hard in the stomach with the pointy end of his boot.

"We're closed," he growled.

"Fitzgerald?" Dr. H asked. "Is that you?"

"Huh?" Fitzgerald said, leaning down to peer out the window.

"I didn't know you worked in the food-service industry!" Dr. H sounded delighted. "Does this mean you've decided on a more meritorious career path than stringing old men up by their wrists?"

"*Meri-what?*" Fitzgerald tried to slam the window shut, but Dr. H must have shoved something under the screen.

"I haven't finished giving you my order yet, young man," he said with his trademark cheeriness. "I'd also like a number three combo with beef—"

I was pretty sure Fitzgerald had broken, or at least bruised, several of my ribs. I pushed past the pain and yelled, "Dr. H, evacuate the libra—"

He kicked me again in the same spot. I cried out in pain.

"What was that? Not the pollos, I hope!" Dr. H laughed merrily. The pain in my ribs stole my voice, but I silently willed him to run far away.

"We're closed," Fitzgerald said again.

"If you're closed, why would you pull into my library?" There was now an edge to Dr. H's voice.

Fitzgerald and Dickens looked to Gonzalez. "What do we do?" Dickens whispered, holding his gun down by his side.

Gonzalez ran a hand through his black hair. "That old man has to go. Get out and pull him in. What's one more?" He said this like he was adding another item to his to-do list. He really was insane.

Fitzgerald threw the back of the taco truck open. Bright light streamed into the dark cabin, temporarily blinding us. Without thinking, I took the opportunity to throw myself at Dickens' exposed ankle and bit down like I was Cujo. He cried out in pain and dropped his gun, but not before kicking me in the cheekbone. I felt the bones in the side of my face crack like an egg.

Kevin, the only one of us whose hands were not bound, grabbed the gun and swung the barrel around till it pointed directly at Gonzalez's heart. "You killed her!" he shouted, his hands shaking with rage and fear. He blinked back his tears. "I loved her and you...you—"

Before he could finish his sentence (or pull the trigger), I heard a voice call from the outside of the van: "DEA—drop the weapon, and put your hands on your head!"

It was Ajay.

"I get up every morning at nine and grab for the morning paper. Then I look at the obituary page. If my name's not on it, I get up."

—BENJAMIN FRANKLIN

CHAPTER 41

A few days later, I stood outside the federal building in Richmond with Ajay—or whatever his name actually was. Holman and I had just been through a lengthy debriefing, and I was still struggling to piece together all that I'd learned since my near-death experience inside the taco truck. I was exhausted not only from the meeting, but also from the pain medicine I was taking for my shattered cheekbone. My left eye was puffed up and red from where the capillaries burst when Dickens' boot made contact with my face. It hurt, and while I didn't like taking medicine, I didn't like being in excruciating pain even more.

Ajay, who had not been a part of our debriefing, met us after it was over and offered to walk us out of the building. Once we were outside, true to form, Holman said, "I think you two need some time to clear up all the lies you told each other. I'm going to go find a vending machine."

We both kind of nervously laughed as he walked away, and then an awkward silence settled around us. He broke it first. "Are you in much pain?" Ajay touched his own face at the same place mine was injured.

"It looks worse than it feels." I shrugged, playing the part of the stoic hero.

"C'mon now." He arched one of his eyebrows. "Is that full disclosure?"

I laughed and the tension receded. "Speaking of that," I said, "Ajay Badal isn't your real name, is it?"

Ajay shook his head, the ghost of a guilty smile on his face. "It's Jaidev Burman. I go by Jay, though."

The DEA agents we had spoken to in our debriefing were far more interested in getting information from us than in giving it out, so I knew some of what had happened but not the whole story. From what I was able to piece together so far, Ajay Badal—or rather, Jaidev Burman—was a DEA agent working the case against the Romeros. The Feds had suspected Romero was involved in his uncle's criminal activity, specifically drug trafficking, for a long time. About four months ago, they started to believe that Tackett was also involved but were having a hard time proving it, because Mateo's operation was so well insulated. So they decided to send in an undercover agent to gather intelligence locally. Enter Ajay Badal.

Turns out Jay really was a certified forensic geotechnical scientist, and he really had been teaching classes at Cardwell College, as well as acting as an explosives consultant for the sheriff's department. That much was true. But he was doing all of that to get into position to either be recruited by Tackett into the organization or to find someone who could inform on him. Jay had tried to connect with Jordan when it became clear she was investigating Tackett's arrest records. He said his higher-ups had told him to befriend her and see what information he could glean. But he hadn't been able to learn much before she was killed.

"I'm sorry I had to lie to you," Jay said.

I shook my head to indicate that it was no big deal. "I understand. You were just doing your job."

As it happened, his job was not going particularly well until I bumbled onto the scene. More specifically, when I managed to get myself kidnapped by Kevin Monroe.

"I'm not sure how much they told you in there, but we weren't even sure Monroe was involved until you'd been taken hostage," Jay said. "It was our first big break in the case."

Holman had the brilliant idea to call Ajay as soon as he found out Gonzalez had Ryan and me in that warehouse. Obviously, Holman had no idea Ajay was DEA, but he'd come up with the crazy idea of strapping the meth to a bomb and thought Ajay could help because of his explosives background. And because of his feelings for me. It was really all just dumb luck. It terrified me to think of what would have happened if Holman hadn't called Ajay. We'd all probably be dead right now.

But being who he was, Ajay/Jay didn't hesitate. He called in his DEA team, seized the meth, set up the dummy bomb with the live timer, and set up the phone—which of course had a tracking device implanted in it, so the DEA was watching our every move. No one counted on Gonzalez going rogue and deciding to kill us all and blow up the library. The plan was for him to let Ryan and me go free, and then Holman would lead them to the meth, where the authorities would be waiting. But when Gonzalez made up his alternate plan, they tracked us to the library and sent Dr. H in to distract our captors long enough to evacuate the library and surround the taco truck.

"I'm still a little confused on what was really going on. I mean, I get that Gonzalez was selling drugs for Mateo out of the trucks, and Tackett was smoothing their way, but how exactly was Kevin involved?"

"Yeah," Jay said, "so that's interesting. Monroe, as the

county prosecutor, was taking money in exchange for not bringing charges against certain people who were arrested for guns or drugs. See, Tackett had a side business selling the weapons collected from evidence on the black market. So when Tackett arrested someone for illegal possession of a firearm or small quantities of meth or oxy, he'd just 'forget' to log the evidence, call Monroe, and Monroe would make sure not to file charges, effectively making whatever they confiscated disappear without a trace. Then Tackett got to keep the stuff, and Monroe could extort cash payments in exchange for no charges."

"So that explains why Jordan had been checking the evidence logs from the sheriff's department."

Jordan had been on the brink of busting open the biggest corruption scandal this town had ever seen. But she'd put her faith in the wrong person. If only she'd gone to Holman instead of Kevin. But knowing what I know about Jordan, I could see why she didn't. It made perfect sense that she'd go to her boyfriend first, particularly since he was the prosecutor, and going directly to him meant she didn't have to share any credit for the discovery. The Jordan I'd known was competitive as hell. It was one of her best qualities.

"So what happens now?" I asked. "The guys inside wouldn't say much."

"Well, it's early days, but I can promise you that Fausto Gonzalez will be locked up for a long time," Jay said. "We have him dead to rights. We're working on getting him to roll over on Mateo." Jay explained that Mateo, at the top of the food chain, had put into place measures to ensure that his involvement would be difficult to prove. "If we can get Juan Pablo Romero to officially press charges, that would help a lot."

"Will he?" I asked. I still found it hard to believe that Mateo's nephew was an innocent in all of this.

Jay shook his head. "I doubt it. Family is family. He claims he had no idea what was going on, but my gut is that he chose to look the other way so he could claim plausible deniability. That way, he doesn't have to implicate his uncle."

Two men in gray suits walked past us to enter the building and we fell silent. Jay looked down at his watch. "You look tired, Riley," he said kindly. "Anything else I can clear up for you before I get back in there?"

This conversation, while enlightening, hadn't provided any of the answers I had really wanted from Jay. "Um..." I screwed up my courage and forced myself to ask the one question I hadn't yet, "are you really married?"

Jay laughed, his wide smile lighting up his handsome features. "No," he said. "Some guy named Ajay Badal is, though. When you confronted me at your house that night, I scrambled to make up an excuse that wouldn't blow my cover."

"I see," I said, feeling an embarrassing mixture of hope and relief. "That's good. I mean, I guess. I mean...whatever."

He suppressed a smile. "Actually, I have a confession to make. I didn't ask you out as part of the investigation."

My belly flipped.

"I joined Click.com as Ajay Badal to connect with Jordan but hadn't had a chance to deactivate my account after she died. Then I saw your profile pop up." He put his hands into his pockets, a gesture I was beginning to notice was common for him. "Regina H thought we'd be a good match. I guess maybe I did, too."

"So you used government resources to ask Riley out on a date?" Holman walked up. He'd been eavesdropping on our conversation.

"Hey, Will," Jay said. "Find anything good?"

"Payday." Holman held up his half-eaten candy bar. I noticed that he was looking at Jay the way a twelve-year-old girl would look at Taylor Swift. I think he'd developed a man-crush on Jay after he swooped in and saved our lives. I could relate.

"So where will you go now that the case is over? Back to Jersey?" I asked, trying to hide how invested I felt in the answer.

Jay shook his head. "I think they're going to keep me in the area for a while longer. For a sleepy little corner of the world, Tuttle County has some vigorous criminal activity."

"He's right," Holman said. "That's why you should come to work with me at the *Times*. We'd make a great team. Right, Jay?" Over the last few days, Holman had been begging me to quit working for the library and come work with him at the *Times*. Said Kay Jackson had already okayed it. But I had yet to give him an answer.

Jay looked at me for an extra beat and then turned to Holman and said, "I think Riley would be an asset to any team she chooses to join."

My belly flipped again, and I felt a blush beginning. It wasn't an intimate compliment, but it wasn't wholly unintimate either. It was somewhere between *I like your purse* and *I'd do the three-legged race with you any day.*

I smiled instinctively and tried to think of something clever to say in response. I think what I came up with was, "Thanks."

"All right," Jay said, a patch of scarlet blooming on his own cheeks. "Go get some rest. I'm heading back in. See you around."

Jay had already turned to walk inside before I got out

the words "I hope so." I wondered if I would see him around or if our moment had passed. Maybe there were just too many extenuating circumstances for us to try again. As I watched him walk into the building, I couldn't help but think that was a shame.

Chapter 42

It was a bright, cloudless day that was lacking the usual humidity, and the air felt pleasantly warm and comfortable. A gentle breeze blew across the front lawn outside the First Methodist Church in downtown Tuttle Corner. I swept my bangs away from my eyes and looked at the groups of people walking toward the entrance dressed in somber clothing.

It seemed like the entire town of Tuttle Corner had turned out for Jordan's funeral. Mr. and Mrs. James had pushed the service back a few days after the DEA told them the real story behind Jordan's death. They needed some time to process the new information. Despite their devastating grief, I think they took some solace in the fact that Jordan had not left this world by her own hand. It wasn't much, but at least it was something. I could imagine that knowing that it wasn't suicide would provide comfort in the years going forward. I think a part of me still hoped that someday I'd be able to prove the same about Granddaddy.

Kevin Monroe was being held in jail awaiting his trial. He'd been charged with conspiracy to commit extortion and abuse of public trust. But I knew that whatever the judicial system had in store for Mr. Monroe, it was nothing compared to the hell he was putting himself through.

Sheriff Tackett had been transferred to a jail in another county, as the judge deemed he wouldn't be safe in the same jail where he'd sent most of the inmates. According to Carl, who had been appointed acting sheriff, the case against Tackett was strong, and in addition to the corruption charges, he was going to be charged with conspiracy to commit murder. Apparently, Gonzalez had given him up like a bad habit in hopes of making a deal for himself.

Nothing would bring Jordan back, but I felt a deep sense of relief that at least the people responsible for her death would pay.

"Have you given any more thought to my offer?" Holman's voice cut across my thoughts. He was like a dog with a bone about this job thing.

I rolled my eyes, but the truth was, in the past few days, I'd done little else *but* think about his offer. Part of me wanted to take the job, and part of me wanted to stay in my safe, comfortable job at the library. It was the only job I'd ever had, and even though I'd stayed there mostly through inertia, I'd miss working with Dr. H, and maybe even Tabitha. So when I hadn't been in DEA interviews, or explaining everything to my parents, or passed out from exhaustion, I'd been thinking about whether or not to go to work for the *Times*. I'd sworn I'd never work in the newspaper business after Granddaddy died, but there was a definite excitement to the work. Plus, look at how much good we were able to do! Because of our investigations, some really bad guys were going to prison. It felt good knowing I'd been a part of that. Kay Jackson also intimated that as a part of my work, I'd be able to work the Obits desk, such as it was. I had to admit I liked the sound of that.

"I'm still thinking it over, Holman."

"'Don't think. Do.' Yoda said that."

"No, Yoda said, 'Do or do not. There is no try.' They're going to revoke your nerd card if you can't even properly quote Yoda."

"You're avoiding the subject."

"Very good, Sherlock."

Out of the corner of my eye, I thought I saw Hal Flick leaning against a tree in front of the rectory. "What's he doing here?"

Holman's eyes followed mine. "I know you two have a complicated history, but I think you've got him wrong, Riley."

I scoffed. "I don't think so."

"You know, when he heard you were taken hostage, he was frantic. He insisted on being involved in the rescue plan."

"Wait—what?" This was the first I'd heard of that.

"Yeah, I thought I told you. Flick was the one who urged me to call in Ajay, I mean, Jay."

"I thought you said you came up with the plan."

"I did. After Flick gave me the idea." He blinked at me in the birdlike way of his and waited for me to respond. But I was too taken aback. It had been Flick who suggested involving Jay? It was Flick's idea that saved our lives? How did Flick even know Jay? Or about Jay and me?

When I asked Holman that, he shrugged. "Flick seems to know a lot about a lot of things."

"Well," I said, brushing it off. "So what if he did. I'm sure he would have done that for anyone."

"I don't know, Riley," Holman said. "I have a feeling there is more to Flick's story than we know. I know you swear he gave up on your granddad after his death, but something tells me he hasn't."

My eyes snapped up to Holman's. "What makes you

say that?"

He shrugged. "Investigative reporter."

It was an interesting theory. Flick had shut me down time after time when I'd tried to talk alternatives with him after Granddaddy died, but what if he knew more than he let on? Could he have been involved in some way? When I looked back for Flick, he was gone. I didn't know if he'd gone inside the church or simply disappeared, but once again, Hal Flick had fled the scene.

Holman didn't seem to have noticed. "Are you ready?" he asked, looking through the doors to the crowded church.

"As I'll ever be."

"You'll do her proud, Obit Girl." Then in a very uncharacteristic gesture, he moved to put his long, spidery arms around my shoulders.

Not exactly sure what was happening, I asked, "Are you trying to hug me?"

"Yes. I'm comforting you during this difficult time."

Oh. It felt like being embraced by a weeping willow. I relaxed into the strange embrace and allowed him to provide me with comfort during this difficult time. For about three seconds. "Okay. I think we're done here."

Holman stepped back and smiled. "Think about my offer, okay?"

I nodded, and he turned to walk inside.

My parents waited for me at the side of the massive arched door. I took a deep breath. Then another. And then another. *I could do this. I would do this. I needed to do this.* I took the note cards out of my pocket and looked them over once last time. When I sat down to write after learning the truth of what happened, the words had come easily, and I already knew them by heart. I was honored when her parents asked me to read them during the service.

Just before I walked inside, I saw Ryan walking up with his parents, who both hugged me before going into the church.

"How are you really?" he asked once they'd gone.

"Okay, really." My face was starting to heal, and I'd been able to stop taking the pain medicine days ago. My ribs were still sore to the touch, but that was the worst of it. I considered myself lucky.

Ryan looked handsome in his dark slacks and pressed white shirt with French cuffs, the cuts on his face making him look more rugged and masculine. His sandy blond hair was neatly in place, and although he was wearing Ray-Bans, I could imagine his baby blues behind them, the same color as the sky.

We'd talked several times in the past few days, our near-death experience drawing us closer together in some ways and further apart in others. Either way, it had changed us both. Ryan seemed older now, more mature. It was like he had a new air of purpose. I really believed he was going to put all his energy into being a good father to his unborn child and stop acting like a victim of circumstance. And I was proud of him for the first time in a long time.

"Listen," he began, "I wanted you to know that Ridley is moving to town next week."

"Oh," I said, not sure how to react. It was going to be really weird to have Ryan's baby mama living down the street. There'd be no avoiding her in a town this size. I guess I'd just have to find a way to coexist.

He paused. "We're still not together-together, you know." He took off his sunglasses, and I could see a dim glimmer of hope in his eyes, the right one still purplish-yellow underneath.

But for me, there was no hope for a future with Ryan—at

least not romantically. A part of me would always love him, but there was too much water under our bridge to go back to how we were.

"You never know, maybe things will change for you guys." I said. "Remember what they say about the best laid plans of mice and men?"

"God, I *hated* that book!" Ryan said, laughing. "In fact, if I remember right, I think I sweet-talked you into writing my essay on it in Mrs. Adler's class." A mischievous, hand-in-the-cookie-jar grin slid across his face.

"That sounds about right."

We stood there as friends on the lawn of the church where, for most of my life, I believed we would be married one day. The best laid plans, indeed.

"I love you, Riles."

"Love you, too."

Then he hugged me, and in sharp contrast to Holman's twiggy feeling, Ryan's hug felt like being wrapped in a warm blanket. His arms would always feel safe to me, but for the first time since Granddaddy died, I was starting to believe that maybe I wanted more out of life than just safety.

Before I walked inside, I pulled out my phone and texted Holman: *I'm in.*

Dear Ms. Ellison:

I am so sorry to report that Ajay257 has deactivated his account on Click.com. I suppose that means that two of you did not "click," as I had hoped you would. But please don't lose faith. As Celine says, your heart will go on and on. #sadsongssaysomuch

Speaking of sad songs, I'd like to make you aware of a special playlist that Click.com has available on iTunes for just this sort of occasion! For a one-time cost of $13.99, you can download our exclusive Heartbreak Harmonies playlist, which is like having the best of the best singing directly into your soul: Celine, Adele, Gloria Gaynor, Lady Antebellum, Sinead O'Connor, Alanis Morissette, and Eminem feat. Rhianna, to name just a few. The songs are ordered from sad to fierce, so that by the end of the soundtrack, you will feel empowered and ready to get right back onto that horse! #youwillsurvive

I realize that you may not be quite ready to move on (especially since you haven't yet listened to our Heartbreak Harmonies), but I did want to make you aware that another Click.com member has recently asked to place an arrow in your quiver! JayFed is an avid reader who likes to spend his free time hanging out in libraries. He is a dog lover, especially German shepherds, and says his ideal date would consist of themed cocktails—not beer—long walks in the park, honest conversations, and passionate kisses.

If you'd like to accept JayFed's offer, please let me know. Although, I hope you don't mind me saying that JayFed sounds a little too specific in his tastes, which could make him difficult. And (I'll just say it) it sounds like he might be unemployed. Libraries? Parks? Conversations? Hmmm. That is all well and good, but a girl can't live on passionate kisses alone! #justsaying

I would understand if you'd rather pass this one up and purchase Heartbreak Harmonies instead. Either way, please know that I have full confidence you will land on your feet and find love! #carpediem #thatmeansseizetheday

Best,
Regina H, Personal Romance Concierge, Click.com

ACKNOWLEDGMENTS

First, to my superstar agents, Emma Sweeney and Margaret Sutherland Brown. Thank you for your enthusiasm, hard work, and patience. I could not imagine having a better team behind me. A special shout-out to Margaret for all the extra hand-holding. I owe you a vat of Nutella.

To Colleen Dunn Bates at Prospect Park Books. Thank you for believing in this book and in me, for your sharp editorial eye, and your patience with my mega-emails. Please know I'm working on brevity (not here, of course). Thanks to Susan Olinsky for the gorgeous cover design, and to Nancy Nimoy for the brilliant illustration of Riley. And thanks to Caitlin Ek, Dorie Bailey, Margery L. Schwartz, Amy Inouye, and everyone else at Prospect Park Books who has worked behind the scenes to launch this book. PPB may be small, but it is mighty, and I am so very proud to be among its ranks.

Thank you to my mother, F.E. Nortman, for a lifetime of unconditional love, support, and hugs. And to Jack Nortman for taking such good care of her. To my father, Neal Rosenfeld, for giving me his love of words and showing me what true dedication looks like. (I hope I made it look easy.) A million thanks to Scott and Cheryl Orr, for being my second set of parents and never once saying no when we asked you to babysit.

To my writing beasties, Ann Breidenbach, Nina Mukerjee Furstenau, Jennifer Gravley, Laura McHugh, and Allison

Smythe. You guys make writing—and everything else—fun.

To my Highland Park buddy and mentor, Steve Weinberg. Thank you for your support and faith in my writing. You are a true writer's writer.

To all the friends who have listened to me talk about this dream for so long, and have been there through so much with me these past few years: Shoshana Buchholz Miller, Stacia Coughenour, Beth Dunafon, Heather Flanagan, Karen Grossmann, Shauna Henson, Melinda Jenne, Chrissy Meyer, Julie McDermott, Jennifer Montgomery, Tia Odom, Lindsey Rowe, Julie Ryan, Nicky Scheidt, Amy Sprouse, and Kaisa Wallis. I love you, ladies!

And now for a tale of three sisters:

To my sister-in-crime, Laura McHugh, you have been both mentor and friend, cheerleader and therapist, coach and cupcake-eating buddy. I could not have done this without you.

To my sister-in-law, Dawn Orr, for your steadfast and loyal support, the way you make everything fun, and your general awesomeness.

And to my sister with whom I actually share DNA, Allison Fiutak, you are my lifelong role model and very best friend. Thank you for always being there.

To my children, Fletcher and Elliette, I want you to know that you are not just mentioned here because you're my kids and I love you, though you are and I do. But you were both genuinely helpful in the writing process. Not only do you have great ideas, but you are generous with them. Thank you for being the best cheerleaders. You have my whole heart, and I am so proud to be your mom.

And to Jimmy again, because your sublime Jimmyness deserves mentioning more than once. If I could fill ten books with acknowledgments of how much you mean to me, I would. #iloveumore #iwinbecauseitsinabook

ABOUT THE AUTHOR

Jill Orr lives in Columbia, Missouri, with her husband and two children. *The Good Byline* is her first novel. Learn more at www.jillorrauthor.com.